CELEBRATING LOVE

SAINTS PROTECTION & INVESTIGATIONS

MARYANN JORDAN

Cover design: Cosmic Letterz
ISBN ebook: 978-1-947214-01-9
ISBN print: 978-1-947214-05-7

There are times when readers make suggestions to an author about what book they should write. Sometimes it correlates with the author's ideas and sometimes, the author has to punt the suggestion.

My readers did not want the Saints' series to end and I decided that I would like Nick to have a chance to find happiness as a Saint after a frustrating FBI career. One of my readers added a simple sentence in a thread from a FB posting (in my Alpha Fan Group). She said, "I'd like to see Nick with Bayley, Blaise's sister."

Boom! A book pairing was born. One that I had not thought of and probably would have never considered. But it's perfect. So, this dedication is to my readers, who read my books, love my books, talk to me, share with me, and even give me ideas.

Author's Note

I have lived in numerous states as well as overseas, but for the last twenty years have called Virginia my home. Many of my stories take place in this wonderful commonwealth, but I choose to use fictional city names with some geographical accuracies.

These fictionally named cities allow me to use my creativity and not feel constricted by attempting to accurately portray the areas.

It is my hope that my readers will allow me this creative license and understand my fictional world.

I also do extensive research on my books and try to write on subjects with accuracy. There will always be points where creative license will be used to create scenes or plots.

every bit the couple out for a fun night. *And here I am, sitting in the corner, nursing my drink.*

As his gaze roamed the crowded club's inhabitants, he began to categorize the patrons. There were the women, trying too hard—wearing either heavy make-up, overly tight clothes, or working their plastic surgery —but with a desperation in their mannerisms. High-pitched giggles. Hands on the man buying them a drink. Opting for a coy expression.

Then there were the older men, standing tall as a woman walked by. Checking out the ones they thought they had a chance with. A few with a white ring of skin around their finger where a wedding band would have been—before they ditched it as they entered the club.

And the young men, certain they had all the answers to the world's problems and on the hunt for an easy lay. As much as Nick gritted his teeth at their actions, he knew they would have no problem finding what they were looking for—a no strings attached night's plea-sure…or just a quick fuck against the back wall.

Sure, there were some that appeared to be there to have a fun time with friends but, on the whole, Nick was harsh in his jaded judgements having spent years with the FBI. He loved investigating, but the latest director was appointed for political reasons only and had managed to create an atmosphere where the right hand had no idea what the left hand was doing. Missions were failing. Appropriations of funds were not going to the most needed sections. And the idea that they were all working for the same end goal had eroded. The only reason he was here tonight was to assist a team, shorthanded since one of the agents went on paternity leave.

Terrorists…something on the evening news for people to get jacked-up when something happened, but who had no clue of the thousands of man-hours of investigations to combat the threat living right among them. *And with the money the drug cartels were filtering through to terrorists—*

Nick's sardonic musings came to a complete halt as his gaze settled on a woman sitting at the other end of the bar. Golden-blonde hair, naturally falling down her back in waves and pouty, ruby lips wrapped around a straw as she sucked a fruity drink. Her red dress fit her curves and, while it was hard to see how tall she was from where he was sitting, he could imagine her legs going for miles.

The whole package captured his attention, but what held his gaze was her eyes. Summer-sky blue. They were clear. Sharp. And definitely taking in the scene. He did not get the feeling that she was on the prowl—more like…*studying?* It looked as though she was studying the scene laid out before her. He watched her fiddle with her cell phone before she took a few selfies at the bar. Shaking his head, he wondered if she was waiting on someone or stood up by someone, although he could not imagine what fool would stand her up.

Knowing he needed to be watching the crowd for a possible meeting of one of the cartel members with the terrorist that the team had their eye on, he forced his gaze back over the people crowding the dance floor.

Rubbing his hand over his face, he wondered how they could stand the loud music. *God, when did I get so old—*

Janice approached the bar, standing next to him as Tom paid their tab. Speaking cautiously, she said, "We're leaving. It appears our suspects are not making the contact tonight."

As he lifted his drink to his lips, he nodded slightly, saying, "I'll follow shortly." Watching them walk out using his peripheral vision, he kept his attention on the crowd. The energy flowing from the dance floor left him more tired than when he arrived, the past few sleepless nights making staying awake for a late night stakeout even more difficult. Unfortunately he knew when he left the club his mind would probably continue to work over his cases and sleep would be elusive once more. A sudden movement to his right startled him and he jerked his eyes over as someone began to speak.

"Hi! I've been watching you and I swear, you look like you'd rather be anywhere else but here. Well, maybe not anywhere…I mean, it would have to be somewhere much quieter and maybe brighter. Not too bright…just maybe less neon-ish. Although, neon-ish can be really nice, depending on the colors. If it's red and green, well, that seems more fitting for a department store at Christmas. Pink and purple are great, but kind of femi-nine…don't know how much guys like dancing with baby-doll colors flashing all around. But pink and dark blue gives off a great vibe and since the name of this place is Neon, I guess you just have to go with it, if you're into that sort of thing which, by the way, you seriously look like you could give a rat's ass about the vibe of this place."

Nick blinked slowly—twice—but the loquacious apparition was still standing next to him. Giving a mental shake, he recognized the gorgeous blonde from the other side of the bar but, for the life of him, he had not noticed when she approached.

His eyes dropped to her fuck-me heels, up her long, tanned legs, to the way the red dress hugged her hips. Dragging his gaze continually upward, he viewed the tantalizing tops of her breasts peeking out from the dress' scooped neck. Just a hint of cleavage…not enough to give away the whole package, but enough to make a man want to drop at her feet to slowly peel the dress from her body, revealing the treasure beneath. His gaze finally landed on her face, the blue eyes mesmerizing as they stared back at him. Her red lips were curved in a wide smile as she placed her hand on her hip before throwing her head back in laughter.

"Good grief, mister," she said. "You gonna just stare or ask me to have a seat?"

Startled out of his revery, he stood quickly and offered her a hand up onto a barstool. Even in her heels, her eyes only came to the level of his mouth, surprising him. She had seemed taller while throwing sass his way. The whiff of something fruity—*lemony*—wafted by as her hair moved over her shoulder. The delicate scent, so understated, was in contrast to the effervescent woman and he leaned in slightly to inhale once more, before sitting back on his stool.

"Uh…can I buy you a drink?" he offered, uncertain

what to say. Not one to hang out in bars, he assumed an offer of a drink was acceptable protocol.

"Nah, but thanks anyway," she said, her eyes still pinned on him. Shrugging, she added, "I can tell this is not your thing."

"My thing?"

Waving her hand around, she explained, "You know...being here...in a club. Anyway, it's not really my thing either." Leaning forward, she whispered, "I'm here for research. I know I could probably get the same info from a Google search or watching a video on YouTube, but this gives me such a feel for the place. Not that I haven't been in clubs before, but that was back in college when I was like most students—young and stupid!" Laughing again, she placed her hand on his arm and leaned in close. "But I've been watching you. And you've been watching the crowd, just like me."

Bristling, he refuted, "I don't know what you mean. I'm just here having a drink."

Lifting one eyebrow, she tapped her fingernail on the back of his hand. "Uh huh. Yeah, right." Suddenly, both eyebrows lifted in surprise. "Oh, wait, you probably think I'm going to blow your cover or something." Leaning in again, she said, "Don't worry about that. You look much more natural sitting here with a woman than you did by yourself pretending to drink."

Nick stared at the beauty, uncertain if she were sincerely smart or a talkative goof or both. Clearing his throat, he repeated, "I appreciate your company, but I'm afraid you have me pegged wrong."

"Hmmm, I wonder," she smiled. "Well, anyway, it's

nice to have someone to talk to besides the bartender. Who, by the way, seems to be shooting glares at me since I moved from his section." Laughing again, she said, "He never had a chance, poor guy." Turning her full attention back on him, she said, "Like I said, I haven't been in a club in ages, so this is research for me."

Unable to keep up with her conversation bouncing from topic to topic, he simply asked, "Research?"

"I'm a writer." Scrunching her nose, she corrected, "Well, a part-time writer. It's really hard to break into making serious money as a full-time writer, but I'm working on it."

"Writer?"

She stared at him a moment, the corner of her mouth quirking up. "Yeah, you know…I sit down at a computer and type words onto paper that all come together to make a story?" she replied with a glint in her eyes. "But are you just going to parrot what I say? If so, that's a boring conversation."

Her silky hair swayed, capturing his gaze, as her laughter filled his ears once more. He opened his mouth to tell her he knew what a writer was, but she did not give him a chance.

"But, alas, I still write on the side while working in a bookstore. A bookstore that keeps me busy." She threw her hands to the side and expounded, "Well, bookstore, coffee shop, and writing extravaganza!" Her expression suddenly serious, she leaned in closer again, her eyes pinned on him, "But let's talk about you. Catching any bad guys tonight?"

Feeling the heat of a blush rising to his cheeks, Nick

grimaced. "Miss, I'm afraid your imagination has run wild. I'm simply here to enjoy my drink." Feeling like he was melting under her stare, he continued, "But since my drink is almost finished, I'll bid you goodnight."

A brilliant smile erupted on her face as her eyes landed on his mostly-full glass. "Finished? If you say so but, please, don't leave on my account." She twirled around on her barstool and stared out over the crowd. "What I was looking for tonight was the chance to see people interact, pick-up lines, dancing, even the way people dressed. To quote my dear Agatha Christie, 'Curious things, habits. People themselves never knew they had them.' I love Agatha, don't you?" she asked, her smile wide.

Nick blinked again, unable to produce an instinctive response to her question but, before he could ponder her rapid-fire train of thought further, she continued.

"Now, take that woman over there. Hot body, but the faint lines around her eyes tell me she has a bit of age on her and, yet, her boobs are really sitting up high. So, boob job. Unless, of course, she's got a really amazing bra but, I gotta tell you, I've never seen any bra that could hold up ta-tas that size, that high!" Throwing her hands up, she quickly continued, "Hey, no judgement here. Just an observation. And that man over there at the edge of the dance floor? He sucks his stomach in every time a woman walks by." Giggling, she added, "That's like doing an ab-crunch every minute or so. He's gonna be sore tomorrow!"

Nick turned his attention back to the enigmatic woman, torn between wanting to keep staring at her beauty and shutting her up with a kiss. *Whoa...no kissing strange women you meet at a cheap nightclub...no matter how kissable those lush, ruby lips are.*

"And see the tall, redhead on the dance floor...the one in the itty-bitty dress that is halfway up her ass due to that guy behind her grinding his crotch against her? Well, she's not into him. You can tell because her ass may be getting down and dirty with the dude behind her, but her eyes are on that blond, beachy-looking guy over to the side." Taking another sip of her drink, she turned her eyes back toward Nick. "That's why I knew this wasn't your typical scene," she added. "There's a bit of desperation here, don't you think?"

It did not matter that her assessment of the club was exactly the same as his. He kept silent, tossing back the rest of his drink.

"But, then, there are those here just out to have fun, I suppose. I've got friends who go to nightclubs all the time." Leaning over, she wrinkled her nose as she added, "But I just can't get into the dancing. I'm not very coordinated but, then again, dancing nowadays just seems to be for girls to shake their ass around a lot and guys to get their crotch rubbed on." Offering a slight shrug, she said, "I've been to some nice ones, but still they're just not my favorite place to be. I'd rather curl up with a good book."

"So why pick this place? Can't you do your research at a nicer club?" he asked, thinking that one with more security would be preferable.

"But my story is about a couple that meets under unusual circumstances in a cheap night-club. So, I needed to come here. Of course, I did some research on clubs in the area first. I wouldn't dare go to one in a bad side of town. I'm all about research, but I'm not stupid. And I didn't want one that was too close to the university, filled with frat boys looking for a quick fuck up against a wall or ugh, in a bathroom." Pinning her eyes on him again, she said, "Now, that's something I just can't see doing. Do you know how many germs are in the typical public bathroom? And to just drop your panties and have your bare ass on a sink? Nope, not me! I have to pee a lot, but I try to hold it when in a place where dubious activities have been going on." She flashed her grin at him and added, "You men can just use a urinal, but us girls have to think about what we're sitting on." Laughing, she amended, "Or hovering over."

Nick was nowhere close to drunk after only having two watered-down drinks, but his brain struggled to keep up with the verbal barrage coming from her mouth. He was a man of few words— carefully thought out words— and he knew it. His friends knew it. Hell, even his co-workers knew it. But, as maddening as she was, there was something endearing about her.

Before he had a chance to figure her out, she slid from the stool and teetered for a second in her heels. His hand automatically shot out steady her.

Blushing, she assured, "I'm not drunk, I promise. It's been a while since I've traipsed around in heels this high, but I figured I needed to blend into the environment." Beaming her white-toothed smile directly at him, she added, "But it's nice to see chivalry isn't dead!"

Leaning over, she patted his arm, "I had you pegged as a gentleman from the get-go."

Turning around, she held up her phone and took several more selfies as she turned in a circle. Placing her phone back in her purse, she smiled. "I'm not really this conceited. I hold up my phone like I'm taking a selfie and then turn it slightly. That way I get lots of pictures all around, but no one gets creeped out." Seeing his brows draw down, she explained, "For my research, of course. I can go back home and when I need to describe something, I look at my pictures!"

Straightening, she grabbed her purse, threw some bills onto the bar, and said, "Well, I'm off. It was nice talking to you."

"Wait, let me walk you outside," Nick said, suddenly fearful for her to be outside alone. "Just to be safe."

Assessing him, she nodded slowly. "Sure...thank you."

Throwing more bills onto the bar, he walked at her side, using his left hand to part the crowd while his right hand lightly rested on the small of her back. Stepping past the bouncer at the door, they were hit with the night air, clean and fresh after the overly-warm club interior.

"Prissy's parked around the corner," she said, smiling up at him.

"Prissy?"

"My car—Prissy."

"You named your car?" he asked, his brows lowered.

"Of course! Don't you name things in your life that are important to you? Think about it. She gets me wherever I want to go. If there's an emergency she's there. I'm not so good about remembering to get her oil changed and things like that, so I guess that makes me a poor Prissy owner, but my brother helps out—he makes sure I'm right on schedule taking care of her."

Once more uncertain how to respond, Nick stared at the animated woman smiling up at him.

"Here's Prissy and, as you can see, I parked right under a street light."

Nodding his silent approval while still wrapping his head around car-naming, he noted her blue Prius parked in a well-lit space. His fingers continued to press gently into her back, tingling at the feel of her soft dress. Stopping at her car, his eyes scanned the area as she unlocked and opened the driver's door.

Turning, she smiled up at him, saying, "Thank you for walking me to my car. And for talking," breaking into a chortle, she amended, "or rather listening to me tonight. I hope I didn't keep you from catching your bad guys." Seeing him about to protest, she stopped him with her palm on his chest. "Don't deny it." Lifting on her toes, she placed a quick kiss on his cheek before quickly sliding into her seat and closing the door.

Hearing the door locks click, he watched as she wiggled a finger wave toward him before pulling into the street and driving away.

Left standing underneath a street light outside a gaudy nightclub, Nick wondered what the hell just hit him as the scent of lemons hung in the air.

Lazlo Gruzinsky stood in the shadows of the alley next to the club, one hand resting on the back door of a white, panel van, his eyes pinned on the blonde woman getting into the car. The one he had been eye-fucking for the last hour when he wasn't doing his job. The one who had been inside taking a lot of pictures, and may have taken one of him. Or the girl he now had. And now that same blonde stood smiling up at some man who had to be some kind of cop, or worse…a Fed. Nobody goes to Club Neon and just sit drinking watered drinks. The man looked around too much and not at the women in the place. Grimacing, he slapped the back of the van, giving it the high-sign to pull away.

Moving in the shadows toward his car, he watched as the blonde climbed into her vehicle and drove away.

2

The quiet greeted him as an old, comfortable friend. Walking into the neat apartment, he reveled in the clean and organized space. Order and peace. Everything in its place. Just the way he liked it.

Nick lived on the third floor of his apartment building, the modern construction offering security, a night watchman, and a first-floor gym. While located just outside the city, it was still conveniently located to the Bureau's local office.

Locking the door behind him, he pulled off his tie on the way to his bedroom, passing the neat lines of the minimalistic furnishings in his living room and pristine kitchen. In his obviously masculine bedroom with its navy and gray bedspread paired with dark wood furniture, he walked to his closet, hanging his tie on the tie rack as he toed off his shoes. Placing his shoes on the shelf at the bottom of the closet, he hung up his suit jacket. Giving it a sniff, he shook his head. Sliding the coat hanger to the far end, he hung his pants next to it, adding a trip to the dry cleaners to his list of things to take care of tomorrow.

Moving into the bathroom, he stripped as the water heated, dropping his shirt and boxers into the hamper. Stepping into the pristine, white, tiled shower, he allowed the water to stream over him, washing away the sweat, cheap nightclub smell, and the thoughts of the case. Instead of his job, the beautiful—albeit talkative—woman who had invaded his space at the bar was now invading his mind as well. *And I didn't even ask her name.*

As soon as that thought crossed his mind, he stepped out of the shower, shaking his head to dislodge the regret, but all he managed to do was sling water droplets over his mirror. Irritated, he grabbed another towel from the linen closet next to the double sink and began wiping the water from the glass before it had a chance to dry, leaving spots. Wrapping the towel around his lean hips, he stood with his hands on the counter and stared into the mirror.

Dark hair, neatly trimmed. Tall, muscular in shape. The physical training at the FBI academy years earlier had stayed with him and he enjoyed working out every day. *Well, almost every day.* Lately, his desk job had taken precedent and, while he appreciated the responsibilities, he missed field work. And that was why he had gone with Janice and Tom to stake out the club. *But it got us nowhere.* Rubbing his hand over his face, he jerked the towel from his hips and finished drying before folding it neatly and hanging it over the bar.

Stalking into the bedroom, he pulled on a pair of loose-fitting shorts and wandered into his kitchen. Grabbing a water bottle out of the refrigerator, he guzzled the contents, letting the cool liquid slide down his throat. Moving to sit at the table, he pulled up his laptop. Checking his emails, he then typed the notes from this evening so he would not forget anything. They had spotted a few low-level cartel members, but did not see anyone identified as working with the terrorists. Sighing, he saved everything and closed his laptop. Placing the bottle into the recycle bin, he began his nightly checks.

Front door locked. Security system alarmed. Stove off. Toaster and coffee maker unplugged. Laptop and phone charging. Lights off.

Turning the covers down, he reclined in his bed, leaning against the pillows on the headboard. Taking the latest book he was reading off the nightstand, he opened up to the bookmark, but before he read one word, his mind shot back to the woman at the bar. A writer…doing research…who works in a bookstore during the day. He wondered if she had lied about her vocation, knowing many people made up stories about what they did when they met someone in a bar. But as the thought ran through his mind, Nick dismissed it. He considered his bullshit meter to be good, so, he was sure she really did what she said.

Irritated that she was on his mind once more, he slammed the book closed before placing it carefully on the nightstand, precisely where he had left it the night before, and slid down in the bed after rearranging the pillows. Turning off the lamp on the nightstand, he closed his eyes willing sleep to come. But he waited in vain. Her plump, glossy lips came to mind...*and how I'd love to see them sliding up and down my cock!*

The semi-erection he had sported since he first laid eyes on her was now rock hard and not going away. Slipping his hand down his boxers, he fisted his aching dick and pumped to the thought of her mouth on him... his mouth on her...and then sliding into her slick sex. Closing his eyes, she was all he could see. Grunting, the muscles in his neck tightened and corded as his balls pulled up. Teeth clenched, he came until he was emptied and lying limp on the bed.

As the fog of lust lifted and rational thought came back to him, he opened his eyes, looking down at the mess over his stomach and his sheets. *What the hell?* Hand jobs were relegated to the shower where the results could be easily cleaned. Irritated that this woman had invaded his mind, his thoughts—*and my good sense*—he jumped up and stalked to the bathroom. After washing himself, he grabbed clean sheets from the linen closet and headed back into the bedroom.

Fifteen minutes later, with soiled sheets rinsed out and in the laundry room, clean sheets on the bed, and lights back out, he lay down once more.

Sleep came, but his dreams were restless...filled with blue eyes and ruby-lipped smiles.

"I didn't even get his name!"

Bayley Hanssen walked up the stairs to her apartment, juggling her purse in one hand while fishing for her keys, kicking off her shoes and bending over to pick them up with her other hand while balancing her phone between her shoulder and ear.

The phone slipped, bouncing onto the floor of the hallway. Dropping her shoes to scramble for her phone, she cursed, "Shit! Sorry, Daphne, dropped my phone. But yeah, I didn't get his name. We just talked. Well, I talked and he sat...kinda quietly, actually, while I prattled on."

Managing to get her door unlocked, she continued, "But damn, I could have just stared at Mr. Tall, Dark, Mysterious, and Beautiful all night."

"Shouldn't he be tall, dark and handsome...or gorgeous? You could call him TDH or TDG!" Daphne enthused.

"Mmmn, nah," Bayley disagreed, shutting the door behind her, entering her small apartment. "Beautiful is the word for him. Gorgeous is such a superficial word, usually just referring to appearance or even enjoyability. Handsome is also so much about appearance, or generosity. But beautiful? It's not just about looks, but about delighting the senses. Having a very high standard." Leaning back against the door for a moment, the image of him in her mind, she smiled. "Yes...tall, dark, mysterious, and beautiful is just the perfect description of him."

"Well, you're the writer and Mr. TDMB sounds like

one of your characters," Daphne said. "One of your really good characters."

"That's exactly what I thought, too," Bayley agreed, tossing her shoes by the door and her purse on the knotted pine kitchen table with the mismatched chairs, where her keys skidded off, landing on the floor. Kneeling, she petted the dark grey cat that slinked out to meet her. "I don't know what he was doing there, but I'm sure he was on some kind of stakeout, so I'll never see him again. But I'm going to remember him, just so I can write him into my next book!"

"Oooh, sounds good, but I gotta go. It's late and I've got to be at work early tomorrow. My boss is such a stickler for being on time!"

"Shut up," Bayley replied lightly. "I'm your boss and when did I care?"

Daphne laughed, "See you tomorrow!"

Disconnecting, Bayley walked into her tiny kitchen, glancing at the clean dishes on the dishrack. She was great about washing immediately, but rarely dried or placed them back in the cupboard. Snagging a cup, she filled it with tap water and drank thirstily. Pouring a little cat food into the bowl on the floor, she smiled as Mr. Lickers ran over, crunching the morsels. Lifting her hands over her head, she stretched. Tired and feeling dirty, she stepped around the counter and down the slight hall through her bedroom, stepping over a few piles of clean laundry that had not made it to the closet, entering the bathroom. Turning on the water, she listened as the pipes groaned a few seconds before the water began to pour. Stripping out of her red dress, she dropped it to the floor, and stepped into the bathtub, letting the shower water wash the nightclub odor off her.

Squirting shampoo into her hand, she washed her long hair, leaning her head back to let the water continue to sluice through the strands. As the warm water relaxed her body, her mind stayed firmly on Mr. TDMB. Easily the most intriguing man in the crowded room, she remembered the instant she first saw him.

Smiling as the memory assaulted her, she continued to glide the fragrant sponge over her body, wishing they were his hands. A giggle erupted at the thought of how out of place he appeared. *Had to be police...or FBI...or someone keeping an eye on something.*

The water began to cool, so she stepped out, grabbed a towel and dried off before tossing it haphazardly on the shower curtain bar. Standing in front of the mirror, she stared at her reflection.

Her light-blonde hair, now wet and dark, lay slicked back from her heart shaped face. Her cheeks were rosy but the black mascara she wore now streaked trails down her face. Grabbing her makeup remover, she rummaged in a drawer for a cotton pad. Pulling out the plastic bag, she realized she used the last one the previous night and had forgotten to put it on her mental shopping list. Tossing the bag, she pulled some toilet paper off the roll and wadded it up before soaking it with makeup remover. The cheap paper shredded as she rubbed her face, leaving little muffs of white over her cheeks.

Somewhat mascara free, she grabbed a bathcloth

and washed her face again. Staring into the mirror, her blue eyes scanned her body, critically assessing each curve. *Is my stomach poochier than it was yesterday?* After turning side to side several times to see if her extra pounds were an optical illusion or not, she gave up. *Fuck it! I bet men don't stand at the mirror and criticize their bodies!* Grinning, she thought of her mystery-man standing in front of his mirror. Shaking her head, she brushed her teeth before grabbing her dress off the floor, then padded back into the bedroom.

Her bed, still unmade from the previous night, looked inviting as she hung up the dress. Giving it a sniff, she grimaced at the stale odor from the club. Taking her coat hanger over to her window, she hung it over the curtain rod, deciding a little fresh air would be perfect. Opening the window slightly to let the evening breeze flow in, she smiled at the thought of saving a dry-cleaning bill.

Slipping under the covers after tossing the pillows in a haphazard pile onto the floor, she stretched her body, feeling the last of the kinks from the evening slip away. Jumping up suddenly, she hurried to the front door to throw the deadbolt. Her brother preached home security to her, but she often left the deadbolt unlocked, although she had trained herself to think of it before she went to sleep.

Back in bed, she grabbed her eReader and continued the story she started last night. The sexy romance soon had her squirming in the bed, erotic thoughts filling her mind. Tossing the eReader to the nightstand, she opened the top drawer and pulled out her battery-operated-boyfriend. With BOB in hand, she put it on her favorite setting and worked her body until she cried out her release. Tossing BOB to her nightstand, she frowned. Sure, she had her physical release, but it was a poor substitute for the real thing. And it had been a long time since she had had the real thing.

"Mr. Lickers!" she called, watching as the cat walked stealthily into the room, hopping up on her bed. He curled up next to her hip, closing his eyes almost immediately. Turning off the light, she fell into slumber, her last thoughts of what Mr. TDMB had been doing in the nightclub. *Who is he and what was he after?*

Outside her apartment, Lazlo stood in the shadows, illuminated by the flare of his lighter. Once his cigarette was lit, he inhaled deeply before letting the smoke curl out from his mouth, creating a halo effect. Seeing the lights go out, he waited until the last puff was completed before dropping the butt onto the sidewalk and grinding it under his boot. Pulling up his collar, he stuck his hands in his pockets and sauntered down the street.

Prying her eyes open, Bayley slammed her hand down on the alarm clock blaring country music. Normally one to jump out of bed, she regretted the late night now that it was morning. Forcing her body to a sitting position, she realized why her room seemed darker than normal—the red dress hanging over the window blocked most of the sunlight. Giving a shiver in the cool room, she stared longingly back at her pillow.

Fighting the urge to sleep in, she stood and padded over to the window, closing it before sniffing the dress. *Not bad!* Grinning as she hung it back in her closet, she headed into the bathroom, staring at the mess in the mirror. Bed-head. A pillow wrinkle down her face. A smudge of mascara that eluded the face scrub with toilet paper last night.

Flipping on the TV as she poured a bowl of Lucky Charms, she watched the news for a few minutes. Weather. Stock market. Ads.

Rinsing her bowl in the sink after finishing the last crunchy marshmallow, she placed it in the rack and walked back into the bedroom just as the news changed to an update. She missed the special report on a missing girl, last seen at a downtown nightclub.

Finishing his early morning workout before most of his neighbors had woken, Nick drank his protein shake before showering, then dressing, and finally fixing breakfast while listening to the news. As he plated his scrambled eggs, bacon, and toast, the newscaster was just announcing another missing girl, this time from a nightclub downtown. As he heard the name of the nightclub, his fork halted on its way to his mouth.

Turning the sound up, he listened as the reporter gave the information on the missing woman.

His phone pinged an incoming text and he turned from the screen to grab it—**8am mtg, Janice**. Sucking in a deep breath, he leaned back, his breakfast forgotten, as he realized his morning had just gotten complicated.

3

_____

Her green eyes stared back at him.

Nick sat in a meeting in the State Capitol District FBI building, having chosen the seat directly across from the large screen on the wall so he would have a direct view of her face. Amy Willis. Young. Red hair cut in a short style. Only eighteen years old. As much as he tried, he did not remember seeing her. What he would not admit to was that the only woman's face he remembered was the entertaining blonde who had talked to him.

Inwardly cursing, he was stunned that he had been so distracted by a beautiful face that he did not keep his eyes peeled while on the stakeout.

"Isn't that right?" Pause. "Nick?"

Startling, he realized all eyes were on him and Janice had asked him a question. "Sorry, what was that?"

"I explained that we were there to specifically watch for the cartel and ISIS groups. We weren't watching for young women in a packed bar full of women. We could have seen her but it would not have registered."

Nodding, he agreed, "The place was dark and crowded, making it almost impossible to lock in on anyone's face. It makes the perfect place for drugs to be sold, deals to be made, any kind of connection between two people who don't want to be noticed." Grimacing, he added, "And, of course, for someone to be taken. Drinks are flowing, the dance floor is packed with everyone in a moving mass. Too damn easy for someone to be taken."

Special Agent Harlan Masten rubbed his face. Nick observed the older agent, his hair still cut in the high and tight military haircut of his younger days in the Marines before joining the FBI. "This is the third missing girl, taken from a night club, in the past two months. What insight we have is that we may be dealing with human trafficking, but we've got little to go on."

"Any video from the club?" Nick asked.

"Their security is shit," Harlan stated. "We obtained and reviewed the tapes but the quality is poor and the cameras are not placed in the optimum locations to observe. The one near the front door is the best. We did get a hit on her arrival at about a quarter past ten. She came in with two other girls, but they soon lost each other in the crowd. We don't have a definitive time of her leaving, but if she were drugged, her face would be down and, believe me, there were a ton of drunk girls staggering out by closing time."

Nick's gaze shifted around the table to the fellow agents assigned to the missing girls' cases. He did not envy their assignment and regretted not being able to offer any assistance. The thought flashed through his mind that the enigmatic woman he met had been at risk for being kidnapped, just by being there. A sudden gasp escaped his lips, drawing the attention of the others. With a shake of his head, he forced his mind to the case at hand and not the woman invading his thoughts.

"We're trying to identify some of the people at the club last night to see if anyone took pictures that might have caught something. People are always taking selfies to load onto social media at places like that."

Selfies? Selfies! Now the blonde came slamming back to mind, but this time it was for the case currently discussed. He remembered what she had said: *"I hold up my phone like I'm taking a selfie and then turn it slightly. That way I get lots of pictures all around, but no one gets creeped out."*

Looking at the others, Nick said, "I'm not sure I can find her, but I talked to a woman last night who took a lot of pictures. Let me work on it and I'll get back with you."

Harlan stared for a moment, his intelligent eyes piercing Nick, before he pronounced, "Nick, you're at the end of filling in for Janice's case and I want to reassign you now, rather than a week from now. If you've got anything on this case that can help, then we're going to want you on it full time."

"But he's been assisting on our case for two months! He knows more about it than Lenny does. We could really use his help. We're close, I feel it," Janice protested, her face scrunched in frustration.

"Yes, but I've got other agents who can work with you. This was only ever temporary—until Lenny got back from paternity leave. Right now, we've got the Governor breathing down our neck telling me if we can't find these girls, he'll call in outsiders."

Nick knew who the governor was referring to—Jack Bryant's Saints. Saints Protection & Investigations. Jack, while still in the Army Special Forces, had worked with a team of highly trained members, making up a multi-task force consisting of SEALs, SF, CIA, explosive experts, and others. Finding the team worked well together Jack re-created the idea of an exclusive multi-task force once he was a civilian. He recruited from SEALs, FBI, SF, ATF, DEA, and CIA for his new team. Top of the line equipment, weapons, security systems, vehicles, and computers—everything the Saints Protection & Investigations could need was at their disposal. And as Jack liked to say, they took on the jobs nobody else wanted or could solve.

That arrogance used to piss Nick off—until he worked with them. Then he understood. The Saints managed to skirt around the bullshit that hampered the police or FBI. Nick found himself irritated and, at the same time, awed at their abilities. He had worked with the ten Saints for the past year and their tenuous relationship had grown into a friendship. Jack had offered a place on his team to Nick but so far, he had refused although, there were times when the chance to investigate, unfettered by bureaucracy, pulled at him. The temptation to forego the rules and structure with his work that he strived for and relished in his personal life was strong. He was definitely a man at odds with himself and he wasn't sure he was ready to face that little fact just yet.

"Nick, what do you want to do? You should have some say in all this. You've got reports and files on our case," Janice pressed.

As he carefully considered the situation, the reality was that any other competent agent could take up his reins easily and, a company man, Nick had always gone where assigned, so he was ready to be moved to a new case simply because his supervisor wanted it. Looked like finding the missing local girl and possibly shutting down the ring of kidnappers loomed ahead. *Okay, and finding the blonde again...* Perturbed that he made this personal, Nick shook his head, "Yes, sir. I'll take the reassignment."

Janice tossed a glare in his direction as she exited the room, Tom offering an apologetic nod as he followed her. Lifting his gaze back to Harlan after scanning the table of other agents assigned to the new case, he said, "I'll let you know as soon as I find the woman with the pictures, sir."

"And then he walked me to my car."

Daphne sat on the stool behind the counter, watching and listening as Bayley walked and talked, waving her hands around as she described her experience from the previous evening. Leaning her elbows on the counter, she groaned, "You have all the luck. If I went to a place like that, I'd get stuck with an OGP instead of TDMB."

"Huh?" Bayley asked, halting her pacing as she looked over at her friend.

"Obnoxious, Grinding, Prick instead of your guy."

Throwing her head back in laughter, Bayley assured, "Well, I saw plenty of OGPs on the dance floor!"

The bell over Bayley's Books & Nooks sounded as their first customer of the day entered. Bayley greeted, "Good morning, Sally. Here to do some research and writing?"

The older woman smiled as she nodded, "Absolutely. Let me get my laptop set up and I'll be over for some coffee."

"Daphne'll take care of you. Just let us know if you need something else." Bayley watched with pleasure as Sally made her way over to one of the many writing nooks the store offered. The old building retained much of the restored glory of its original beauty, including the brick walls and heavy wooden bookshelves. The back held a small employee workroom plus the storage room, and a set of stairs that led to Bayley's office in a hidden loft.

The idea for her unusual business came to her when she first started writing and lived in an apartment shared with three other women. Crowded and noisy, it was never a good place to write. She discovered the bookstore three years ago when the old owner was looking to sell. Falling in love with the building, she managed to get a loan with the help of her parents. Desiring the concept of a bookstore and writing nooks for authors, she created her business...*and haven.* She now had almost twenty authors that paid a small, monthly fee to use her facilities, which not only included the space and research materials, but was also used for author groups and author critiques to meet.

The bookstore was incredibly popular with a separate room for the children's section, where Daphne would host weekly reading times so the moms and dads could shop or write.

Once Sally was situated, Bayley walked over with the steaming cup of coffee in her hand, setting it carefully on the table next to her. "So, what are you working on today?"

Sally pushed her glasses down slightly so she could peer over the top at Bayley. "I was going to ask you about your research last night. How was the club?"

"It was crazy-loud and crowded," Bayley said, "but I met a man that I'm sure was a detective staking out the place!"

"Well, maybe he's looking for whoever is snatching girls from clubs!"

Cocking her head to the side, Bayley stared at Sally. "What girls?"

"My dear, it was all over the news this morning! This makes the third woman that's disappeared from a night club in the area. And she was with friends last night at Neon."

At the name *Neon*, Bayley's smile dropped from her face as her heart rate sped. "Neon? Neon the nightclub Neon?"

Nodding, Sally opened her laptop as she took a sip

of her coffee. "Yep. You'd think in a place filled with so many people, someone would have noticed something. How could a woman be dragged out of a place with no one noticing?"

Leaving Sally in peace, she forced a smile at several more patrons in the store as she made her way back to the front counter, her heart pounding as dizziness threatened to overtake her. "Daphne," she whispered hoarsely as she leaned close, "did you know about the girl taken from Neon last night?"

"No," Daphne replied, eyes wide. "You know I hate listening to the news. It's too depressing." After a quick pause, she added, "Oh, I wonder if you could have seen something and never realized what was happening right under your nose!"

Rolling her eyes, "Thanks, Daph! That makes me feel so much better," Bayley moved to her laptop in the nook by the tall window. Googling the news, she scrolled through the reports about the latest incident. She stared at the pictures of Amy Willis. *Jeez, she looks like half the women there last night.* Not recognizing her, she finished reading the article before clicking over to her work-in-progress manuscript, but found her mind continually roamed to the previous evening. *I wonder if TDMB was there watching out for a kidnapper? And I distracted him!* Immediately contrite, she closed her laptop, knowing no other words were going to come today.

With a knock on the doorframe, which garnered the attention of the room's occupant, Nick took a step inside. Harlan stood, shaking hands with him before motioning him to a seat. "Nick," Harlan said, "I'm real glad you agreed to be reassigned to this case. I know it's not easy to switch horses mid-stream."

"When I got back from Alaska, Janice asked if I would mind assisting on the case she was heading up since she had an agent out on paternity leave. I knew my time working on her team was almost up and I'd be heading up the mid-Virginia office. Your case is in my jurisdiction and it interests me."

"And you don't remember seeing Amy Willis?"

Shaking his head, he admitted, "No, but I want to look at the tapes. There was a woman I talked to that was taking a ton of pictures. She said it was research for her books." Shrugging, he added, "She may have been bullshitting me, but she did take a lot of pictures. I wanted to try and see if I can ID her and then get ahold of her phone."

Harlan leaned back in his seat, his elbows on the arms of his chair as his hands came together, his forefingers raised against each other. He quietly studied Nick before saying, "I've got to tell you that there's pressure from above and things are changing. Do you know Richard Tillman?"

Nick nodded slowly as he answered, "Yeah. Real go-getter and doesn't mind who he steps on to get to the top."

Harlan chuckled. "That sounds about right."

"What's this about?"

"Richard's angling to get moved up to the D.C. Bureau and not just as an agent. He's been getting political backing from state senators, and is already rubbing elbows with some bigwig D.C. politicians."

"This got something to do with this case?"

Nodding, Harlan let out a long sigh. "I've only got about two more years to retire. Been a career agent. Seen a lot of hotshots come and go, but Richard unnerves me. Make no mistake, Nick. He wants results on this case and he wants them fast. He'll be thrilled that you're on the case and that says a lot about you. But...watch your back. He doesn't like anyone going rogue and he'll cut you off at the knees if you give him half-a-chance."

"So, investigate and no cock-ups, right?"

Harlan added, "I just want to make sure you know he'll be breathing down your neck. You're a real by the books guy, but he doesn't want the governor to call in the Saints. I know you're friends with them."

Giving a little shrug, Nick said, "I like the idea of working on this case. There's a strange sense of responsibility, having the scene at a location near where I live. One where a kidnapping took place, so close, and I didn't know it. I'd like to work to make that right. But Harlan? Even following the rules, I'll use whatever means I need to so that this case can be resolved. And if the governor calls the Saints in...I'll work with them just like before."

Grinning, Harlan nodded, "You'll have no problems with me, so welcome aboard, Nick. You'll keep working on it from your local office and report in to me. I'll send whatever you have up to Richard. And if I can keep him off your back...I will."

"Pass the bread, please."

The family sitting at the dining room table smiled at each other as the mother served breakfast. The two adult sons, Lazlo and Grigory, as well as their sister, Agnes, joined their parents, Milos and Chessa Gruzinsky.

"How is Portia?" Chessa asked, eyeing her eldest, Grigory.

"She's fine, Mama," he replied, shoveling more cheese dumplings onto his plate. "She says her father is ready to discuss the wedding now that the preliminaries are out of the way."

Milos narrowed his eyes at his son, spitting, "He should be grateful for you to cast your eyes on his youngest. We are a family to be envied." He pounded his fist on his chest in emphasis. Chessa placed her hand on her husband's arm, patting it calmly.

"I think her family is more in awe of us than against us, Papa," Grigory stated calmly, looking up from his plate at his parents. "She'll be fine once we're married. I have no doubt of her complacency."

"Well, we won't talk of family business when she joins us for meals," Chessa declared.

Grigory's fork halted on its path to his mouth. "Mama," he spoke, hesitation in his voice as his eyes darted toward his brother. "My bride and I will not be eating here every morning as we are now."

"Bah," Chessa spat, waving her hands dismissively. "My children will always be at my table."

No rebuttal came and the only sound for a few minutes was the clattering of cutlery as they continued to eat. Agnes sat quietly observing, as she did every morning, her eyes darting between her parents and brothers.

Setting his fork down, Milos looked at his youngest son, lifting his eyebrows in question. "So, Lazlo, I noticed our new addition this morning. Did you find anything else last night?"

"There was a woman, a blonde, taking photos. I followed her, so I know where she lives."

"And?" Milos prompted, impatience in his voice.

"Why follow her? Surely other people were taking photos too," Grigory asked, still chewing as he reached for more porridge.

"She was not drunk...not participating. The others were too busy drinking or dancing to notice. But this girl," Lazlo replied, "her eyes were sharp. And then she was talking to a man at the bar...he had to be a Fed or something. The man just had a look about him...didn't trust his eyes."

Lips pinched, Chessa huffed. "I said last night was not good. Did I not say last night was not good?" Darting her gaze toward her husband, she repeated, "We risk it all for another red-head?"

Shrugging, Milos sipped his dark, thick coffee. "You know the demand. We supply."

Slapping her hand down on the table, Chessa barked, "You don't lecture me on our business. Remember who my family is." Jabbing a finger at her chest, she claimed, "I'm the one who checks to make sure our girls are clean. I'm the one to organize their schedules. I'm the one who keeps an eye on them."

Patting her hand, Milos turned his fond gaze on his indignant wife. "Yes, yes, my *zhena*. You hold us all together."

Calming, she looked at her boys, all ignoring her tirade as they continued to eat. Picking up a platter, she stood, dishing out more food onto Grigory's plate. "Eat, eat. I'll not have it go to waste."

Milos lifted his gaze to Lazlo, catching his son's eyes. "I'll send Johan to the girl. See what she knows—"

"No!" Lazlo answered loudly, then softened his voice. "I'll check on her. I can find out what she knows."

Chessa's sharp eyes landed on her youngest son. She cocked her head to the side as she peered at Lazlo. "You have some interest in the girl?"

"No," Lazlo protested. "She caught my eye and I've already followed her. She went home alone. I want to be the one to see what she knows. Johan has a...heavy hand. This girl needs to be handled delicately." Hearing Grigory snort, he glared at his brother.

"Johan can handle the job," Milos stated, drawing a frown from Lazlo. "I've already talked to Gavrill. They are sending him now that he is back in the country."

"I can do more than just snatch the girls," Lazlo protested.

Milos interrupted, his voice hard, "Let Johan do this.

You need to keep your face from being recognized. She may have seen you last night, as it is."

The family stopped eating as they stared at their father. "Our family business may be small, but it is part of a much bigger organization. We need to proceed carefully. Unwarranted risks are foolish."

Lazlo said nothing, hiding his emotion as he stood taking his now-empty plate into the kitchen.

"And what if the girl suspects something? What if she already suspects?" Chessa protested.

"Bah," Milos dismissed. "She is a girl. A stupid girl hanging out at a nightclub. What could she possibly know?"

Agnes hid her smile as she sipped her coffee. She had plans that went far beyond just marrying someone her parents picked out for her and doing nothing more than having more sons for the family business. She planned on gaining control of her destiny and had no problem working for it. Glancing at her brothers, she recognized their weakness…the same weakness her relatives in Norfolk had—they stuck to the old ways. Lucky for her she did not have that same problem.

4

Nick poured over the video from the front entrance of Neon, scanning the faces as he looked for the blonde. Shaking his head in frustration, he had to admit the video was poor quality and the camera was hung at an awkward angle for obtaining clear shots of who was entering the club.

"Told you it was crap!" A hand slapped down on his shoulder and Nick twisted to see another agent walking into the room, sitting down at a nearby desk.

"Hey, Mike." Turning back to the video, he continued scanning for several more minutes. Stopping the feed, he leaned closer to the monitor.

"You think you got something?" Mike asked, moving to look over Nick's shoulder. "Damn, is that the girl? Fuck, you didn't say she was gorgeous!"

"She's just a person of interest who might have inadvertently taken some relevant pictures," Nick groused, irritated at both Mike's comments about the blonde and at himself for feeling a bolt of jealousy fire through him.

"And you didn't get her name? Man, I woulda got that first thing."

Fighting the urge to punch Mike in the mouth, Nick just said, "I was there on a job, not to pick up some random girl."

Throwing his hands up, Mike laughed, "Hey, it woulda made finding her a lot easier. Do you even know what she does or where she works? That'd help."

As Mike walked out of the room, Nick continued to stare at the monitor, viewing the grainy image of his blonde, wondering why he had just considered her to be *his blonde*, while admitting the poor video did not do her justice…and would not give him enough for facial recognition.

Rubbing his head, he wondered where he would find a writer, before remembering she said she worked in a bookstore. *How did she describe it? A bookstore, coffee shop, and writing extravaganza.*

Moving to a computer, he began searching for bookstores in the area, narrowing his search to those with coffee shops attached or within. Eyes wide, he was stunned at the number of bookstores offering coffee. Hearing someone come in, he looked up and smiled. "Margery, just the person I need. How the hell does the search work on this program?"

Margery smiled and shooed him out of his seat. "That's why you come to me first instead of wasting your time trying to figure this out on your own." Settling into the chair, she said, "Okay, what do you need?"

"I want to search bookstores in the area that have coffee shops. I came up with this huge list—"

"No shit, Sherlock," Margery exclaimed, twisting her head to look up at him. "Most bookstores have coffee shops in them now."

"Oh," Nick said, his eyebrows down as he thought this through. "I never noticed."

"You never get coffee when you're prowling through a bookstore?"

"No—what if someone spills coffee on the books?" He shook his head in derision, hating the idea of the ruination of a book. Nick continued to think through what the blonde had said as Margery sat patiently. "Is there a place where someone would go to write a book?" he asked.

Cocking her head to the side, she murmured, "Hmmm. You mean like all three? A place that sells books, serves coffee, and where people write?" At his nod, she laughed and answered, "Hell, Nick, that would be horrible. What if someone spilled their coffee on their computer while they were writing and then it dripped onto their books?"

"Shut up and search," he groused.

Still chuckling, her fingers began to fly over the keyboard as she entered in code to find what she was looking for. "I don't know, Nick. Anyone can write while in a bookstore or coffee shop. I'm not sure what you're looking for."

"What about a writing extravaganza?" he said hesitantly, feeling heat rising to his face.

Margery's fingers stilled over the keyboard, a smirk on her face, as she repeated, "Writing extravaganza?"

"The woman I'm trying to find said she worked in a bookstore that was…and I'm quoting here, a bookstore, coffee shop, and writing extravaganza. Unquote," he added.

"Well, I'll be damned," Margery breathed, her eyes pinned on the monitor. "I swear if you'd entered all that into a Google search, I think you'd have come up with the same thing I just did with my fancy, investigative program." Laughing, she said, "I've got a hit on a bookstore in the city that bills itself as a place for writers to call home. Hmmm, let's see. The business is a licensed bookstore and coffee shop, but also advertises that it has designated spaces for a small monthly fee for authors to have their own writing nook and they also offer writing groups. Bayley's Books and Nooks." She twisted her head around to look at Nick again. "Does that sound like what you're looking for?"

Dubious, Nick said, "Who works there? Can we see that?"

Shaking her head, Margery stood up from the seat. "That, my dear, you can find out on your own."

Nick sat back down and searched, quickly finding the website for Bayley's Books and Nooks. The screen filled with a picture of an older building, a green awning over the front door.

Looking for your favorite books? Look no further. Bayley's Books and Nooks has a wide variety of books of all genres.

Moms and dads - need a break while you search

for your own books? We feature a children's room with a weekly story time.

Authors – would you like a quiet nook to write, always available to you, with multiple writing programs, critique groups, research facilities? Monthly rentals on writing nooks available.

Whatever your reading or writing needs are, Bayley's Books and Nooks is here to serve you! Come by, check us out, have a cup of coffee, and stay for a while.

After reading the blurb, he clicked to the pictures showing the inside of the store and viewed a warm, inviting space that appeared to be just as it advertised. And in one picture, an older lady sat at a desk with her laptop open, a woman standing over her shoulder. The woman was blonde. Smiling. Beautiful. *Bingo —found her!*

With an uncommon jaunt in his step, Nick hustled out of his office building with the directions in his hands...and a just as uncommon smile on his face.

"What's the best way to poison someone?"

Bayley smiled at the young man sitting in one of her writing nooks, his fingers no longer typing on his laptop. "You can always do a simple search, but isn't your book set in the old west in the 1800's?" Obtaining his nod, she motioned him to follow her as she led him to a stack of research books she kept on hand for authors. "Here are a couple of old medical books, a few of them from the early 1900's, which will give you an authentic feel for the times."

His eyes wide, he dove into the bookshelf, his attention now diverted to his research.

"Bayley?" Daphne called out, as she walked into the back room where the nooks were located. "You've got a visitor out front." Leaning in, with a twinkle in her eyes, she whispered, "And he's also a TDMB. Damn, girl, I need to hang out with you more often if you keep meeting these guys!"

Tossing Daphne a curious glance, Bayley walked toward the front of the store, spying a tall man standing with his back to her. "Hello, I'm Bayley. May I help you?" As the man turned around, she gasped, "You?"

Nick's gaze landed on the woman—Bayley—from last night and, for a second, his professionalism slipped, and he gawked. He thought she was beautiful when seen in the garish neon lights, but seeing her standing in the bright sunlight streaming through the front window, he found it hard to breathe.

Golden-blonde hair framed her face like a halo. Flawless skin with a hint of makeup. Rosy cheeks, matching her lips. An unadorned green sweater paired with navy slacks and on her feet, little flat shoes that reminded him of what a ballerina might wear. But it was her eyes. Just as large as last night. But even more bright. Even more blue. And then there was her smile. It was the last that sent electric shocks through him.

Swallowing, he shook his head wondering what the

hell was wrong with him. Holding his badge in one hand for her perusal, he stuck out his other hand, saying, "Nick. Agent Nick Stone, ma'am. And yes, we did meet last night. I was wondering if there was somewhere we could talk."

Taking his hand in her much smaller one, her eyes widened. "I knew it! I just knew you were after someone last night! You were there, all business-like, and you had your eyes pinned on the crowd, scouting everyone out." Suddenly, she reared back, sucking in a quick breath. "Oh…is this about the missing girl?"

He let go of her hand, but missed her touch as soon as he pulled back. Clearing his throat, he asked, "Please, ma'am, can we speak privately?"

"Absolutely. We can use my office." Leading him toward the back of the store, she began to ascend an L-shaped staircase leading to a loft. She opened the door and entered, ushering him to one of the leather-padded chairs.

He glanced at the space, impressed with her office and her style. The floor gleamed with the waxed, original, wooden planks. Two of the walls were lined with wooden bookshelves flanking a large, wooden desk. Tall windows filled one wall, allowing in natural light giving the office a warm glow. The fourth wall was made of windows overlooking the bookstore below. "These windows are interesting," he commented, walking over and looking down at the bustling store.

"Aren't they great?" she enthused, standing next to him. The shop owner before me wanted a way to keep an eye on his employees without them knowing about it. So, he had this window put in that provides a way to look out, but the picture on the other side looks like a wooden panel. It matches the wooden interior of the store so no one knows it isn't really wall, but whoever is up here can look down." She stepped over next to him and smiled. " 'It is clear that the books owned the shop rather than the other way about. Everywhere they had run wild and taken possession of their habitat, breeding and multiplying, and clearly lacking any strong hand to keep them down.'" Seeing his blank expression, she laughed. "That's from Agatha Christie's book, *The Clocks*. Isn't it a great quote? I love to think of my bookstore as the books owning the shop instead of me. But alas, I'm the one who has to pay the bills."

He turned, his gaze landing on her as she pointed to a chair. "I admit when I came here, I didn't realize you were the Bayley of Bayley's Books and Nooks."

Leaning her head to the side, she perused him, deciding he was much more handsome than she originally thought. *He could be a TDMS-B—tall, dark, mysterious, super-beautiful!* Blinking, she realized he had spoken to her. "I'm so sorry. Can you repeat that, please?"

"I was just saying that I didn't realize you were the owner. Your shop seems very nice."

Beaming, she nodded. "Thank you. I truly think it's my life-blood! But how did you find me? And why? I'm assuming you must have some secret spy software that can pluck an image from the sky and it totally gives off someone's name. Of course, that seems like such an invasion of privacy, but then I guess you have to employ all kinds of super-duper ways to investigate."

Blinking, as he attempted to follow her running dialog, he said, "As to the how, I remembered you described working in 'a bookstore, coffee shop, and writing extravaganza.' There were a ton of bookstore coffee shops, but when I put in writing, this place popped up."

"I'm in your secret spyware?" She clapped her hands at the thought, then sobered with his explanation.

"Uh…no. You actually came up on a Google search."

"Oh," her face fell for a second before she smiled again. "Well, that's not nearly as exciting, is it? But, then, it's nice to know the Google analytics are working for my business!"

"As to the why for my visit, I was hoping you could help me."

"Of course. What can I do?"

"I was, in fact, at the club last night on a case, but," he held up his hands to still her verbal barrage until he could get his request out, "not on the kidnapping case. It just happened that was where it occurred. Therefore, I and my co-agents, were not focused on anything other than our suspects. But you took a lot of pictures…uh… random pictures and I thought you might have caught something without realizing it."

Eyes wide, Bayley said, "Brilliant! Here, let's look." She opened the bottom right drawer of her desk and pulled out her large purse. Seeing his lifted brow, she laughed. "You must not have a sister…or a girlfriend… or a wife. We take little bags out when we party or go to bars, but for our daily lives? Bigger is better."

Rummaging around in her purse, she began to pull out an assortment of items, placing them on her desk.

Keys. Ponytail elastics along with a large hair clip. Fat wallet with several coins spilling from the half-zippered compartment. Looking up, she said, "Coins are so silly, aren't they? I mean, we hardly use them anymore." Her head back down, she continued to pull out items. IPad. Cosmetic bag. Sunglasses. Measuring tape. Gun.

"What the hell? Do you have a—"

"Stop right there, Mister. Don't patronize me. I have a permit and, I might add, I'm an excellent shot." Seeing him snap his mouth closed, she continued to dig. Her fingers landed on her phone and she pulled it out, unnecessarily declaring, "Found it!"

Nick felt the corners of his mouth curving up as he viewed her unadulterated pleasure at holding her phone. "May I look at the pictures from last night?"

"Sure," she easily complied. Opening the photo-gallery app, she handed the phone to him.

As he began to scroll through the pictures slowly, his gaze scanned the scenes she captured, carefully looking for any images of Amy Willis. "How many pictures did you take last night?"

"Almost forty," she replied, right into his ear, as she leaned around his arm to peer at the photographs as well.

"Jesus!" he jumped. "I didn't hear you move."

Her soft giggle caused his dick to jump and his lips tightened in irritation. Hating to lose control, he tried to focus back on the pictures. The phone was too small to be able to clearly see the individuals in the background but he knew Margery would be able to analyze the images. Looking up, he said, "I really need to take these back to my office...to have them isolated and enlarged for our investigation. He readied himself for her anger at having her phone confiscated for a few hours.

Nodding, she smiled as her blue eyes lit. "No problem."

Shocked, he pulled his head back a little. "Uh...thank you. I can have it back to you tomorrow." Reaching into his pocket, he pulled out a business card. Starting to hand it to her, he hesitated, wondering if he should include his personal cell number. Giving himself a mental shake, he held out the card. "Here's my card. You can call me if you need anything or think of anything else."

Her fingers reached out, taking the card while brushing against his at the same time. Warmth spread up her arm and she smiled. "Thank you. Um...does that mean I get to see you tomorrow? I mean, I'd hate for you to make an extra trip, but I'd love to see you again. If you'd like to—"

"Yes," he interrupted. Smiling down at her, he added, "We can meet tomorrow and I can return your phone to you." He turned and moved out the door, hearing her footsteps lightly on the stairs behind him. At the front door of the store, he nodded his goodbyes and stepped out onto the sidewalk. Pursing his lips as he climbed into his vehicle, he sat for a moment before he began to smile at the thought of seeing her again.

5

"**D**amn, girl, it's the day for a man alert in here!"

Bayley looked up as Daphne ran a hand over her hair, smoothing back the wayward strands, before greeting the new visitor with a brilliant smile.

"Can I get you something? Coffee? A latte? A good book suggestion? My phone number?" Daphne called out.

The dark-haired man stopped in his tracks, his eyes widening as he looked at the two women behind the counter. "Um..."

Laughing, Bayley said, "Don't mind my assistant. She gets overly eager when a new customer comes into the shop."

His white-toothed smile met hers as he approached the coffee counter. "Thank you for the warning." Glancing over to Daphne, he said, "I'll take a cup of coffee...black, if you please."

"Sure thing. Coming right up."

Smiling at the new customer, Bayley turned to

Daphne saying, "I've got plans this afternoon so I'll see you tomorrow." Throwing her bag over her shoulder, she stepped past the man and walked out the front door.

Daphne fiddled for a moment in hopes the handsome man would spend a few minutes in the store with her, perhaps giving her enough time to engage his interest, but then she frowned slightly as she watched his eyes follow Bayley. As he turned back to her, it was apparent by the drawn-down brows, he was interested in Bayley. Offering him her best smile, she handed him the coffee cup. His gaze landing back on Daphne, she preened as his lips curved ever so slightly.

"I'm Daphne," she said. "And you are?"

"Lazlo," he offered, an unexpectedly sensuous smile in place.

"Yep, he took my phone!"

"Will he give it back soon?"

Bayley smiled at her sister-in-law, Grace, sitting comfortably on the sofa, nursing Bayley's nephew. "Actually, I'll see him again tomorrow. He said he'd bring it by the store."

"So, he was good-looking?" Grace asked, wiggling her eyebrows at Bayley.

Laughing, she said, "I nicknamed him Mr. TDMB for tall, dark, mysterious, and beautiful. Silly, I know, but I honestly think that doesn't do him justice! Today, in the bright sunlight, he was positively breathtaking!"

"So, he's looking for pictures of the missing girl. Tell

me again why you were at that place? What if it had been you?"

"I was doing research and needed to get a real feel for describing a low-class nightclub. One of my main characters needs the money, so she gets a job as a bartender." Shrugging, Bayley said, "I wanted to go, hang out at the bar, and take a bunch of random pictures." Seeing Grace about to protest, she quickly added, "And I kept my drink with me and didn't leave the bar. No one could ruffie me."

"I wish you'd called Blaise. You know your brother would have taken you to the club and made sure you were safe."

Rolling her eyes, Bayley protested, "I couldn't ask Blaise. You guys have a baby, and I know you still don't get tons of sleep!"

Readjusting her bundle, Grace retorted, "Well if Blaise couldn't do it, you know any one of the Saints would have accompanied you."

"Oh, my God. That's just what I need—a big babysitter who would scare everyone away and blush at the thought of my *research*," Bayley grinned.

"Well, I thinks it's cool that you're a writer and I love your books."

Sighing, Bayley added, "I hate that romance books sometimes get such a bad rep. I love the stories I create."

"You know, I'm not the only person who reads your books. Almost every woman I know loves them, too."

"Really?" Bayley grinned.

"Absolutely!"

Grace placed little Ben on her shoulder, adjusting

her shirt. Rubbing his back, patting lightly, he let out a burb, eliciting a giggle from Bayley. Wiggling her fingers, Bayley said, "Can I hold my nephew?"

"Of course," Grace replied. "In fact, I was just going to lay him down so I can nuke some dinner before Blaise comes home. Will you stay and eat with us?"

Bayley held the precious baby bundle close to her heart and cooed. "Auntie Bayley wishes she could stay with you, little Ben." Kissing the soft fuzz on his head, she lifted her eyes over to Grace. "Thanks for the invite, but I've got a writers' group tonight at the store." Following her sister-in-law into the kitchen, she sat at the table, still cuddling Ben as Grace took a casserole from the freezer and stuck it in the microwave to thaw.

Grace laughed, saying, "Right now, this is the best I can do for dinner. But the other Saints' women all brought food over. Thank goodness they spread out the meals so that I didn't have to fill up the freezer all at once. Plus, your mom brought over some food."

"Well, good! New moms shouldn't have to worry about cooking right away. Or housecleaning!"

"Oh, that reminds me! I forgot to tell Blaise that you gifted us several months of a cleaning service. He got caught the other day when he walked downstairs in his underwear and surprised two women cleaning."

Bayley hooted loudly, then was immediately contrite as Ben jumped at the noise and scrunched his face up. Cooing, she jiggled him as she laughed as quietly as possible. Looking at Grace, she asked, "Do you remember when Mom and I came by, not knowing you were here with Blaise? You had that kitten in your arms that scratched you as it tried to get away and you fell backwards over his dog? That was so funny!"

Grace, unable to keep from laughing, shook her head. "I couldn't believe that was my introduction to Blaise's family!"

As if on cue the door from the garage opened and Blaise walked in. Tall, Nordic, he could have walked off the pages of a Viking romance. He smiled as Grace bounded over to offer him a kiss, then, as she moved back to the oven to check on the bread, he bent to place a soft kiss on his son's head. Lifting his gaze, he greeted quietly, "Hey, sis."

Bayley looked fondly at her big brother and whispered, "Go get in some comfortable clothes and then I'll give Ben to you."

He was only gone a few minutes before striding back into the room clothed in a sweat shirt, sweat pants, and a burp cloth over his shoulder. "I'm ready," he proclaimed.

Transferring the sleeping baby to him, Bayley kissed his cheek. "I've got to go to my writer's group, but I had some excitement last night and today. I'll let Grace fill you in."

With a hug to Grace, she bounded out the front door, hustling to Prissy, knowing she would just make it to her shop in time to meet the others in her writing group.

Nick sat in the chair next to Mike and Margery, closely studying the photographs on the computer screen from Bayley's phone. Shot after shot clearly showed the inside of the club.

"Hell, she's good at this," Mike admired, his eyes pinned to the screen. "You said it looks like she's taking selfies, but instead of herself, she manages to capture what's behind her."

Nick grunted his agreement, his gaze searching for some evidence of Amy Willis. "There," he pointed, seeing a woman with short, red hair near the bar.

Margery zoomed in using her photo-enhancement program, making it easier to identify the woman in question. "Yes, that's her. You can tell by the light-blue shirt."

"Time?" Nick queried.

With a few clicks, she replied, "This was at about eleven thirty."

Mike commented, "No one else is around her, but she's buying more than one drink."

Nick looked at the bar in front of Amy, observing two drinks. "So, she's buying them for one of her friends or she's met someone new."

"If it was a man, wouldn't he be buying the drinks?" Margery asked.

"Not in this day and age," Mike said, gaining a quizzical expression from her. "Could be she wants to be in control and is keeping an eye on her drink, instead of giving someone the opportunity to drug it."

"Never thought of that," she said, shaking her head. "It's been many years since I was in the single scene and that was back in college about thirty years ago. Lots of changes..."

As Mike and Margery continued to talk, Nick focused his attention on the stream of photographs. He saw Amy in two other pictures. On the dance floor with a dark-haired man behind her, but he was facing away from the camera, and one with her head leaning on the same man's shoulder who was, once again, facing away from the camera. Pointing, he said, "Get what you can on this guy. Amy is about five feet, seven inches, so this guy isn't over six feet."

"What if she were wearing heels?" Margery asked.

Shaking his head, Nick cursed. Standing with his hands on his hips, he ordered, "Go back to the picture of her at the bar."

Margery complied and once more, Nick studied the photograph, slowly nodding. "Bar's about 4 feet tall. Compared to where the bar is coming against her front, I'd say she had only about three inch heels on. So, that still makes that guy just about six feet tall."

"Impressive," Mike whistled as he sat down at his computer and began typing. "I'll see if I can pull up anything on him entering the club, but with that dark jacket, I don't know if I'll recognize him."

A frustrating hour later, the three leaned back in defeat. "Well, we know she was still alive at almost midnight," Mike surmised, "but we don't know the identity of the man she was with."

Replacing Bayley's phone in his pocket, Nick added, "I'll get Ms. Hanssen's phone back to her tomorrow. I'll also point out what we've looked at to see if she has any more information." Walking out of the room, the frustration of not obtaining a definitive facial recognition of the man in question was mixed with the eager anticipation of seeing Bayley again.

Seeing the small smile cross Nick's face as he left, Margery grinned before turning back to the bank of computers.

"You might want to consider adding in a little more blood and gore."

Bayley continued to read the paragraph in front of her as she engaged her critique group. The four other writers sat at the round table, each reading and critiquing as well. The manuscript she was studying was for a new author writing in the horror and suspense genre. Bruce had excellent characters and his writing was very professional, but she felt as though he was holding back.

Looking up at the young man, his dark eyes intently staring at her from behind his wire-rimmed glasses, she smiled. "Are you nervous?"

Chuckling, he replied, "Yeah, I guess I am. I really want to get the first chapter right so that it will be ready for sending to an agent."

Nodding, she smiled. "Well, for what it's worth, I really like it. And, if you can't get a publisher or decide you don't want to go traditional, then I'll help you self-publish."

Pushing his dark blond hair from his face, he smiled warmly. "I appreciate your help, Bayley—"

"Hey," she interrupted, holding up her hand, "we all have to start somewhere. Glancing to the clock on the wall, she announced to the group, "I didn't realize the time—we need to finish up."

The others stood as they packed up their laptops, slinging bags over their shoulders, and with goodbyes ringing out as they left, Bayley locked the front door behind them. Quickly checking the store to make sure it was ready for opening the next day, she set the alarm and stepped onto the sidewalk, jiggling the door handle, ascertaining it was properly locked.

Turing toward Prissy, she heard heavy footsteps coming rapidly from behind. Whirling around, she startled when a dark-cloaked figure approached, leaning over her. Stepping back, a gasp slipped from her lips as his hand snatched out to grab her upper arm. Wincing, she jerked back, her eyes narrowed in anger.

"Let go of me," she bit out, but his grasp only tightened. Heart racing, she glanced around, desperate for a passerby to assist, but only the dark night illuminated sporadically by streetlights greeted her. Cars honked in the distance, but none came down the street. The bookstore was located in an older section of the town, not near the center where trendy restaurants and bars had moved in. Instead, her business neighbors consisted of an insurance company, an attorney and accountant offices, and a bank. All steady businesses that she figured helped her customer base, but none opened at night.

Shifting her gaze back to his impassive face, her mind categorized his features. Small eyes, close set. Dark, with a hint of amber from the streetlight over Prissy. Leathery skin with large pores, as though years of smoking had sucked all the oxygen from his body. His nostrils enlarged and the scent of old cigarettes assaulted her senses. His hair was hidden behind a fedora, but what she could see was greasy or slicked with an old-fashioned gel. He was much taller than her, but his body was thin, wiry, angular.

"Where is it?" he growled, his husky voice cutting through her analysis.

Blinking, she narrowed her eyes. "What? Where is what?" Shaking her head slightly in confusion, she added, "I think you have the wrong person, whatever you're looking for."

His thin lips slid into a grin, showing yellowed teeth, as his gaze slid over her face. "I got the right one, and you'd do well to give me what I want."

Jerking back on her arm once more, she repeated, "What? I don't know what you want!"

His gaze dropped down to her purse and he held up his free hand. "Your phone, princess. Give me your fuckin' phone."

Her eyes widened as her mouth opened, but her words halted as his fingers squeezed harder. Wincing, she protested, "You're hurting me! And I don't have my phone anyway!"

"Well, you'd better get it quick or—"

Approaching footsteps, sounding on the sidewalk from around the corner, halted his threat. With a quick look over his shoulder, he dropped her arm and ran into the darkness just as Bruce rounded the building, his frown widening into a smile as he saw her.

"Bayley! Thank goodness you're still here. I can't find my car keys and think they must have fallen out of my pocket."

As he approached her, his steps slowed, his brow knitted. "Hey, are you okay?" he asked as his gaze moved to the shadows of the street where she was staring.

She turned, dragging in a shaky breath. "Yes, I'm fine, but thank God you came back. A man just accosted me but he ran away when he heard you approach."

"Fuck, Bayley," he gasped, reaching his hand out to her shoulder. "Are you alright? Should we call the police?"

Still in shock, Bayley did not reply, but she instinctively knew the assailant was tied into the same case as Nick. He had to be, asking for her phone like that. It couldn't just be coincidence. Looking up sharply, she shook her head. "No, no. Not the police. But don't worry," she assured as he was about to protest, "I've got a contact that will be interested."

"Oh yeah, your brother."

Bayley simply nodded as she moved to the front door of her shop again, giving him the indication that Blaise was who she intended to talk to. Inwardly cringing at the thought of telling her overly-protective brother, she swung the door open, after a few failed attempts with the keys due to shaking hands, and urged Bruce to enter quickly. Locking the door behind her, in case the man returned, they searched the back room for a moment before Bruce headed to the men's room, coming out with his keys proudly in his hand.

"Sorry for the trouble," he said, "but I'm glad I had to come back."

Sucking in a deep breath, Bayley agreed as they headed back outside. Scanning the area quickly, Bruce walked her to Prissy and stayed until she was safely locked inside her car. She insisted on following him to his car and they pulled out onto the street at the same time.

Neither saw the tall man as he stepped from around the side of the building, his eyes pinned on her retreating automobile, face lit by the red glow from his cigarette.

6

The card felt firm between her fingertips, as though the personality of the name printed on one side could offer comfort.

Nicholas Stone

His agent title, phone number, email address, and the FBI logo made up the rest of the simple print.

Sitting in her living room, she noticed her fingers still shook slightly, as they held the card. She had rushed from her car, up the stairs to her apartment, unlocking the door with speed as she sent furtive glances over her shoulder.

Now, pinching her lips together, she looked at the old telephone hanging next to her kitchen counter. It had originally belonged to her beloved grandmother and, when she died, Bayley could not part with the outdated phone. Her family thought she was nuts to pay for a land-line when she had a cell phone, but to Bayley it represented a different way of life. The long, spiral cord, twisted out of shape from years of her grandmother's walking around her kitchen while talking to one of her church friends or neighbors, still hung from the wall. Now, she was glad she had the extra way to communicate.

Sucking in a fortifying breath, she pressed the buttons on the old phone, dialing Nick's work number. Hearing his official voice message, she recorded, "Nick —uh, Agent Stone. This is Bayley Hanssen. I had someone, well, a man who I didn't know, come up to me tonight. Come up and grab me. I was outside my store and he approached. He kinda rushed over before I had a chance to react and grabbed my arms. He kept demanding my phone and wasn't too happy that I didn't have it. Um...I thought you'd want to know since it probably has to do with your investigation. Um...I guess you can call me back and I'll be at work tomorrow." She rattled off her home number before quickly adding, "Um, goodbye."

Feeling foolish, she shook her head as she placed the handset back in its cradle. Her fingertips rubbed her forehead in a feeble attempt to still the burgeoning headache. Leaning back against the sofa cushions, she kicked her shoes off as she lifted her feet to the scuffed coffee table, a deep sigh leaving her lips as a tendril of hair escaped her ponytail.

Now that the shock was wearing off and the adrenaline rush had passed, she rolled the event over in her mind. Not wanting to forget any details, she opened her laptop and settled into a stool at her counter. Clicking onto her notes page, she began typing what she could remember. The man's height, features, voice. Closing her eyes, she wondered if she would be able to pick him out of a lineup. Solidifying the image into her mind, she reviewed what she had written. Blowing out a deep breath that puffed her hair away from her forehead, she hoped it would be enough for Nick to use.

As she slid off the stool, she eyed the open blinds on her third-floor window. Never one to worry about someone peeking in, she felt a rush of chills over her body. Nervous, she approached the window cautiously, sliding to the side to hide from sight if anyone should happen to be in the street below. Grasping the pull-cord in her hand, she jerked the blinds down, cutting off all views into her apartment. As her eyes moved back to her front door, she threw up a thankful prayer that even though she was shaken when she entered, she had locked and bolted the door.

After she finished in the bathroom, she lay in bed, her tumultuous thoughts running, with Nick Stone still firmly in the mix. Heat infused her cheeks as she remembered BOB doing the work last night as her thoughts ran rampant with the image of the enigmatic FBI agent. *And tonight?* She rolled over and punched her pillow as thoughts of her assailant interrupted any thoughts of Nick.

Flopping to her back, Bayley began clearing her mind using the technique her grandmother taught her as a child. Imagining her brain as a tub, overfilled with thoughts, she pulled the imaginary plug and allowed the thoughts to run out. Her eyes grew heavy as her concerns slipped away and soon sleep overtook her.

Plopping heavily into the seat behind his desk, Nick watched his coffee slosh to the edge of his cup, thankfully not splashing over. His papers and files were neatly stacked from the evening before and he placed his cup squarely next to his laptop. Firing up his computer, he pressed the button on his phone to listen to his messages as he waited for his computer to come to life. Lifting the steaming cup to his lips, he startled at the voice.

"Nick—uh, Agent Stone. This is Bayley Hanssen. I had someone, well a man who I didn't know, come up to me tonight. Come up and grab me—"

Jerking as Bayley's message sank in, the hot coffee hit his chin. "Shit!" he cursed, grabbing a tissue from his desk, dabbing at both his face and the desk as he placed the cup back on the desk.

"—Um, goodbye."

Hitting the playback, he listened carefully again, inwardly cursing this time. "Mike!" he barked, seeing the young agent just sitting down to his desk.

"Yeah?"

"Get me the home address of Bayley Hanssen. Now."

Eyes wide, Mike asked, "The bookstore owner?" His fingers were already flying over his keyboard, as though anticipating Nick's response. "What's up?"

"She left a message—said she was approached and a man grabbed her last night wanting her cell phone."

"Damn," Mike cursed before pointing to the printer. "It's coming off now."

Snagging the address off the printer as he grabbed his jacket, he made sure he had her cell phone in his pocket before hustling out of the building. "Call Harlan and tell him I'm going to her house. I'll check in as soon as I know anything."

Calling the phone number she left as her land-line, he growled as it went to an answering machine. "Bayley, it's Nick...uh, Agent Stone. I'm on my way. Don't leave the house and don't let anyone in."

Rattled, he cursed the traffic as he made his way across town. Hitting every red light, the underarms of his shirt were wet by the time he finally pulled into a parking space in front of her building. Jogging up the three flights of stairs, he rounded the corner and pounded on her door. When she did not answer, he looked at his watch. Only seven-thirty. *Where can she be?* Pounding on the door once more, he ran his hand through his hair, causing the ends to stand up.

Considering breaking down her door, his breath left him in a rush as he heard someone fiddling with the locks from the inside. Suddenly the door was thrown open and his gaze landed on her dripping wet form, water droplets sliding down her legs and pooling onto the floor. A short robe was haphazardly tied around her waist and her hair was wrapped in a towel, still allowing more water droplets to drip into her face. Blinking her blue eyes, she looked at him in surprise.

"Wow, Agent Stone, I didn't expect you so early. What time do you get into your office?"

"I came as soon as I got the message," he said, forcing his eyes to stay on hers, fighting the desire to allow his gaze to roam down her body, sure to be naked underneath the robe. "Are you all right?"

Smiling, she stepped back, motioning for him to come in. "I'm fine, but admit I was scared last night."

"Did he hurt you?"

Shaking her head slightly, she replied, "No, not really—"

"What do you mean? You said he grabbed your arms." Nick knew he was losing objectivity, so he fisted his hands to keep from reaching out to hold her. To make sure she was not injured.

"My upper arms are bruised," Bayley admitted, "but honestly, I bruise easily. Sometimes I just run into a table and will end up with a big, ol' bruise the next day." Holding the front of her robe closed to maintain modesty, she slipped one sleeve down, exposing her shoulder and upper arm, covered in faint, blue bruises matching finger marks.

Nick stepped closer, the lemony scent wafting off her sending his senses reeling, as his gaze dropped to the bruised skin. Reaching up, he touched her gently, his finger barely tracing the bruise.

"Bayley, I'm so sorry—"

"What the hell?" a man yelled from the doorway.

Nick's hand jerked away from Bayley as she twisted quickly, her feet slipping on the wet floor. Her arm swung out to keep her balance as Nick grabbed her around her waist, pulling her tightly to his body as her robe slid open exposing the tops of her creamy breasts.

"Blaise?" Bayley and Nick said at the same time, each looking at the tall, muscular blond stalking closer before jerking their gazes back to each other in surprise.

"Nick? Sis? What the hell is going on here?"

Nick, steadying Bayley's feet as she tried to pull the gaping edges of her robe tighter around her body, shot his gaze between her and his friend. Blaise was one of the Saints and he had worked with him on several cases. *Sis? He called her sis?*

"Nick? What the hell are you doing with my bruised sister, half-dressed in your arms?" Blaise growled.

"Blaise! How dare you come in here yelling!" Bayley argued.

Swinging his face toward Blaise, Nick said, "I had no idea she was your sister—"

"So that makes this all right?" Blaise glared, his eyes landing on Bayley's arms.

"This? No, this is not what it looks like," Nick began.

"You've got no say—" Bayley began.

Ignoring her protestations, Blaise stepped toward the couple, his anger palpable. Bayley inserted herself between the two, much-taller men, shouting, "Blaise! Look at me!"

Fists planted on his hips, Blaise dropped his glare down to his sister before lifting his eyes back up to Nick. "You want to tell me why I find you here, early in the morning, with my sister almost naked, bruises on her arm—"

"You seriously think I put those bruises there?" Nick bit back, his hands resting on Bayley's shoulders.

"Stop! Once and for all, shut up and listen to me!" Bayley shouted, chest heaving in frustration. Gaining

Blaise's attention, she pointed to the sofa. "Go sit down and I'll tell you what's going on. I've got to make a statement to Nick anyway, so you might as well hear it at the same time."

"Are you all right?" Blaise asked, his voice now flush with concern.

Throwing her hands to the side, she quipped, "Oh, now you're ready to find out what's going on instead of just making assumptions?" Looking over her shoulder at Nick, she said, "Go get some coffee while I run and throw some clothes on—I take mine with lots of cream and sweetener." With a last glance at Blaise, she added, "And you can just sit on the sofa and stew!"

7

No words…just glares.

Nick sat in the chair opposite the sofa, his coffee in his hands, still angry that Blaise would think the worst of him. Blaise sat on the sofa, his anger having morphed into an expression of confusion as he darted glances at Nick.

Bayley walked back into the room five minutes later, her hair still wet but combed away from her make-up free face, and wearing pink yoga pants paired with a slouchy sweatshirt, sporting a faded lion's face on the front. She halted suddenly as she observed the two men filling the room with their silent presence, before settling her gaze on Blaise. "Well, I see a few minutes of calm hasn't made you more agreeable!"

She turned toward the kitchen counter where a cup of creamy coffee sat waiting for her. Unable to stifle a grin at the way Nick prepared her coffee just the way she asked, she carefully carried the hot cup over to the coffee table and sat on the opposite end of the sofa.

Twisting her body so she faced the two men, she tucked one leg underneath her bum and took a sip of coffee. Closing her eyes, she purred as the sweet liquid slid over her tastebuds.

Nick's attention was focused on her lips as the sound of appreciation escaped, when a loud meow interrupted his scrutiny. His gaze dropped to Bayley's feet, where a cat circled her legs. Eyes wide, he stared at the creature, unused to being in close proximity to a cat.

"So...where shall we begin?" she quipped, drawing both men's attention to her. Looking at Blaise, she continued, "Shall I start with how I just met Nick the other evening? Or maybe how I've now become involved as a possible witness to a kidnapping?" She threw her hand up as Blaise startled at her words. "Oh, no buddy, you just listen right now."

After another sip, she said, "Of course, I had no idea I was a witness to anything. After all, one doesn't walk around expecting a kidnapping...or a bank robbery, for that matter. These things just occur and if you happen to be in the vicinity, well then, there you are." Shrugging slightly as she took another sip of coffee, she added, "And in this case, I had no idea about any of that going on until Nick came into the store looking for me." Her gaze landed back on Blaise as she said, "We had met the night before at the club, but only casually. I interrupted him as he was on a stakeout and I was there doing research for another book."

Blaise's narrowed eyes widened with each word from Bayley's mouth. "Kidnapping? What the hell,

Bayley?" Turning toward Nick, he said, "Please make some sense out of all of this."

Nick growled, "You done with thinking I'm here debauching your sister—"

"Debauching? Oh, my God, Nick, that's hilarious!" Bayley hooted, drawing dark looks from both men. "No one says debauching anymore, but I love that word. I must work it into the book I'm writing." She leaned over and grabbed a pad of paper lying on the coffee table and began to scribble.

"You know what I mean," Nick argued, his gaze piercing Blaise.

Throwing his hands up in front of him, Blaise admitted, "I'm sorry, Nick. I know what kind of man you are, but hell, I walk up to my sister's apartment to find you and her all tangled up together and her half-naked—"

"Earlier you said 'half-dressed,'" Bayley complained. "So, which is it? Half-naked or half-dressed? I, personally, think they have two very different connotations. But then, I can see where you wouldn't make that distinction."

Nick leaned back against the chair, his breath leaving him in a rush. His only consolation was seeing the same exasperated expression on Blaise's face. Calm, quiet, intuitive Blaise. *How the hell can they be related?* Shifting his eyes between the Nordic blondes in front of him, he admitted, so alike in appearance, it was easy to see the familial resemblance.

"Sis, I love you, but if you don't sit there and keep

quiet just long enough for Nick to tell me what the hell is going on, I'll tape your mouth shut!"

At that, Bayley blinked, pursing her lips together tightly. Huffing, she leaned back, cradling her cup of coffee mumbling, "This is my house, you know."

Blaise turned his attention back to Nick and, with raised eyebrows, quietly waited for him to speak.

Nodding, Nick explained, "I met your sister at a club where I was on stakeout for another assignment. She was taking a lot of pictures for her book research. The next day, I was re-assigned to the kidnapping case, which I'm sure you've heard of, and realized Bayley may have inadvertently taken pictures we would need to see. I found her and she voluntarily gave me her phone for a day."

The room was silent for a moment and she realized both men were staring at her. Lifting her shoulders while giving a little sniff, she said, "Well, that's fine if you just want the bare-bones story, with no embell-ishments."

"Bare-bones is good by me," Blaise groused, still looking at Nick. "So, this morning?"

"Bayley left a message on my work phone last night and I just heard it this morning. She was accosted as she left the store—"

At the word *accosted*, Blaise leaned forward, his brow drawn down, and asked, "Bayley? Why the hell didn't you call me? Fuckin' hell, sis! What's wrong with you?"

"Wrong with me?" she repeated, meeting her broth-er's glare with one of her own. "There is nothing wrong with me! I came home quickly, locked the door, and called Nick. I was safe here. And there was no way I was going to call you, considering you and your wife have a new baby!"

Standing suddenly, Blaise said, "That's it. Pack a bag. You're coming home with me."

Hopping to her feet, she planted her hands on her hip. "I most certainly am not going home with you! I have a life to live, a business to run, and you, brother dearest, have a family that does not need to be dragged into this. It was scary last night, I'll admit it. But today it doesn't feel like that big of a deal."

"It doesn't feel like that big of a deal?" he asked incredulously. Taking a deep breath, he looked her straight in the eyes. "Okay. I'll make you deal. I'll go to Jack and the Saints will provide your protection—"

"Nope, nope, nope," she argued, "I'm not staying with any of them either."

Nick lifted his hand, rubbing the back of his neck as he listened to the two siblings argue back and forth. Speaking before he had time to talk himself out of his offer, he proposed, "Let's compromise." Gaining the attention of Bayley and Blaise, he said, "I need to interview Bayley and you need to stay for it, Blaise. Then I'll take Bayley to the office with me, because I need her to see if we can identify the man from last night. Blaise, you talk to Jack and arrange to have a Saint be with her when she is not with me."

Bayley's lips curved slightly at the thought of spending more time with Nick and, for all her bravado, she had to admit the idea that the Saints were keeping an eye on her and her shop was comforting. Nodding, she agreed, "I can live with that."

Blaise nodded as well. "Okay. Let's hear about last night and then I'll call Jack."

"Well, my, my," she cooed as they sat back down. "All friends again?" Looking at Nick, she said, "To explain about last night, I had my writers' group. It's a group of published and aspiring writers who meet at the shop and we critique each other's work as well as spend time writing." Pushing her drying hair back from her face, she continued, "We finished about nine o'clock. I locked up after them and spent a few minutes making sure the area was clean for business opening the next day...uh, well now I guess it's already today. I stepped out onto the sidewalk and locked the door from the outside." Cutting her eyes toward Blaise, she added, "And I checked to make sure the door was locked, just like you are always telling me. Then I was walking to Prissy, which was parked underneath a streetlight as always."

Seeing the men still staring intently, she said, "I heard footsteps approaching quickly and turned. A man got right up into my space and grabbed my arms, demanding I give 'it' to him. Not knowing what 'it' was supposed to be, I asked. That, apparently, did not make him very happy."

Nick took careful notes as his jaw ticked in anger.

"Jesus, Bayley," Blaise moaned.

Continuing, she said, "He was wearing a dark trench coat and a fedora over greasy, slicked-back hair, which I found to be completely unimaginative. You know, like he watched *The Godfather* movie, because he probably never read the book. I know I shouldn't make judgements, but he didn't look like he spends his downtime reading. Anyway, he looked like he watched the movie and dressed like the mafia-muscle that Michael Corleone had in the second movie. Only not as big... that guy was kinda thick, but the guy last night was leaner."

Nick's pen halted as he looked up. Over the years, he prided his perfect FBI interview face—non-expressive, almost blank, encouraging witnesses to talk while not indicating that he agreed or disagreed with them. At that moment, he realized the FBI face was gone, obliterated by Bayley's rambling descriptions. Looking at Blaise's face, he knew it his own mirrored as he observed the open mouth, wide-eyed expression.

"Do you have any idea how much danger you were in?" Blaise asked, his voice now soft with an undercurrent of fury.

Heaving a sigh, Bayley shook her head. "I'm not stupid, Blaise. Yes, I was scared. Terrified, not knowing what the man wanted or what he would do. Without a cell phone, I felt vulnerable, but thank God, the man ran away when one of my writing group members came back to get something he left inside the shop." She twisted her almost-dry hair into a sloppy bun and grabbed a pencil sitting on the coffee table, tucking it amongst the tendrils, holding them mostly in place. "I had Bruce check out the area and he walked me to my car. I made sure he got into his and we drove away at the same time. I watched in my rear-view mirror and was not followed. I locked my doors the instant I got inside the apartment and called Nick with grandma's old phone—which, I might add, you thought I was silly to keep and pay for a land-line."

Seeing Blaise about to protest once more, she leaned over, placing her hand gently on his leg. "I promise, I would have called you if I felt as though I was still in danger. But I felt safe, called Nick and knew he would get to me today." Grinning, she said, "I underestimated how quickly he would come, hence I was still in the shower. When you walked in, I had just opened the door, after seeing who it was, and was showing him the bruises on my arm. Period. End of story." She leaned back against the sofa cushions, a satisfied expression on her face as she sipped more of her coffee.

The silence that followed sounded unusual to Nick, considering that the loud voices ever since Blaise had appeared in her apartment had barely stopped. He looked back down at the notes he had taken, making sure to have her detailed description. "Anything else about the man last night? His voice?"

"Yes!" Bayley admitted, slapping her forehead with her palm. "He smelled like old cigarettes and his breath was soured from years of smoking and his teeth were stained and yellow. His voice was husky and low." Her nose scrunched as she thought and she added, "If it was not my imagination, I swear there was a Slavic accent."

Nodding, Nick jotted the last information down before scrubbing his hand over his face. Looking up, he grimaced as he said, "I'm so sorry this happened to you and because I had your phone, you were in more danger last night. I won't make an error like that again."

Reaching into his pocket, he pulled her phone out, but added his personal number before handing it to her. "It's charged and ready to go. I've added my office and personal numbers to your contacts. I did not delete any photos, but we have copies of them."

"Did you find anything?" she asked, leaning forward in anticipation.

Dragging his gaze from her blue eyes and partially opened, pink-tinged lips, he answered, "Yes, you had a few shots of Amy Willis. We do not have a definitive identity of anyone with her."

Leaning back sharply, the breath left her lungs in a whoosh.

"I'm calling Jack," Blaise said, standing as he pulled his phone from his pocket. "You want in on this?" he asked Nick.

"You know I can't right now," Nick said. "The Governor hasn't called for assistance from the Saints and I can't discuss this anymore with you than I already have."

"Got it, but I'm telling you the damn rules'll kill you," Blaise said, stepping into Bayley's kitchen.

Watching Blaise pace while talking on the phone as Bayley walked into the kitchen to pour another cup of coffee, Nick fought the urge to pull her into his arms to make sure she was safe. *The Bureau's rules are already hampering me. And in ways I never imagined.*

8

An hour later Bayley sat at a grey, metal, functional desk as an agent named Mike had her flip through picture after picture, in an effort to identify the man who accosted her last night. She had called Daphne to tell her that she would be late, but now the excitement of going to the local FBI building and working on the case had dwindled as the mind-numbing parade of thugs made her eyes cross and her nerves frazzle.

Nick leaned over and asked, "Can I get you another cup of coffee?"

She leaned back, stretching her aching neck as she looked up into his face. Snorting, she replied, "Nick, if I drink any more coffee I'll be running to the bathroom with an even greater frequency than I already am."

He had noticed she had excused herself twice already to go to the lady's room, but put it down to nerves. Without thinking, he placed his hands on her shoulders and kneaded the tight muscles. "I know this is boring, but keep at it for just a little while longer, if you can."

Smiling, she groaned as his fingers worked magic on her neck. "Oh, my God, that feels good. I could let you do that all night."

Nick's hands stilled at the sound of her groan, the blood rushing to his dick as thoughts of what he would like to do all night with her rushed through his mind. His eyes shot over to Mike, the smirk on the younger agent's face causing Nick to jerk his hands off her. Clearing his throat, he said, "Right...well, uh...keep at it and let me know if you find something. I've got to talk to Harlan."

Watching him leave, her gaze landed on several framed photographs on the wall behind Mike's head. Seeing Nick in one of them, she stood and walked over. It looked like a picture from a retirement party and she recognized Mike, Margery, and Nick.

Mike looked over and grinned. "It's hard to get a picture of Nick and he rarely goes out with anyone. That was taken last year when Harlan was leaving this office."

Looking at Nick standing next to the distinguished, military looking gentleman, she admired the image of the man holding her attention.

Down the hall, Nick stepped into his office, sitting down in his chair before picking up the phone, placing a call to Harlan.

"I hear you've got the woman in with Mike looking at photos. Any luck?"

"No. She's given us a good description though, so my gut tells me we may be dealing with either the Russian mafia or a subsidiary of them."

"Local family?"

"Maybe. I don't know of any specific Russian dealings in this area yet, but I know we might have individual families working on their own." Nick leaned back, his chair creaking with the strain. "I don't like the idea of them in our district, so we're going to focus on them."

"If they're working on their own, good chance they're tied in to a larger group somewhere else. My guess would be Norfolk, if it's the Russians. I'll pass this on to Richard and have him check with our offices in the Virginia Beach area. They may be transporting girls there to ship them out worldwide."

"Will their office share readily?"

Harlan snorted. "I'll see if I can get Richard to light a fire underneath them, but you know jurisdiction plays a part in all this. They'll want our information to see how it plays into their investigations."

Disconnecting, Nick sighed heavily, the burden of knowing what was happening in the area bearing down on him as well as the discontent of jurisdiction battles. *Everyone wants to be the fuckin' hero.*

"Hey," Bayley's melodic voice startled him out of his musing. He looked up, seeing her leaning against the doorframe to his office. She smiled and he returned it, feeling the burden lift slightly.

"I thought I'd let you know that I wasn't able to identify the person from the other night." Her smile drooped as she added, "I'm really sorry."

Standing, he stalked closer, fighting the desire to have her smile curve back. Instead, he stopped several feet from her, his hands fisted at his sides. "It's okay, Bayley. We may have to widen our search base. It's possible that he came in from somewhere else and is now working this area. Did you take a look at the artist's drawing?"

Nodding, she said, "Yeah, although the computer image he created just seems to be lacking something."

An idea formed and before Nick could dismiss it, he blurted, "Would you be willing to meet with someone else? Someone who has a knack for...uh...pulling out of a witness things that others can't seem to obtain?"

Her brows drew down as she questioned, "Sure? Another artist?"

"Yes. Just one who's unofficial." Motioning her to a seat, he said, "Let me talk to Blaise first."

"You don't need my brother's permission—"

"No, but I need his input." Sitting back down in his chair he dialed Blaise's number.

"Good grief! Look at this place!"

Nick, driving with Bayley in the passenger seat, continued up Jack's lane as they made their way through the security gate toward the Saint's compound.

As they came out of the woods along the driveway, an enormous log home stood against the backdrop of the Blue Ridge Mountains, a long porch gracing the front. Nick pulled up and parked next to a multitude of other vehicles.

"This is amazing. I want to take pictures but I have a feeling that Jack would never allow it! I knew about this place from Blaise but I've never been here." Bayley's head swung around as she looked out her window, to the front windshield, then to Nick's window. Twisting in her seat, she looked out the back window as well. "I love the mountains, don't you? Majestic...well, obviously, the Blue Ridge Mountains aren't as massive as the Rocky's or even the Smoky Mountains, but still...very impressive to live right at the base! To have this view every day...good grief, it must be fabulous."

Her babbling halted as Nick placed his hand on hers. "You ready to go in?" Before she could answer, Blaise stepped out onto the massive front porch, his hands on his hips as he stared at them. "Guess that's our cue, whether you're ready or not."

Giggling, Bayley squeezed his hand before hopping out of the vehicle. As she rounded the front, Nick stepped in her path. "When you're with me, wait until I can open the door for you," he ordered gently.

"Hmmm, I do seem to remember how gallant you are," she smiled. Looking at her brother, she recognized his impatience. "We'd better go before Blaise pops a button."

The pair walked up Jack's front steps, Nick and Blaise shaking hands after Blaise leaned down to place a kiss on his sister's forehead.

"Come on in, the group is here," Blaise invited.

Stepping inside the foyer, leading to the exposed beamed ceiling of the living room, Bayley's gaze landed on the two-story stone fireplace with floor to ceiling windows on another wall. "Holy moly, Blaise! Your boss has a gorgeous home." Seeing the others in the room stand, she threw her hands up in front of her, closed her eyes, and called out, "Wait! I've got to cement this in my brain!"

"Jesus, Sis," Blaise grumbled, but was quickly interrupted.

"No, no," she countered, opening her eyes. "With a structure like this, I need to memorize it so that later, when I need a creative way to describe a mountain cabin, I can recall the house that Jack built!" Laughing at her own joke, she appreciated the chuckles coming from the gathering. Opening her eyes, she swept her gaze at the men in the room. "And you all...I think I could write a book about each one of you." She watched a bearded man approach, his outward appearance resembling a logger, but his eyes showing the discerning intelligence of a man used to analyzing everyone in his path.

"Miss Hanssen, I'm Jack Bryant. Welcome to my home...and the Saints' compound."

"Mr. Bryant, please call me Bayley. It's nice to finally meet you. I know my brother has the utmost respect for you," and as her gaze swept the group of men and women, added, "and the rest of you, as well."

"Nick," Jack greeted, his hand extended in a shake. "Glad you brought her to us." Nodding toward Bayley, he said, "Come in and let me introduce you to the rest of us."

Bayley made her way around the room, introduced to Cam, Jude, Monty, Chad, Patrick, Luke, and Marc.

"Lordy, I'm in man-heaven!" Bayley cackled, drawing more laughs from the group.

"Bayley, I'm Charlotte, Luke's fiancé, but everyone calls me Charlie. I'm the lone woman Saint around here.'

She smiled at the pretty, dark-haired Charlie, before moving to the last Saint, a tall, muscular blond with his arm around a petite, dark-haired woman, she smiled as her eyes met the woman.

"Hello, I'm Faith and this is my husband, Bart. I understand I'll be working with you today."

Nodding, Bayley sobered as her gaze moved over the room full of her brother's co-workers and Nick's friends. A feeling of warmth spread over her, chasing away what remnants of nerves existed.

Nick watched as Bayley's smile slowly morphed into a determined expression, her lips thinning. Without thinking, he placed his hand on her arm, offering a squeeze. "You got this, Bayley. Just talk to Faith the way you did to Blaise and me." His gaze narrowed to her blue eyes twinkling up at him, missing the raised eyebrows of her brother and the knowing smiles from the others in the room.

Bayley sat on the floral cushion of the comfortable rattan chair in the sunroom at the back of Jack's house. She watched with fascination as Faith's pencil furiously scratched on the pad of paper she held in her delicate hands. Faith's hair was pulled back from her face with a white headband, keeping the tendrils from falling toward the page. She bit her lip as she concentrated on her creation.

Bayley fought the desire to lean over and see what Faith was producing, knowing that she was unable to write when someone leaned over her computer. Beginning to fidget, she shifted her weight several times.

Faith looked up, her eyebrows lifting from concentration to amusement. "Tired of sitting?"

"I'm so sorry," Bayley gushed. "I'm always a bit of a bouncy-sort."

"I think my child is going to be that way, also," Faith admitted. "He'll take after his father. Bart always has a lot of energy."

"Oh, I had no idea you had children. Do many of the Saints have kids?"

"Several," Faith admitted. "They're all either married or engaged, with kids or some on the way. The group has changed in the past couple of years."

"I remember wondering if Blaise would ever find someone," Bayley laughed. "He always liked animals more than people."

"Grace is a wonderful friend."

"And a wonderful sister-in-law," Bayley added. Sucking in her lips, she leaned forward slightly. "So, uh…can I see it now?"

"Yes, but remember what I told you when we first came out here. I...well, I not only listen to your description but I tune into your emotions...fright, anger. I can...see all of that when you speak and use it to create a picture of who you saw."

"You have a gift, don't you?" Bayley said, her voice now soft with awe.

Nodding slowly, Faith confirmed, "Yes, although not everyone believes."

"Oh, I believe," Bayley whispered, her desire to see the picture even greater. As Faith turned the pad of paper toward her, Bayley gasped, her hand coming to her throat. Dark eyes stared back at her from an angular face shadowed by a fedora. A gnarled hand reached toward her from the page as stained teeth grinned underneath a slightly crooked nose.

"That's him...oh, Faith, that's him!"

The Saints lounged in the living room with Nick, listening to Jack discuss his latest phone call with the governor.

"Nick, I know this sucks since you just got assigned this case, but the governor has put me on alert that he may want the Saints to work the investigation as well." Holding up his hands in protestation, he continued, "It's got nothin' to do with his faith in the FBI, and everything to do with his re-election coming up next year."

"I know," Nick admitted. "There's not much I can tell you about this case, since I was just assigned to it yesterday, but as much as it sucks," he spared a glance toward Blaise, "Bayley being approached may have been just the thing to get us what we need."

"We'll work with you," Jack promised, "and you'll have all we can offer at your disposal. We've got a couple of cases we're working right now, but we can fit this one in. Although I did tell the governor that we were stretched at the moment and would only be available to assist your office's investigation."

Before Nick had a chance to respond, Faith and Bayley entered the room. He caught her bright-eyed expression as Bayley's gaze landed on his immediately. Refusing to analyze the warmth that rushed over him at the realization that she sought his eyes first, he watched as she hurried to him.

"Nick, she's a genius, an absolute genius! Faith just listened and listened as I talked and the next thing I know, she's got this picture and it's him. I swear it's just like she took a photograph of him!"

Meeting her grin, he lifted his gaze over her head to the art pad Faith was holding up. Staring at the man who accosted Bayley, he felt his blood run cold. *Fuckin' hell.*

"Nick? Nick, what is it?" Bayley asked, her brows drawn down as she took in his face. Not receiving a response, she jerked slightly on his arm.

Swallowing as his looked around the room to see the Saints all watching him closely, he dropped his gaze back to Bayley, seeing the concern in her eyes. Finally, focusing on Blaise, he confessed, "That's Johan Serkov.

He's a known enforcer for the Russian mafia. He hasn't been sighted in the U.S. in two years, having fled back to Russia. He was last seen working for the Volkov family, out of the Norfolk area."

The Saints broke into a cacophony of cursing, but Bart was the loudest, as he moved to tuck his wife into his embrace. "Nick, before you were with the Bureau here, I...well, we worked a case in that area and had dealings with the Volkov family. This was over a year ago. They were newcomers and, by that, I mean new to this country. No background to guide them. No elder at the helm. Gavrill Volkov is their head. We were told that they came to America about five years ago and each year they become a little more ruthless."

"That's it!" Blaise stated, his voice belying his fear as he turned toward Bayley. "You're moving in with me!"

Facing her brother, with her hands on her lips, Bayley shook her head slowly. "Blaise, I can't. I can't possibly bring this to your doorstep...not with your wife and baby."

Nick's breath caught in his throat but before Blaise could argue, he spoke up, "I've got her." He watched as the other Saints nodded, no doubt showing on their faces.

"Nick—"

"No, Blaise. She'll be at my place until you can get her apartment and shop secure and up on your grid. I've got a spare room and I'll have agents keeping an eye on her apartment and on her shop. My building has coded access and security. Plus my apartment has added security." He turned toward Jack and asked, "While investigating, can you spare some eyes on her?"

Jack was already nodding as the other Saints pledged their agreement. Nick dropped his gaze to the woman standing in front of him, her slight smile indicating she accepted his protection.

9

"We're here." Nick pulled into the parking garage of his apartment building, sliding into his assigned space. Bayley was quiet and he glanced to the side, wondering what she thought.

"I guessed that," she said, leaning forward to look around, just as a long meow sounded from the back seat. "Mr. Lickers, I'll get you out in a few minutes."

With a nod, Nick exited the SUV, grabbing her overnight bag from the back as she took the cat carrier and litter box. The elevator took them to the third floor and he continued to glance at her, as she was unusually quiet.

"You okay?" he asked, as they walked down the hall to his door. She was never this quiet and he found it unnerving. Her nod was the only reply he received.

Opening the door to his apartment, he stepped back, allowing her to enter first, watching as she moved cautiously into the space.

Halting, Bayley looked around at the large, pristine,

living room, a black sofa against the wall facing a large, flat-screen TV. Two chairs sat at angles to the sofa, both covered in a grey material. The walls were eggshell-white with no adornments. She could see the dining room table to her right and as she moved forward, the kitchen came into view. Sparkling appliances. Empty countertops. A blank hall opened directly in front of her, leading to what she assumed were bedrooms.

Twisting back around, her brow knitted as she asked, "I thought we were going to your apartment? I had no idea you were bringing me to a safe house."

Nick blinked in confusion, but before he could reply, she continued. "I mean, this is cool and all, but do you really think this is necessary?" Her eyes widened, "Oh, jeez, am I in that much danger? This is crazier than I thought." She bent over and set the litter box on the floor before opening the cat carrier, letting Mr. Lickers run out. He began to sniff as he low-crawled around the furniture.

Nick spied the cat warily before he dropped his gaze to the covered-litter box now sitting in his foyer.

Bayley kicked off her shoes on the way to the kitchen, leaving them in her wake as she pulled off her jacket and dropped it over the back of a dining room chair. "I guess the FBI never knows who might need to be stashed in a place, but you'd think they'd have a few kitchen items for us to use." Opening a cabinet, she discovered cups, plates, glasses...all perfectly stacked. Pulling on a drawer, she found the cutlery, neatly placed in holders as well. "Okay, it looks like they've got stuff here."

Tossing her purse to the kitchen counter, a few items skidding out and along the surface, she turned to open the refrigerator. Water bottles, lined in straight rows, sat on the bottom shelf. Fruit and vegetables filled the bottom drawers and the shelves contained other food items and plastic containers neatly stacked. "I can use some of this for my research...you know, nothing specific, but just little details about what a safe-house might look like—"

"Bayley," Nick interrupted, as he walked over and picked up her jacket. Hanging it in the closet, he bent to line her shoes up neatly next to the front door. "Bayley," he repeated a little louder when she didn't respond, approaching the kitchen counter and placing her fallen items back into her bag and moving it to the side.

"Yeah?"

"This isn't a safe-house."

She turned and stared at him, waiting for him to continue. He opened his mouth a couple of times, but words did not come. Understanding dawned on her, eyes widening in surprise. "This is your house? You live here?"

Clearing his throat, he replied, "Yeah...uh...yes. This is my apartment."

"Oh, wow...it's nice...well, a nice space." she admitted. "You must have just moved in, since it's so blank. I just assumed no one lived here since it's got nothing personal in it. Oh," she added, slapping her forehead with her hand, "It was furnished, wasn't it? Of course! Well, once you've added your own touches, it'll really be nice."

Nick watched as she beamed her smile up at him and he hesitated. He shifted his gaze around, trying to see it through her eyes. Neat. Clean lines. *Just the way I like it...but not to her taste. Since when did I care what someone thought of me?* Blushing slightly, he rubbed the back of his head. "Actually, it is my furniture." Shrugging, he added, "I like things neat, I guess. Not much into clutter."

"Or color!" she laughed, leaning over to pat his arm. "Hey, it's fine. It's your place. But," she said, her gaze now wandering around, "maybe a few, little, homey touches wouldn't be too bad. A couple of throw pillows with some color would brighten up the living room. Maybe a few pictures on the walls." Walking over to the bank of windows in the living room, she smiled. "The view really is gorgeous. I'm envious of this. My little apartment is on the third floor too, but only overlooks the parking lot. You must stand here a lot and just look out at the vista. You can watch the sun set over the mountains...wow, it must be glorious!"

Her words jolted him. Walking over, he stopped next to her, looking out the window as well. He liked the view with the city not too far off and the Blue Ridge mountains rising in the distance, but he had never spent any time noticing the sunsets. He took note if it looked like inclement weather was coming, but not the beauty. Unsure what to say, he remained quiet, but had to admit, the sun settling over the mountains, shooting out rays of red and orange, did look impressive.

Twisting her head up toward his, she asked, "So, gonna show me the rest of the place? I need a place to put Licker's litterbox since I'm pretty sure you don't want it by the front door."

He wondered what she would think of the other rooms, but plastered a smile on his face as he nodded his agreement about the litter box. "You can put it in the guest bathroom." Pointing to the front, he said, "You've seen the dining room and kitchen. Uh…behind the door is a closet…for your coat."

"Seems you've already hung it up," she laughed, following him toward the hall.

Opening the first door on the right, he said, "Here's the guest bathroom," showing a small bathroom, its interior supporting a sink, toilet, and tub. The walls were white, matching the fixtures. A white towel hung on the rack, perfectly folded and centered. She scooted the litter box next to the toilet.

The next door on the right was opened, and he motioned with a wave of his hand, "Here's the guest room. I apologize, it's kind of junky…just a place for me to store a few things."

Curious, she peeked inside expecting to find boxes and household oddities—the things people have but can never find a good place to keep. Instead, her gaze rested on a daybed sofa against one wall, the navy cover providing the only color. Underneath the window in the room sat a desk, a pen holder and a few books, neatly stacked, the only items on top. One piece of furniture sat in the corner, completely out of character for the lifeless room—a wooden rocking chair, complete with slightly worn, green cushion, its ties attaching it to the back. Before she had a chance to ask about it, Nick moved in and set her overnight bag on the bed.

"It's not much—" he began, strangely uneasy with her evaluating his living space and wondering if she found it lacking.

"It's absolutely perfect," she rushed, placing her hand on his arm, staring warmly into his face. "I know this is weird for you. Certainly not something you were expecting. I'll be perfectly fine here for a day or so until we know my place is safe." Sucking in her lips, she added, "It will just be a day or two, right?"

Rubbing the back of his neck, in a motion that she was already recognizing meant he was uncertain, he admitted, "I have no way of knowing right now. But I want you here until we know you're not in danger."

Nodding, she smiled. "Hey, you had some good things in your refrigerator, why don't I cook dinner?"

Shaking his head, "No, no. No way. You're here as a guest, Bayley. I don't expect you to do—"

"I know," she interrupted. "I don't feel obligated, honestly. But I like to cook and my kitchen is small. I'd love to fix something for us."

He peered closely, seeing nothing but honesty in her eyes. "Okay...sure...uh—"

Laughing, she patted his shoulder as she moved past him into the hall. "Go relax and I'll whip up something easy. If it makes you feel better, you can do dinner tomorrow."

Convinced she was telling the truth, he moved into his bedroom, slipping off his shoes before placing them onto his shoe-rack. Tie, jacket, pants—all hung up.

Dumping his shirt into his laundry basket, he listened as the clatter of pans in the kitchen sounded foreign and, strangely comforting, all at the same time. Deciding to take a quick shower, he emerged from his bedroom twenty minutes later, dressed in jeans and a dark green, long-sleeved t-shirt, eagerly moving toward the tantalizing smells coming from the kitchen.

Rounding the corner, he jerked to a halt at the sight in front of him. The sink held two dirty pans, with two more on the stove. His chopping block was out, the remnants of cut vegetables scattered on top as well as on the counter. His gaze landed on three knives on the counter as well. Various food items, including a rotisserie chicken package, lay on the counter. As he examined the kitchen disaster, he noticed what appeared to be flour on the counter and floor, and as she turned around sporting a big grin, her face was smeared with the white powder as well.

"Hey!" she beamed. Her gaze slid down his body, landing on his bare feet sticking out from his jeans. Fascinated with how sexy his feet were, she finally moved her eyes back up to his face. "I decided to make chicken pot-pie since you had all the ingredients. I heated it all on the stove before putting it into the oven, so it's about ready. Once the top crust is brown, we can eat."

Dragging his eyes from his messy kitchen to her face, his lips curved into a smile, meeting hers. "Sounds great," he admitted, as his stomach growled, deciding he could clean later. "I'll get the plates."

Fifteen minutes later, they sat at his table, diving

into the pot-pie. The pastry topping and thick sauce seasoned perfectly with chunks of chicken, carrots, onions, and potatoes had him moaning in delight. He did not consider himself to be a slouch in the kitchen, but comfort food was not his forte and if a messy kitchen was the price to pay for the delicious meal, he would accommodate.

After a meal accompanied with small talk—Bayley's small talk and Nick's occasional nod—she began to clear the table. He watched as she opened the dishwasher to place items in without rinsing.

"I'll do that," he offered, hoping she would move into the living room.

"Oh, I've got it," she said, continuing to load the dishwasher.

"Uh…we should rinse those first."

"Nah, you've got a really good dishwasher. It's one of those that'll clean anything. Plus, I have to wash by hand at my house, so this is a treat."

"But you really should—"

"Okay," Bayley said, her voice unsure as she looked over at Nick. Stepping away, she watched as he took the dishes out and rinsed them first. Turning to hide her grin, she grabbed a dishcloth and began wiping down the counters.

"Oh, here, use this," Nick said, handing her a different cloth.

Looking down at the replaced cloth in her hand, she cocked her head to the side. "Was something wrong with the one I was using?"

Nick saw the uncertainty in her face, so unlike her

normal smile, and hated that he put it there. "Sorry...I guess I'm just used to living by myself. Um...why don't you go put your feet up since you fixed dinner."

Nodding in understanding, her smile slid back into place, as she said, "I'll take a shower, if that's okay?"

"Absolutely," he enthused, and watched as she headed down the hall. His gaze dropped to her ass, stunning as always in the cute dress she was wearing. Once she disappeared into the guest bathroom with her hands full of personal items from her overnight bag, he shook his head. His mind drifted to his upbringing and he knew his habits were ingrained and unlikely to disappear.

Singing met his ears, startling him from his musings. Grinning as he moved to stand outside the bathroom door, the sound of water running mingled with loud, slightly off-key, singing was totally...*adorable*. Unable to remember the last time he thought anything was adorable, he chuckled.

Moving back to the living room, he sat on the sofa, heaving a sigh as he leaned back. A strange noise was coming from underneath the window so he turned his head to see what it was. Mr. Lickers was sitting on the floor, one back leg lifted high, as he licked his—*what the fuck is he*—as if the cat could hear his thoughts, he raised his head, tongue still hanging out as he stared at Nick.

The water, and the singing, had stopped and before he knew it, Bayley bounded into the room, smelling of lemons and sunshine. Her scrubbed, make-up free face was grinning. He tried not to stare at her delicious body clothed in baggy, flannel pants decorated with tigers all over them and a t-shirt with a large penguin on the front. An outfit that should not be sexy was sending the blood straight to his cock.

"That shower was phenomenal," she gushed. "You've got great water pressure here. My place? Not so much. It takes forever just to get the shampoo out of my hair, but with your shower, it was easy. Of course, I think you've got great pipes as well. My building has old, copper pipes and the water is hard." Stopping for a second, she looked at Nick's face, contorted in a combination of a grimace and wide-eyed surprise. "What's wrong?"

"What is that cat doing?"

Scrunching her face as she walked past the sofa, she burst into laughter at the sight. "Oh, Nick, you goof! He's licking his little willie. How do you think he got the name Mr. Lickers?"

Closing his eyes for a second, Nick wished he could get the image of the cat out of his mind, but its posture was burned into his brain. That, and the fact that he earned the name Lickers, had Nick shaking his head. "You named your cat after his dick-licking activities?"

The sofa dipped as she sat down next to him, still laughing. "All cats do that and, usually when there's company, they do it right in front of everyone. Haven't you ever had a cat?"

"Good God, no!"

"A dog?"

"No."

Bayley's mirth left as she wondered about the uptight agent's childhood. "So, no pets at all?"

Nick's mind slid to the past, the memories of his parents not as strong as he would have liked, but he was grateful for the old photo album on the bookshelf. He felt the sofa cushion move as he lifted his gaze back to Bayley, who was shifting around to face him, tucking her legs up underneath her. Her face, usually full of excitement, was pensive as she stared at him. Offering a small smile, he replied, "No...no pets."

She reached over, placing her hand on his arm, "I'm sorry, Nick. My babbling seems to have struck a sad note with you. And I'm sure having me and Lickers here is putting a real crimp in your lifestyle."

"Not at all," he assured, although secretly he had to admit Lickers was a bit much to take. "Don't apologize —I just want to make sure you're safe."

With that, they fell into silence as Nick turned on the TV, flipping to the news. Bayley leaned back, her eyes on the TV but her thoughts on the man sitting next to her. She wondered about TDMB, especially the M part. *Mysterious. Where did he come from? Where was his family? Were they so uptight also? The man needs a pet!* Her tumultuous thoughts about her host had her shifting her gaze toward him, staring at his profile, now concentrating on the B. *He is beautiful.* His features were straight, almost angular, with deep-set, dark eyes and a straight nose. High cheekbones and firm jaw. The stubble of whiskers was showing, giving an almost dangerous look, but she knew they would be cleanly shaved off the next morning. His lips drew her attention and the desire to run her tongue over them almost had her leaning his way. *Steel and satin,* she decided. *That's what they'd feel like.*

Nick felt her perusal and shot a glance her way. Hair drying, pulled back with a few angelic tendrils framing her face. Her eyes, so big and blue, enticed him and as he dropped his gaze to her lips, pink and plump, he fought the desire to lean over and kiss them. *Soft and silky,* he decided. *That's what they'd feel like.*

They both moved, ever so slightly, toward each other as the magnetic pull proved difficult to resist. The sound of a cat scratching litter in the distance and then a bolt of fur-lightening flew across the room, followed by the odor of—

"What the hell?" Nick asked, his body jerking in surprise.

"Oh, God," Bayley exclaimed, jumping up. "Lickers just pooped in the litter box and he likes to run like a demon when he finishes!" Rushing into the kitchen, she grabbed a plastic bag and hustled to the guest bathroom, where she scooped out the offensive item. Tying the bag, she dumped it into the trash and searched underneath the sink for room-freshener spray. Finding it, she gave the living room a heavy dose of rose scented spray before sniffing. "Better?" she asked hopefully.

"Sure," Nick lied, trying not to choke on the cat-shit-floral odor now lingering. Standing, he turned off the TV, saying, "I guess it's time to turn in. I'll see you in the morning."

A smile hiding her disappointment, she nodded. "Yeah…tomorrow's just a regular day in the shop. I'll open and one of the Saints will be there."

Bayley climbed into bed, leaving the door cracked in case Lickers wanted to sleep with her. It did not take long for him to do just that, curling at her legs, purring loudly. She reached her hand out and rubbed his head, the fur soft underneath her fingertips, and her thoughts went to the man across the hall. Raised by a strong father and with an alpha brother—who worked with other alphas—she had tried to avoid them, figuring she did not need another in-control man in her life. Thinking she needed to be with the opposite type, she tried dating authors or artists, but found no one who rocked her world. Lying on her back, she stared at the ceiling. She knew the difference between a man who had to be in control and a man who took care of others, especially the ones he loved.

Smiling, she thought of Blaise with Grace, and now their son. Her memories of her father's no-nonsense, loving firmness filled her mind. *Maybe I've been looking in the wrong direction...maybe I do need someone like him.*

Later, lying in bed, Nick thought of the bewildering woman in his guest room. Funny. Smart. He had had more conversation that day than in the past few weeks put together. Sexy. Whether dressed up or in PJs with tigers on them, she was beautiful. As his thoughts brought his dick to attention, he forced his mind to safer traits of hers. *She's disorderly.* Rolling over, he focused on the mess in the kitchen…*which was easy to clean up and the meal was delicious.* Then he thought of the cat…*which she also took care of quickly.* Rolling back over again, he came to one final thought—one that pushed her lips out of his mind…almost. *She's under my care and therefore untouchable.*

"Johan's made a mess of things!" Chessa shouted, waving her hands at her husband and sons. "I don't want to have to call in my uncle."

Used to her loud tirades, Milos, Lazlo, and Grigory winced before Milos argued, "You will not involve your uncle. You will tend to the girls we have and let us do the planning."

Chessa huffed, turning back to the stove as she stirred lunch. "Agnes," she barked, "set the table while the men work."

"I told you to let me handle things," Lazlo retorted. "I could have gotten close to the girl and would have had no problem getting my hands on her phone. Now, it's going to be much harder to find out what she knows."

"Get rid of her," Grigory said, casually looking at his family, shrugging. "Problem solved."

"Did I raise my eldest to be an idiot?" Chessa cried out. Grigory's lips pinched together as she continued to rant.

"Let me go to the shop," Agnes said, her voice interrupting the family's tirade. The others quieted, turning to look at her. Before her brothers could protest, she said, "No one knows me. No one will suspect a young woman in a bookstore. I can easily get close to her and find out what she knows. Who she's told. Probably even get my hands on her phone. And if need be, get my hands on her."

Licking her lips, she looked up as her parents were still quiet. Her father's eyes were piercing hers while her mother nodded slowly.

"It could work," Milos said. "No one would suspect a woman."

"I'll go too," Lazlo insisted. "There's no way Agnes should be doing this and certainly not alone. We don't want any fuckups. Anyway, I've met one of the women that works there. I can get close to them."

As the others nodded in agreement, Agnes maintained a serene expression, inwardly smiling, knowing it was time to show her family what she was made of.

10

"You have to put all this in a book. This is stranger than fiction!" Daphne exclaimed. "And you get to go home with Mr. TDMB!"

"It's crazy, that's for sure," Bayley agreed, not wanting to admit that the last part of Daphne's statement caused butterflies to beat their wings wildly in her stomach. She had spent the last two nights at Nick's place and it was getting harder to fight her attraction to him.

"Crazy? That's putting it lightly! You've got FBI agents, gorgeous security men, and kidnappers all at your fingertips."

Bayley smiled at her friend, who gushed while serving coffees to some of their regular customers. As word of her unique shop was spreading, more people came, whether to look at books, sit and type for a while, or bring their children into the reading room. Happy for the business, her focus drifted over to the huge, muscular man sitting near the door, sipping coffee while perusing the newspaper. *Marc...that's his name. Bart was this morning. Chad and Mitch were yesterday.* He appeared casual, but Bayley was learning the Saints' habit of being ever vigilant while exuding a normal air about them.

As Bayley walked toward the writing area, she heard Daphne greet another customer. "Lazlo, hi!" Turning, she grinned as Daphne and the dark-haired young man began chatting. Recognizing him as the customer who came in two days ago, she breathed a sigh of relief, knowing that repeat customers could be the life-blood of a business.

Seeing Bruce at a table with a young woman, she walked over to check on his writing. Smiling, she greeted, "Hey, Bruce." Nodding toward the new customer who smiled up at her, she said, "Welcome. I don't remember seeing you in my shop before." Noticing the woman's cup of black coffee on the table was almost empty, she offered, "Can I get you another cup?"

The woman stood, her hand extended, and smiled ever so slightly. "It's nice to meet you, Ms. Hanssen. I'm Agnes. I was curious about what Bruce was working on and relished the opportunity to meet another writer. He insisted that your shop is the place to come to learn more about publishing."

Beaming, first at Bruce and then at the new customer, she said, "I hope he invited you to our critique group."

"Oh, yes, he did. I'm afraid I don't have any work to

share at this time...I'm still very new to the idea of writing."

"We all have to start somewhere," she said, "so don't be afraid to join us as soon as you do have even just the beginnings of a manuscript. We can critique your ideas to help you get started."

With a nod, she moved away, looking up to see Marc's piercing eyes on her and the two writers she just walked away from. Heading straight to him, she greeted, "I see you're just as observant as the others."

Grunting, Marc jerked his head toward the table and asked, "You know them?"

Stifling a giggle, she replied, "The man is Bruce Dester. He's a fellow writer and has been coming here since I opened. In fact, he's the one who scared off the man from the other night."

"And the dark-haired woman with him? The one with no computer or books in front of her?"

"You are suspicious, aren't you? She's a new customer and said she's an aspiring writer but not ready to join the night critique group yet."

"Hmmm," Marc grunted again, his gaze moving back around the large room. The bell over the door sounded and Nick walked in, his stalwart expression softening as his eyes landed on her.

"Hey," she greeted, her ready smile greeting him. "All good in the criminal-catching world?"

Nick's eyes shifted to Marc, now standing, and met the Saint's smirk with a twitch of his lips. "Everything okay?"

Marc nodded, prompting a pout from Bayley. "I

swear, y'all talk in caveman-speak. A few words and it's all done. What happened to the art of conversation? You know, full sentences. Discussions between people. Even just comments about the weather!"

"Bayley," Marc said, patting her shoulder, "you talk enough for all of us." With that, he offered a head jerk to Nick and walked out.

"Well, how do you like that?" she said, her hands on her hips as she watched Marc stalk to his SUV parked outside. Huffing, she turned to Nick and said, "I don't know whether to be offended or to laugh."

Chuckling, Nick replied, "He wasn't insulting you, just stating a fact." He glanced over the busy shop, taking in the patrons milling about the inviting space. Children and parents. College students. A few writers at the tables. He recognized Bruce, intently typing on his laptop while his companion, with her face away from Nick, appeared to just be sipping coffee.

"You ready to leave?" Nick asked, his focus back on Bayley.

Nodding, she said, "Yeah. I'm having Daphne close tonight and I'll open tomorrow."

Sticking out his elbow, "Then we're off."

"How jaunty of you," she laughed. "Downright cavalier!"

Nick, losing the battle of keeping his lips from curving into a grin, held the door open for her as they walked out into the evening.

Agnes's gaze followed the couple as they left the shop, her lips pinched together as she stood. With a goodbye to Bruce, she was just passing the check-out counter on her way out when Daphne waylaid her. Agnes's eyes continued to dart toward the street, and she heaved a sigh as the couple's vehicle moved out of sight, seeing her brother's car following them.

———

Wide-eyed, Nick stood at the doorway to the hall bathroom, stunned at what he saw. The small, single-sink counter was covered with bottles, tubes, containers—some with their lids off—small brushes, and flat plastic cases filled with what he assumed was makeup. His eyes moved to the shower stall, two wet towels thrown haphazardly over the towel bar and a wet washcloth hanging on the door. Water spots covered the mirror and a hairdryer lay on the back of the toilet.

Fighting the urge to call his cleaning service, something brushed by his pants and he looked down, seeing Lickers weaving between his ankles, purring as he pranced around. Nick sucked in a deep breath through his nose. *It's only clutter. It can be fixed. It's only a cat. He can't destroy the house.* His fingers clenched at his sides for a moment, but hearing Bayley singing off-key in the other room again, made the tightness in his chest relax.

Walking into the kitchen, he was no longer surprised to see the complete wreckage she had accomplished as she dished up homemade lasagna. The scent of garlic-cheese bread sent thoughts of clutter out of his mind.

He eagerly sat down to dinner with her and he realized it had been a long time since he had looked forward to spending time with anyone, much less a woman. It took a moment for him to remember the forgettable dinner date he had had with a woman he met at a conference before the last case took him to Alaska. He could bring her face to mind but could not remember what they had talked about. Shaking his head, he cleared his mind as he stared at the unforgettable woman now sharing his dinner.

"Do you know when I'll be able to go back to my apartment?" she asked.

His smile drooped at the idea that she was looking forward to leaving his place. *No, that's good. No more clutter...no more cat.* Suddenly the idea of being alone again after only a few days of her presence did not appeal to him.

She watched his smile fade and wondered what was on his mind. "I only ask because I know you're probably dying to get Lickers and me out of your hair."

"No," he said, sharper than he meant. "I mean, you're welcome here as long as you need a safe place to stay."

Her smile slid easily back into place as she felt his dark eyes pierce hers. "Even Lickers?"

Chuckling, he nodded. "Yeah...I can't exactly say the cat has grown on me, but at least I'm not afraid of it anymore."

"Afraid? You were afraid of a little cat?"

"That thing has claws. And teeth. And sometimes it looks at me like it wants to make my legs its next meal."

Throwing her head back, she cackled, "Oh, Nick, you're so funny. Mr. Lickers is harmless. I don't even think he would know what to do if a mouse ran by."

Giving in to the smile tugging at his lips, he could not remember anyone ever saying he was funny. He watched her hair swing down her back, his fingers itching to see if it felt as silky as it looked. Her face, animated in laughter, showcased her plump lips, blue eyes, and peachy complexion. All traits he had never noticed with another woman. He wondered if he had ever really looked at someone before her.

As her mirth dissipated, she fastened her gaze on his, her breath now catching in her throat. He was so intelligent, so dedicated. And more beautiful than any man had a right to be. She sucked in her lips, knowing she felt safe with him but wanting so much more.

Clearing her throat, she asked again, "So...when do you think I'll be able to get back to my apartment?"

"Blaise called today to say the Saints have set up security cameras in your apartment and shop, as well as secure locks on your doors and windows. They've got you wired into their system. There's a security firm that works with the Saints. Alvarez Security will have you monitored twenty-four-seven. I'd say tomorrow, as long as you get the all-clear from them, you can move back."

"And my shop?"

"They finished the security system this afternoon...I got the call while you were in the shower."

"Okay, then. Well, uh, I guess Lickers and I'll move out tomorrow. It's been really nice to...uh...be here... with you. All part of your job, I'm sure—" stumbling over her words, uncertainty entered her, an emotion she was unused to experiencing.

Reaching out, Nick placed his hand over hers. "Bayley, it's been my pleasure. You need to know that I've never done this before. I've never had a woman here and certainly not one I was protecting. This was not part of my job. In fact, it's been a...well, let's just say, I've had to convince my superiors that this was in your best interest and wouldn't compromise the case."

Eyes wide, she exclaimed, "Oh, I never thought of that! I hope you didn't get into any trouble."

Remembering the conversation he had with Richard, his lips narrowed in frustration. *If you fuck up this case because you can't stay away from a witness, I'll have your badge.* He had almost told Richard where he could stick his badge, but years of disciplined professionalism kept his mouth shut. "No, no, it's fine," he fibbed.

Smiling once more, Bayley said, "I'm so glad. I really like being with you and would hate to think that you were in trouble over me. But you'd always have a job with the Saints...I know Blaise and the others would love to have you."

Sitting back and clearing his throat, Nick realized that for the first time in his life, he was willing to buck the system—and it was all for this woman.

Unable to sleep, Bayley considered snooping. Her mind was filled with it being her last night in Nick's apartment. Wondering, when she was no longer under his protection, if he'd make a move on her, then considering making a move on him.

Smiling, she climbed out of bed, dislodging Lickers sleeping at her hip. Rubbing his fur as she moved, she turned on the light at the desk. Clean, neat. A few books neatly stacked in the corner. She snickered at what she recognized as his OCD tendencies. Moving to the bookshelf, she scanned the titles. Books on interrogation, detection, police policies, law, investigation techniques. She wrinkled her nose at the topics.

On the bottom shelf, an old photo album lay on the bottom of a stack of other books. Curious, she pulled it out, opening it to the first page. Gasping, she realized she was staring at Nick's childhood photos.

A picture of a couple, the mother, dark-haired and smiling, was holding a baby while sitting in a rocking chair that was in this room. *That's the rocking chair that's in this room!* The father, standing behind her with his hands on her shoulders, beamed proudly toward the camera. Looking at Nick's father, she saw how much he resembled his dad. Other shots, all with the same three, filled the pages and as she continued to go through them, she watched Nick grow from a baby to a child of about eight years old. Tall like his father. Dark-haired, like both of them. Always smiling at the camera. Pages of birthdays, Christmases, bike rides, and picnics.

Then the pictures stopped. No more happy family. After turning several blank pages, she saw Nick's high school graduation pictures. This time he resembled the Nick she knew—stern-faced and serious. His dark hair was trimmed close to his head, dark eyes boring a hole into the lens with a focused and thoughtful expression. *What happened? Where did your parents go?*

11

"We may have a problem."

Blaise's call to Nick early the next morning did not portend good things. "What's up?"

"The governor just called Jack to tell him that there is a high terrorist alert for a meeting that's going on in the capitol and he needs the Saints to provide added security and intelligence. Normally that's not a problem, but it's going to pull some of us away from assisting you and covering my sister—"

"It's no problem," Nick assured in haste. "I've got Bayley covered."

If Blaise wondered about Nick's words and the possible double meaning, he did not let on. "I know you do and I appreciate it. Her apartment and shop are all wired in and we'll be monitoring it round the clock. I'm beating myself up that I had not upgraded her places before a problem happened—"

"This is not your fault, man," Nick said. "But I know how you feel...just like I do about taking her phone and leaving her with nothing to call with when she needed it."

"Well, I'm on my game again," Blaise assured. "But Jack just wanted me to let you know that our resources will be strained for a few days."

"No problem. I've got this," Nick replied. "I'll protect her with my life." The unplanned words rolled off his tongue easily, surprising himself, but he immediately recognized they were true.

"I owe you, man," Blaise said.

"No debt," Nick promised. "She'll want to hear from you so make sure to keep in touch. I'll get her settled back into her place and won't leave until she's comfortable with the security set-up. I'll also make sure she's escorted to and from work until we have a better handle on Johan and where the threat is coming from."

Disconnecting, he heard a noise from the bathroom and, with a quick glance at his clock, he knew Bayley was up early. The sound of off-key singing hit his ears and he thought of how quiet the apartment would feel with her gone. That thought did not settle well.

Stepping out of his room after getting dressed, he moved toward the kitchen, but his attention was captured by the hall bathroom. Flipping on the light, he stared at the pristinely clean room. No wet towels. No makeup, bottles, hair items. It was as though she had never been there and he rubbed his chest, right over his heart, absentmindedly easing an ache. He told himself, this should be good. *My space back to being my own again.* But it was harder to convince his heart of the thoughts he was forcing into his mind.

Nick and Bayley first went to her house to drop off Mr. Lickers and Nick went through the added security system. Once at Bayley's Books & Nooks, he acquainted her with the upgraded security, not leaving until he was certain she knew the codes and was comfortable with the system.

"I'll pick you up again this afternoon," he promised, hating that there would not be a Saint in her store today.

"You don't have to, you know," she replied, pleased that he offered.

"You don't have your car here and I want to assure myself of you getting home all right...at least until you're more familiar with the security."

"I accept your gallant offer," she smiled. Leaning up on her toes, she kissed his cheek, immediately noting the warm tingle that traveled through her lips, causing a faint gasp to slip out.

His breath caught in his throat as her lips touched his skin. Reaching out, he pulled her in, carefully observing to see if she objected. His unspoken question was answered by her wrapping her arms around his neck. Standing in the middle of her shop, they held each other. No words. Only the feel of bodies pressed tightly. Pulling away slightly, he kissed her forehead as he slowly stepped back.

"See you later," he whispered against her ear.

Smiling, she squeezed his arms before letting him walk out of her store. "Whoaaa," she breathed, her heart pounding. With a squeal, she twirled around several times before settling in to work.

Stepping into the room, she swept her hard gaze around, unsmiling as she quickly took in the state of the girls sitting on their beds. The six women, wide-eyes nervously staring at Chessa, all stood quickly. A stale odor permeated the space and more than one of them wavered as though close to fainting.

Chessa moved forward, nodding at their acquiescence, and walked closer. Approaching the first girl, a tall blonde, she eyed her up and down. "Are you eating?" she asked, her words clipped.

Swallowing deeply, the girl said, "Yes. Uh...yes, ma'am."

"Good," Chessa acknowledged. "You were too thin. Men want women with some meat on their bones."

Moving to the next girl, a petite brunette, she narrowed her eyes. "That is unless they want more of a child...and you, my dear, will do nicely for them."

The girl blinked back her tears, her hands shaking as they clutched her shirt.

Stepping down the line, Chessa checked each girl before stopping at the last one in line. "Amy," she said. "Our newest one."

Amy held Chessa's gaze, asking, "What are you going to do with us? You can't keep us here, you know. There are people looking for us, they'll find—"

A slap resounded in the small room as Chessa's hand made contact with Amy's cheek. Leaning close to the tearful woman, she said, "You will learn respect. You will not question me. You are here to do what I tell you, when I tell you."

Walking backwards, she stopped at the door and said, "You all have been given the okay by our doctor to begin working soon. We have a few girls that will be shipped out and as soon as their rooms are vacated, you will fill those positions."

As she left, she shut and locked the door. The six women sat back on the mattresses in unison, each shaking as tears slipped down their cheeks.

Amy looked to the others, her voice quaking as she asked, "Are we staying here or will they ship us out too?"

"Who knows," Bette, the tall blonde, replied. "All of us have only been here a few days."

Amy's insides quivered as she said, "I saw something about this on the inside of a bathroom door. I never...never."

"Saw what?" Selena, the petite brunette asked, as she moved to the sink and wet a cloth. Walking back, she placed it on Amy's red cheek.

"A warning about human trafficking," Amy said, her voice barely above a whisper. "I was trying to watch my drink but someone must have messed with it. I was at a club and then? I have no idea until I woke up here."

The women were silent, each pondering their fate.

"Nicholas Stone? I'm afraid I have bad news."

"Who is this?" Nick answered curtly, anxiety spearing through him.

"This is Doctor Marsden, from the Sevier County Memorial Hospital. Bernard Stone, who we have listed as your great-uncle, was brought into the emergency room last night after a 9-1-1 call was placed. He collapsed outside his apartment. He had a heart attack and is here now. He is stable, but we've had to operate to get him there. You're listed on his doctor's records as being the only kin and point of contact."

Nick sucked in air, choking on the thickness of emotion. "Yes, that's right. I'm his only relative." *And he's my only relative.* Rubbing his brow, he added, "It'll take me about an hour to settle things at my job and another hour to get home to pack a bag. I can drive and be there in about another six hours." Glancing at his watch, he said, "I can be there by seven o'clock tonight."

"That's fine. I'll call this number if there are any changes."

Disconnecting, Nick leaned heavily in his chair. *Great-Uncle Bernard. Bernard Stone. Marine Sergeant Bernie Stone.* No matter what name he went by, his great-uncle was a tough man. *A heart attack. Never thought that would take the ol' cuss down.* Thinking of what all he needed to do, his first thought rushed to Bayley, knowing the timing sucked.

Frustration poured through his veins as he called her cell phone, wondering how to make sure she was protected with him gone.

"Hey, Nick," her sweet voice answered. "What's shaking?"

"Bayley, I've got a major situation. Just when the Saints are stretched thin, I got a call about my great-uncle. He's had a heart attack and I'm his only living relative—"

"Oh, no! I'm so sorry! What can I do?"

Her concern washed over his tangled thoughts and he closed his eyes, relishing in her words. "There's nothing you need to do, but I'm desperate to know that you'll be safe while I'm gone to Tennessee for a few days. I need to be at the hospital, make sure everything is being taken care of, and check with his living quarters to make sure they'll be able to take care of him if… when…he's discharged."

Bayley's heart skipped a beat just as his words stumbled. This man who had offered her all his strength, needed her now. "When do you need to leave?"

Rubbing his head once more, trying to still the headache creeping in, he replied, "I'll need an hour here and then an hour at home to pack a bag. I should be ready to leave about one p.m."

"That's fine. I can be ready by then."

Nick blinked, uncertain of her meaning. "Ready? You don't have to see me off, but I was going to drive by your shop to see you before I left. I just need time here to talk to my superiors and get someone else to watch you, as well as call Jack."

"You don't need to come by the shop. Just come by my apartment to pick me up since I'm on your way to the highway."

"Bayley, I don't understand. Are you leaving the

store to go home early today?" A soft laugh met his ears, gentling his spirit.

"Nick, I'm coming with you. I'm not going to let you go through this alone."

For a second, he was not sure he had heard her correctly, but she kept talking.

"I can get Daphne and my other employees to run the shop while we're gone. I'll leave now and that'll give me time to get Mr. Lickers to Blaise's house. He loves animals and Grace'll take care of him while Blaise is working. Then I can run back and you can pick me up at my apartment."

The phone line was silent as Nick's heart pounded, her words finally sinking in. "Bayley, you don't have to do this—"

"Nick," she interrupted. " 'Never do anything yourself that others can do for you.' "

"Another Agatha Christie quote?" he asked, his headache easing slightly.

Laughing, she admitted, "Of course. Let me come with, Nick. If I stay, I'll just be here being worried. I promise I won't get in your way. You won't even notice me."

Now it was his turn to laugh, knowing there was no way he would not notice her. He debated for a moment —*taking her would keep her safe and away from anyone here trying to get to her. But Richard will not be in favor of this decision.* Sighing heavily, he realized how much he wanted her with him. *I won't have to worry about her. I can be with her. She'll make whatever I find out a little easier to face. All selfish reasons.* "Okay, Bayley...you're going with me—"

"Yay!" she gushed. "Thank God you're letting me go. I'd be worried sick about you if I wasn't there. I know it won't be a fun road trip by any stretch of the imagination, but I'll feel better being with you."

Once more, her words soothed over him. "Listen, I've got to go take care of things on my end. Do what you have to do, but when you talk to Daphne, tell her under no circumstances is she to discuss with anyone— and I mean anyone—about where you are."

"Got it, bossman," she agreed.

Feeling lighter, he disconnected. Knowing he had to face the inevitable, he called Harlan to let him know what was happening.

Questions danced in her head, but Bayley refused to give them a voice.

She wanted to ask why he was the only relative for his great-uncle. She wanted to ask why his family pictures ended at age eight. She wanted to know everything, but shooting a glance sideways, the tension radiating off him was almost tangible. Turning her attention to the vista out the window, she let her mind slide to the past.

"I love the mountains, don't you? I grew up here and we used to go hiking all the time. Dad was big on camping and hiking. He used to quiz us as we went along about the various trees and plants. Not in a bad way, of course, but he'd teach us and then wanted to make sure we appreciated the various aspects of the nature around us." Snickering, she added, "Blaise was always more interested in the animals we came across. And by the time I was a teenager, I just wanted to check out any boys that happened to be hiking at the same time. Poor Dad...I think I frustrated him terribly."

They had just crossed the Blue Ridge Mountains on their way toward Highway 81, which would take them all the way to Tennessee.

Silence.

Bayley shifted her gaze toward Nick driving his SUV, his eyes forward on the road, but she could tell his mind was a million miles away. Unsure if she should question his thoughts, she quieted.

Nick looked over a few minutes later, a crease appearing on his forehead. "Why'd you stop talking?"

"I didn't think you were listening." Shrugging, she added, "It's okay. I know you have a lot on your mind."

"No, no," he protested. "I like hearing you talk."

A laugh snorted from her as she said, "Now you're just being nice."

He reached over and placed his right hand over hers, giving a little squeeze. "No, really. I like it. You're full of...I don't know...interesting things to say."

"I just don't want life to pass me by. Agatha Christie's character, Miss Marple, once said 'Life will not pass her by. Strange and exciting events will surround her.' I always thought she was describing me."

Chuckling, Nick nodded. "I agree...it sounds like you." An easy silence filled the vehicle as the wheels churned down the road. When he spoke again, it was whisper soft, "And so different from me."

Bayley looked over, seeing the faraway expression in his eyes as they stared straight ahead once more and she turned to look out her window, the Virginia farmland passing by. And it was her turn to whisper into the silence. "Miss Marple also says, 'Everybody is very much alike, really. But, fortunately, perhaps, they don't realize it.'"

12

"Again? You've got to stop again?"

"I can't help it...it's just me."

Nick sighed as he flipped on the blinker, turning into another reststop along the highway. So far, Bayley had needed to stop at each one. "Are you all right? Are you car-sick?"

Laughing, Bayley playfully slapped his arm. "No...I just have to go frequently and it's worse when I'm traveling. Blaise and my dad called me Peanut Bladder, cause I always had to go pee. I promise, I'll be back out in a minute. Unless, of course, there's a line, because women can really fill up a ladies' room. I think it's because we have so much more to take care of instead of just unzipping our pants and pulling it out."

Having no response to her declaration, he parked in the space at the rest stop and she hopped out, running inside the building. Swinging his gaze around, he viewed the other families doing the same and, glancing at his watch, realized they were making good time. Her frequent need to stop was not making them late. And true to her word, she emerged a moment later. Her ponytail swung behind her as she hurried back toward him, a bright smile on her face. His heart skipped a beat as it hit him that while she smiled at others around, she beamed at him.

"All better," she announced, climbing back in and buckling up. Turning to him, she asked, "Um, don't you need to go?"

"No, I'm fine."

"But you haven't been at all and we've been on the road for five hours."

Turning toward her, he peered at her quizzical face. "We're seriously sitting here talking about *my* bladder when you obviously have no control over yours? You keep drinking water…no wonder you can't hold it."

Chuckling, she agreed. "Fine, fine. But you know water is so good for your body. It helps keep your complexion clear, helps you to keep from overeating, hydrates your brain so you can think better, and flushes out toxins—"

"Yeah, you got the flushing-out part real good," he quipped.

"Oh, my God! Nick Stone made a joke!" she giggled, settling back into her seat. Looking at the sign for entering Tennessee, she asked, "Where will we stay tonight?"

Rubbing the back of his neck, he admitted, "I haven't even thought of where to stay. He lives outside Pigeon Forge, which is a real tourist town, so there are plenty of motels. I know this time of year there are lots of families and tourists, so we may have to—"

Pulling out her phone, she said, "Leave it to me. I'll find a place. I've always wanted to visit Pigeon Forge and Gatlinburg." Silence filled the vehicle as she clicked away on her phone.

As she searched, she made little 'hmmm' sounds, each one more adorable than the last and Nick's attention was drawn to her mouth just as the blood ran to his dick. Shifting, he tried to ease the discomfort and now wished for a reststop just so he could rearrange himself.

"Got it!" she called out. "I found the perfect place. It'll be fabulous!"

Nick doubted any hotel in a tourist trap location would be fabulous, but he kept his doubts to himself. *As long as it's got a shower and a bed, it'll be fine*. At the thought of a bed, his cock strained even move against his zipper and he cursed under his breath.

Glancing over, Bayley shook her head. Assuming his grumpiness was due to his great-uncle's uncertain health, she stayed quiet, turning her attention back to the rolling hills of east Tennessee. She wanted to ask about his relationship with Bernie...but the emptiness of his childhood photo album played on her mind. Unneeded curiosity had her biting her tongue, thinking it would be best to see what happened when he saw his uncle. Sighing, she heard his phone vibrate and he ignored it. Realizing he had done that for the past three hours, she said, "You know, it's fine for you to talk on the phone."

"Not interested in what the person has to say right

now." He had seen Richard's number and made up his mind before they hit the road that he was not going to take a call until they got to Tennessee. Hopefully Harlan could keep Richard off his back.

"Oh," she said, sucking in her lips. "If you need privacy, we can stop again." Rushing, she added, "I don't need to pee again, but I can always get out and let you talk."

Glancing to the side, he viewed her eager-to-help face. He never knew what she was going to think or say next, and he found it unbalancing, and yet endearing. Smiling at her offer, he shook his head. "Thanks. Really...thanks, but don't worry about. I'll deal with them once we get to the hospital and I know what's facing me."

Following Nick's long stride, Bayley hurried to keep up. Making it to the nurses' desk, he stopped suddenly, causing her to slam into his back. Whirling to steady her, his brows lowered in question.

"Sorry," she mumbled, embarrassed at her clumsiness.

"S'okay," he replied, giving her arms a slight squeeze before turning back to the nurse, who smiled up at him.

Moving around to his side, Bayley made sure she was in the nurse's sight while at the same time wondering why it mattered. *He's not mine to claim.* Casting a smug smile toward the nurse, who was still talking to Nick but sweeping Bayley with her gaze, Bayley stayed tucked closely to Nick.

"Mr. Stone is stable at this time. I know Dr. Marsden was expecting you. I'll page him right now. You may go in to see your uncle—only one visitor at a time."

Offering Nick an encouraging smile, Bayley said, "You go, don't worry about me. I'll run to the ladies' room and then to the cafeteria to grab some coffee. I'll come back up in a little bit and meet you in the waiting room here."

Nick's chest was tight with worry, but Bayley's words slid over him, as they often did, soothing the ache. Giving her arm a squeeze as he leaned over to kiss her forehead, he agreed. Walking away, he wondered about the kiss. *What the hell am I doing?* But with the realization that her presence calmed his fears, he tossed out his doubts. *I'll face them later.*

No change at this time. Wait and see. The next twenty-four hours will be crucial. We'll let you know.

Nick walked out of his great-uncle's cubicle, opened to the ICU nurses' station. The big man, always in control, had laid unmoving, with tubes and wires connecting him to continuously beeping machines. The functional, utilitarian beige walls were covered in plug-ins for equipment, mounted boxes of gloves, and carts containing more equipment. There was precious little room to sit and Nick continually had to jump up from the plastic chair when a nurse came in to check on Bernie.

Nick held his hand, even though Bernie gave no indication he knew his nephew was there, and talked to him over the sounds of beeping, pinging, and whooshing, for the fifteen minutes they let him visit. As he walked out, he could not even remember what he had talked about. *Maybe it doesn't matter...maybe he could just hear my voice.*

Stepping into the stark, empty waiting room, the chairs appearing to be just as uncomfortable as the one he left, he pondered trying to search for Bayley, but knew she would return as soon as she got the coffee. His phone vibrated once more and, seeing the ID, he sighed but, this time, he answered.

"Richard, I know what you're going to say—"

"Agent Stone, you've got no fuckin' clue what I'm going to say," his superior clipped.

Nick grimaced, steadying himself for the onslaught he knew was coming.

"I get a call this morning from Harlan who informs me that you've had to take emergency leave for a family matter. Got no problem with that. But then he proceeds to tell me that you took the Hanssen woman with you. I want to know what the fuck you're thinking."

"Sir, I can't protect her if I'm not near her—"

"You can't protect her? *You?* Who the fuck do you think you are? A one-man-FBI show? You take her to your home. You take her on this emergency trip. Are you fucking her too?"

Fury roared through Nick as red-dots blurred his

vision. "I'm not going to dignify that with an answer, Richard. You know me. You know my professionalism—"

"And I've never had a reason to doubt it until now, so these latest shenanigans have me wondering what the hell she's done to you. You're being led by your—"

"Do not go there, Richard. Do not go there," Nick fired back. "We were working with the Saints, who have been pulled into another job with the governor. I could not leave her to—"

"The Saints? That renegade group of men the governor is so fond of? Is that who you identify with now?"

"My job is to investigate and protect, sir. And that's what I'm doing."

"If you don't get that witness back here asap, you won't have a job anymore," Richard bit out.

Nick stood, his heart pounding as anger coursed through his blood. "Are you seriously threatening to fire me?"

"Damn right, I am. I can have your badge for this and then you'll have nowhere to go, other than those Saints."

"Sir, right now, becoming a Saint is looking better and better!" Nick slung back. Disconnecting, he stared out of the window for a moment before whirling, his hands clenched into fists. "Auggggh!" he growled. At a slight noise from the doorway, his gaze shot up, seeing Bayley standing there, her hands filled with a tray of sandwiches, chips, and two coffees. And her wide, blue eyes staring back at him.

Quiet. The only sound was the munching of chips and the slurping of tepid coffee, more resembling mud than a drink.

Bayley had entered the waiting room and calmly set the tray on the table in the corner. Gently, she had led Nick to a plastic seat and had gone about setting the food in front of him. Taking the seat opposite of him, she asked about his uncle.

"The doctor is supposed to come in and see me as soon as he gets back to the floor. Uncle Bernie's sleeping, so I just sat and talked to him."

"I'm sure that was a comfort, even if he's not aware of it," Bayley said, her lips curving slightly. "And I'm sure it was good for you to see him as well."

Nodding as he chewed, he agreed. "Yeah…"

They continued to eat but Nick barely tasted anything. Richard's words kept swirling around in his head, mixing with worry over his uncle and wondering how much Bayley overheard. *She hasn't said anything, so maybe she just walked in at the end.*

Just then, a tall, silver-haired doctor walked in, his gaze landing on Nick. "Mr. Stone?"

Nick jumped up, wiping his fingers on the napkin Bayley shoved into his hand. "Yes. Dr. Marsden?"

The doctor smiled warmly and said, "Please, sit down." Pulling up a chair, he nodded toward Bayley before turning his attention back to Nick. "I've just been in to see your uncle. I'm pleased with his stable condition but, of course, we will know more in the next twenty-four to forty-eight hours."

"Can you tell me what happened?"

"Pine Arbor, the independent-living facility where he lives, called 9-1-1 when a neighbor saw him fall outside in the common-area yard. He was having a heart attack. He's lucky because he got to us so quickly. If he'd been alone, he might not have survived. We have done a thrombolysis, a procedure that involves injecting a clot-dissolving agent to restore blood flow in a coronary artery. He's responding very well, and we are hopeful he will be awake by tomorrow. Once we're sure he's stable, we will immediately get him up and walking around."

"So soon?" Bayley interjected, surprise plastered on her face.

Nodding, Dr. Marsden said, "Yes, it's essential to recuperation that patients begin moving and walking. It helps with healing, circulation...many benefits to having the patients up and mobile." He glanced down at their half-eaten sandwiches and said, "There's nothing more you can do tonight. I suggest you get some rest and come back in the morning. I have your cell phone number in case we need to get hold of you."

Standing, he shook hands with both of them before walking out of the waiting room.

Bayley looked up at Nick, seeing indecision on his face. Her take-charge protector appeared lost. Her heart ached for his concern and yearned to bring a smile to his beautiful face. She realized that sometime in the past couple of days, he was no longer just Mr. TDMB to her...but a real-life man, full of power and doubts all at the same time.

"Come on," she said, dumping the tray's contents into the trash can. Smiling as she took his hand in her own, she gave a gentle pull. "Let's go to the hotel and get some good food in us and rest. You'll feel better and then we can come back tomorrow when your uncle will, hopefully, be awake."

Nick allowed her to lead him back out to the SUV, surprised at his own acquiescence. And pleased with the feel of her hand in his as they stayed clasped together the whole time.

13

"**W**hat the hell?"

Laughing, Bayley said, "Come on, it'll be fun!"

Nick, following the directions Bayley had given him from her phone, weaved through heavy traffic and turned into the hotel's parking lot, his gaze landing on the sign in front of the eight-story hotel and decorated grounds.

The Christmastown Inn and Holiday Park

The small, fir trees dotting the parking lot were lit with millions of twinkling, red, blue, and yellow lights. Wooden statues of elves, reindeer, and snowmen lined the walk from the lot to the front door, where a doorman dressed as a real elf greeted them.

"Welcome to The Christmastown Inn!" he called out, whistling for a bellman who, also dressed in full red and green elf costume, came rushing forward to grab their bags.

Stepping into the massive lobby, the couple looked

around—Nick in stupefied silence and Bayley in gleeful awe.

"Isn't this amazing?" she gushed, her eyes dancing in the twinkling lights draped around the lobby.

Near the staircase, draped in evergreen, stood a two-story stone fireplace, complete with stockings hanging from the decorated mantle and a massive wreath above. The entire space gave off the feeling of being at the North Pole in Santa's workshop. Staff, in elf costumes, were everywhere, including the restaurant to the right, the bar in the back, and behind the reception counter. Grabbing his hand, she dragged him forward.

"Hi!" Bayley greeted. "We have a reservation. I made it in the name of Hanssen."

"Yes, I see it here. It's a good thing you made a reservation," the female elf said, smiling widely. "There was a water main break at the other end of town a few hours ago, but the hotels on this end were not affected, so we filled our rooms with the out-placed guests." After a few more clicks on her computer screen, she confirmed, "I have a king-sized bedroom, facing the Holiday Park gardens. Non-smoking, with a balcony and whirlpool tub in the bathroom. Breakfast is included in the price and is served a la carte in the restaurant from six a.m. until ten a.m. I'll just need to see a credit card, please."

Confused, Bayley inquired, "What about the other room?"

"What other room?" the elf asked, looking at her computer screen.

"I reserved two rooms…I think…I thought I did. I meant to…" Bayley stammered.

"I'm only showing one room reserved and," the elf looked up at them, "it's the only room we have. We're booked to the roof tonight."

"Oh..." Bayley said, blushing to the roots of her hair. Twisting her head around to Nick, she apologized. "I'm so sorry—"

"We can go somewhere else—" he began but the elf interrupted.

"I'm afraid you won't find anything in the area due to the water issue. In fact, we've been sending people who didn't have a reservation back down to the highway to find a hotel at the next exit."

Nick, mentally exhausted, stood in uncharacteristic indecision for a moment before turning his gaze down to Bayley.

"It'll be fine, Nick. We can make it work. I promise, it'll be fine."

Nodding, he agreed, too tired to try to find another hotel that would only be farther away from the hospital, while wondering how the hell he could handle being in the same room with the woman that filled his thoughts. Pulling out his wallet, he handed his credit card over as Bayley dug in her purse for hers.

"Perfect," the perky elf said, taking his card. Within a few more minutes they were following a teenage boy elf up to the fifth floor and stepping into a luxurious room. Holly and evergreens hung on the fireplace's wooden mantle, as well on the patio door. Pictures of Christmas' past hung on the walls and a small, decorated tree perched on the table in the corner.

Bayley exclaimed in excitement as she walked

around the holiday-themed room, peering out the sliding glass door to the decorated garden below. Nick stared at the king-sized bed, covered in a downy soft, red and green comforter. *How the hell am I going to keep my hands off her?*

Rolling his eyes at the elf flirting with Bayley, Nick rubbed his forehead. The headache that had been building all day from the moment the call about his uncle came in was threatening to implode. The constant perkiness from the endless elves all around caused Nick to reach for his beer, downing more at a time than he should. The hamburger and fries were good and, he had to admit, the food helped.

Looking across the table at Bayley, he was unable to keep a smile from curving his lips as he watched her bright eyes bounce around the room in unabashed delight. Following her gaze, he observed the twinkling lights hanging from every surface—the ceiling beams, the backs of the booths, the holiday trees in every corner, some reaching as tall as fifteen feet or more. Wreaths adorned the columns and windows and holly boughs draped over the doorways.

Staying in theme, the servers were also in full elf costumes, including hats and pointed shoes with bells on the ends. Mr. and Mrs. Santa Claus made their way around the tables greeting the guests. As they neared, Nick noticed they were not wearing wigs nor was Santa sporting a fake beard but, rather, the two appeared as real as their personas.

Bayley turned her excitement to him, saying, "Isn't this place great? As soon as I saw it on the internet, I knew it was the place for you to be!"

"Me?" he asked, surprised at her comment.

"Yes, you! It's your name—Nick. I know you don't work for Jack, but you're good friends with the Saints. Soooo...St. Nick. Christmastown. Holiday Park. Get it?"

Stunned, he stared wordlessly at her, but she didn't seem to notice as her eyes continued to sparkle with the lights reflected in their depths.

"Of course, you're kind of a grumpy St. Nick, but still...it fits you. And this place is so cool. Everyone should celebrate the season...even when it's not the season!"

Staring at the beauty sitting across from him, he noticed a dab of ketchup on the corner of her mouth and fought the desire to lean over and lick it off. Instead, he lifted his hand and gently swiped her lips with his thumb.

Bayley's smile slid slowly as her eyes darkened with lust. Swallowing before she choked, she lifted her beer, taking a long drink. Instead of cooling her off, it felt as though her blood rushed hotter through her veins. "I...I think I'm finished."

"Me too," Nick breathed, standing as he reached for her hand. Entwining her fingers with his, he led them to the elevator.

"Hello!"

Turning, they watched as two elves slid between the closing elevator doors, laughing as they joined Nick and Bayley. The two employees began to talk excitedly about the activities planned for the guests for the next day.

"What will you be doing?" Bayley asked.

"Reindeer games," one elf answered. "We'll have them in the Holiday Park garden right after lunch. You should come."

As Bayley and the two elves continued to chat, Nick loosened his grip on her fingers. Torn that he hated the interruption to their building lust, he knew it was the right thing to do. *Put the brakes on.*

Bayley felt the change come over Nick and by the time they arrived at their room, she sighed heavily. Entering, the king-sized bed loomed large, seeming to have grown in their absence.

Nick opened his mouth, but Bayley beat him to it. "Nick, I know you're getting ready to say that you'll do something self-sacrificing, like sleep on the floor, but this bed is huge. We can easily share." Grinning up at him, she joked, "And I can keep my hands to myself on my side."

Dropping his chin to his chest, he wondered if he could make the same promise. Feeling her hand on his arm, he lifted his head. Her eyes, now warm with concern, held his.

"You're tired…it's been a long day and tomorrow will prove to be long as well. Hospital visits are never easy. Let's get some sleep."

Nodding his agreement, it felt strangely nice to allow someone else to offer comfort instead of expecting him to take charge every second of every day. Upon her suggestion, he showered first and, unsurprisingly, by the time she entered the bathroom, it still looked as though the maids had just visited.

She stifled a giggle looking around at the wiped counter and mirror. His toiletries neatly placed back in his case. As she finished her shower and got dressed, she hesitated, fingering the wet towel she had dropped on the counter. Folding it neatly, she hung it up over the towel bar. Flipping off the light, she glanced at the rest of the counter, her toiletries still exploded over the surface. *Well, there's no reason to turn into a complete neat-freak too quickly.* Exiting the bathroom, she observed the lump in the bed where Nick was, facing away from her. His breathing appeared steady as she tiptoed around the room. Sliding underneath the covers on her side, a sigh escaped her lips. Tired, she lay awake, her mind on the man next to her. Nothing like the guys she had been dating and, yet, proving to be everything she needed. Closing her eyes, she drifted into a fitful sleep.

Hearing her breathing slow, Nick rolled back toward her, viewing her face in the thin stream of moonlight coming from the slit between the curtains. The faint illumination only served to give her face more beauty. Her lips, so often widened in a smile, now lay in rest, plump and slightly open. Her blue eyes were hidden, but it gave him a chance to appreciate her thick lashes laying on her upper cheek. Her nose was pert, slightly turned upward.

Rolling over to his back, he stared at the ceiling, torn between desire for her and maintaining his professionalism. A quandary for which he had no answer. Forcing his mind to his uncle's situation in an effort to stop thinking about Bayley, he heaved a loud sigh. *Tomorrow may not be any better than today.*

Nick opened one eye as the bright, morning light streamed into the room. He tried to move, but a weight was keeping him pinned to the mattress. Lifting his head slightly, he was met with a surprise sight. Bayley's head was on his chest, her face turned up toward his but still slack with sleep. Her left leg was slung over his hips, perilously close to his cock, which was already standing at attention. Her left arm curved on his abdomen, her hand resting on his chest near her face.

His arm began to tingle as circulation desperately tried to travel, but her weight was impeding the flow. Sliding his arm slightly up improved his circulation, but also managed to pull her in tighter. A sigh slid from her parted lips, the warm breath tickling his chest. Bed head, no makeup, sleep messy—and she was beautiful.

He raised his head enough to see the clock on the nightstand. Almost seven a.m. Amazed he had slept all night, he felt truly rested for the first time in a long time.

Bayley shifted, opening her eyes as she stared in confusion at the wall of chest muscle presented to her, a silver pendant in front of her eyes. Pushing her hair out of her face, she lifted her head, staring down at the smiling face greeting her. Realizing her position, she startled before pulling her leg off his hips. "Oh, I'm sorry! Did I keep you awake? I was supposed to stay on my side." She tried to sit up, but her legs and arm simply flailed about, managing to elbow Nick in the pecs as her knee made contact with his groin.

"Umph," he grunted, dislodging her legs while keeping his manhood intact.

Both slid up, sitting in bed with shared blushes on their faces. His eyes dropped to her outfit and he swallowed deeply as he viewed her nipples poking through the penguin t-shirt. Her legs were encased in flannel shorts, adorned with polar bears. He wondered for a second if all her sleepwear had animals on them, but the thought left his mind as she stretched her arms over her head, leaving a sliver of bare skin showing at the top of her shorts. Smooth, peachy skin peeked at him, tempting him more than a risqué outfit from a nightclub.

Giving his head a shake, he jumped from the bed and said, "I'll get dressed in the bathroom and then we can have breakfast before we head back to the hospital." Stalking to the doorway, he stopped and turned around, his expression thoughtful. "You know, you could stay here today. The hospital will be boring...nothing for you to do, since they only let in one person to visit. You could...I don't know...uh...maybe join the reindeer games?"

Throwing her head back in laughter, she exclaimed, "I swear, Nick Stone. This place just might make you less of a grumpy St. Nick after all." Sobering, she added, "But, honestly, I just want to be with you. I've got no problem sitting in the waiting room. I've got my laptop so I can write and my ereader, so I can read. Anyway, I only want to play reindeer games with you."

Unable to keep the smile from his face, Nick nodded before walking into the bathroom, leaving Bayley staring longingly at his back.

14

"Why the hell did they call you?"

"Good to see you too, Uncle Bernie."

Nick was greeted as he walked into his uncle's room before he had a chance to speak. Shaking his head, he smiled as the older man groused in his bed.

Bernie settled his eyes on Nick, his clear gaze piercing the younger man. "There was no reason for them to interrupt your life to come check on me. I'm too ornery to kick off now."

Walking over, Nick picked up the metal chair next to the wall and moved it closer to the hospital bed, making sure to avoid the multitude of wires and tubes. Sitting down, he said, "Even though they didn't need me here, I wanted to be with you. I needed to see for myself that you were going to be all right."

Bernie narrowed his eyes. "So, you just drop everything and come all this way?"

"You could say that."

Bernie shifted, his eyes glazing in pain for a moment

before focusing again. "Well, if you're here, you might as well talk. Get my mind off this confounded place."

"I'd rather hear about you and how the hell you ended up here."

Grimacing, Bernie shook his head slightly. "Just went outside to pull a few weeds from the front and felt a stabbing pain in my chest and arm. Knew it was something but don't remember what happened after that."

"Your neighbor was watching out her window and saw you pitch forward. She called 9-1-1 and they got you here quickly. The cardiologist says they did a procedure that dissolved a clot...or something like that. Says it's supposed to get your blood flowing in your coronary artery. He also says you're doing great and he wants to get you on your feet tomorrow."

Bernie opened his mouth then closed it without speaking. Nick watched him closely, knowing his uncle hated his incapacity. "Sounds like your neighbor saved your life."

"Busybody," Bernie complained. "But, you're right. I guess now I'll have to accept her invitation to coffee."

Lifting his eyebrow, Nick grinned. "She's been hitting on you?"

"Keeps asking me to come over for coffee. I turn her down...what the hell would an old Marine like me have to talk about with a nice lady?"

"So now she's gone from a busybody to a nice lady?" Nick asked, a grin tugging at his lips. "So, which is it?"

"Both," Bernie declared. Sighing, he admitted, "She's a nice lady. I'm just not much of a man to sit with a china cup of coffee balancing on my knee while trying to make small-talk."

"Maybe that's not what I want," came a melodious, feminine voice from the door.

Nick jerked his head around as Bernie stared over Nick's shoulder. A petite, white-haired woman stood at the doorway wearing a flowing skirt, in multiple colors, paired with a blue blouse. A bright green scarf draped around her neck and her feet were encased in blue ballet slippers. For a second, Nick had a vision of Bayley as an elderly woman and he turned back to his uncle, grinning as he observed the light in Bernie's eyes.

"Woman, I'm laying here buck-naked under this sheet with my chest done been cut open and you expect me to entertain?"

Stepping into the room, she stuck her hand out to Nick. "Hello. I'm Vera Higginbothom, Bernard's neighbor."

Nick stood quickly, shaking her hand as he said, "Are you the one who called the ambulance?" Receiving a nod, he said, "Thank you so much, Ms. Higginbothom."

"Please," she waved her hand dismissively. "No thanks needed, but you can call me Vera."

"Why the hell should the boy be calling you Vera?" Bernie groused, pulling the sheet up further on his body.

Ignoring his uncle, Nick offered his chair to Vera.

"No, no. I just wanted to pop by. I slipped in even though they said only one visitor. I'll head back out."

"Actually, I needed to check on a friend and get some

coffee. Please stay with him and I'll be back in about fifteen minutes." Turning to his uncle, he mouthed, *"Be nice."*

As he walked into the waiting room he grinned, seeing Bayley sitting at a table, perched in an uncomfortable plastic chair, bent over her laptop, the ever-present pencil tucked into her hair holding it on top of her head in a semblance of a bun. She heard him enter and searched his face before breaking into a grin.

"Your uncle must be doing all right?"

Nodding as he took the chair opposite of her, "I left because he had another visitor. His neighbor. The one who keeps asking him to coffee and, from what I can see, is definitely interested in him."

"Oh, my," she laughed. "How sweet."

"Well, I hope so. He's in there grumbling and complaining, so she might not stay long. He's not one for open shows of emotion, but I think he likes her too."

Leaning back in her chair, she sucked in her lips. "Can I ask you something, Nick?"

"Sure," he agreed, knowing she had to be curious about his relationship with his uncle, but uncertain how much he felt like saying.

"Do you really hate the Christmastown Inn?"

He startled, seeing the sparkle in her eyes. Chuckling, he shook his head, never knowing what she was going to say next. "No, it's fine. Not the place I would have chosen, but it's growing on me. I didn't even fuss when the elves greeted us this morning or when they served pancakes in the shape of gingerbread men."

Clapping her hands, she said, "That was great, wasn't

it? I've taken so many pictures so I can remember all the details of that fabulous place."

A few minutes later, Vera appeared in the waiting room. Nick stood and hurried over. "I hope Uncle Bernie wasn't too rude."

"Honey, the day Bernard stops being a grump is the day we'll lay him to rest," she replied, her smile wide. Patting his arm, she continued, "Don't worry. We had a nice little chat, but I can tell he's tired. I wanted to keep my visit short but, if you don't mind, I'll come back tomorrow."

"I'd like that very much," he agreed. Seeing her eyes shift over to Bayley, he introduced the two women.

As Vera turned to leave, she looked up at Nick and said, "He may be an old cuss, but I've been inside his apartment. It's bare except for two things. He's got pictures of the days when he was a Marine and pictures of you. I figure those are the two most important things in his life, so it is so nice to meet you."

Nick watched her leave, his breath leaving his body in a whoosh as he felt Bayley's fingers rest lightly on his arm.

"You okay? You look a little off-kilter."

Shaking it off, he turned to look at her, taking in her honest and open expression. "Yeah, fine. Just a little surprised I guess. I never noticed Uncle Bernie taking pictures."

The afternoon sun peeked through the leaves as the Little Pigeon River rushed over the rocks below.

While Bernard rested in the afternoon, Nick drove Bayley up a winding mountain road. Stopping just outside of Gatlinburg, they wandered along a path near the river. Thick trees lined their walk and the sunlight sprinkled down between the leaves.

"This is so gorgeous," Bayley said, inhaling the clean, mountain air deeply. Lifting her face to the sky, she closed her eyes as the sun warmed her skin. Smiling, she said, "It must have been heaven living here." As soon as the words left her mouth, she dropped her eyes back to Nick. "Oh, Nick. I'm sorry. That was so insensitive of me."

Having been entranced by the sunlight on her face, Nick was slow to realize what she had asked. The topic he usually steered away from no longer seemed too painful to share with her. Shrugging, he said, "What do you already know?"

Confessing, she said, "I found your photo album in your guest room the other night. I looked at your childhood pictures with your parents and, then, they just stopped. I...well, I wondered."

Linking fingers with her, they wandered along the path a little further until finding a large, flat bolder overlooking the river. Sitting, he pulled her down next to him, the stone underneath warm from the sun. The woods surrounding the river were thick with foliage, the sound of birds chirping filling the air as well as the rustling of small, woodland creatures in the leaves. The air was crisp and clean, scented by the pines growing nearby.

Nick was silent a moment, his mind rolling through the events of his childhood, something he had not talked about in a long time. Bayley gently rubbed her fingers over his arm, the soothing motion giving ease to his tangled thoughts.

Clearing his throat, he said, "There's really not a lot to tell, Bayley. I grew up on the outskirts of Knoxville, not too far from here. My parents were young when they had me, but by the time I was about six years old, all my grand-parents had died. Both of my parents were only children so I had no aunts, uncles, or cousins. My dad had an uncle though, Bernie, and he was a career Marine. We only saw him when he was between tours. There was nothing bad about my childhood. It was really good, actually. I had friends and a good life, until it all went to shit one night."

The silence settled over the two of them again before he sucked in a deep breath and continued. "My parents were killed in a car accident. Uncle Bernie was at the funeral and afterwards, I overheard him talking with a woman, who I later understood was a social worker, but at the time I had no idea who she was."

"And they were discussing your situation, weren't they?" Bayley asked softly.

Nodding, he said, "After they talked, they came over and told me that I'd be placed with a nice family to live."

Gasping, Bayley's eyes widened as her fingers stopped their gentle touch and grabbed his arm instead. "Oh, my God, Nick. I am so sorry."

Shaking his head, he smiled ruefully. "I was lucky... had a great foster family. I had no idea what to expect, but they were really good to me."

"Were you disappointed that you couldn't live with Bernie?"

"No, not at all. At that age, I had no expectations, but then to be honest, I don't remember much about that time. Bernie was a Marine and had been one for twenty-eight years at that time. He was stationed overseas and came home for the funeral. He'd planned on retiring after thirty years in. I saw him rarely...didn't really know him. When I was older and knew how the foster system worked, I knew there was no choice since Bernie was a bachelor, never been married or around children, so the only decision at the time would be for me to be placed in a foster home."

They sat quietly for a few minutes before Nick continued, "It was weird for me because the Griffey's... that's the foster family, had two kids of their own and two other foster kids. So, we were a big group of seven around the dinner table. My parents had been quiet people and I was too. I admit, I was overwhelmed most of the time in the foster home, having never been around a family that size. But they were good people. They had me in counseling to deal with my parents' death, and that really helped a lot, actually, but I'm not sure I ever got over the feeling that life can change instantly."

"What about Bernie? He came back into the picture, right?"

"He retired two years later, after his thirty years in

the Corps, and moved back to the Knoxville area, settling in Sevier County. He got a job working in a home improvement store—loved working with his hands. He came to visit me at the foster home and something happened—"

"What?" she interrupted, eyes wide. "What happened?"

"The next month, the social worker came to tell my foster parents that I would be moving in with my great-uncle. She said he had a house, steady job and, as next of kin, he would be taking me with him."

"Wow," Bayley breathed, her mind filled with thoughts of young Nick and how his world had changed so drastically as a child, barely getting used to one situation before another one came along.

"I think it just hit him when he saw me there. When he'd been overseas with the Marines, he could pretend all back home was the same. He was used to my parents' quiet home, me being independent and thoughtful. He was a loner, too, when he wasn't with his fellow Marines. I remember him visiting me at the Griffey's house, sitting on the living room sofa, and the other kids playing in the next room, making noise like kids do. It was chaotic. Toys on the floor. Bikes on the lawn. People moving in and out of the room. Just a big, noisy family."

Bayley loosened her grip and began to rub his arm again, listening intently.

"So," he shrugged, "from the age of ten, it was me and Uncle Bernie."

"How was that?"

Chuckling, he admitted, "At first, I was concerned. I only knew him from his visits when my parents were still alive, but in some ways, living with him was also familiar. I realized later, how nice it was to be around someone who knew mom and dad. Bernie wasn't much of a talker, so our lives were rather quiet, which reminded me of my parents' household. It was good... different, but good. But it was a huge change from the foster family, which I had started to become accustomed to. I went to school and Bernie worked an early shift so he got home about the same time I did. I did homework and he puttered in his garage or workshop. We'd have supper and watch the news and then whatever sports were on. But he'd tell me stories about my dad when he was little and things that he remembered about my mom and grandparents. I've come to realize how much those stories meant to me...they were my connection to my family that I would have lost if not for Bernie."

"No toys on the floor?" she asked, gently.

Shaking his head, he smiled. "Thirty years in the Marines and Bernie liked his order." Shrugging slightly, he added, "But it's all good. After living with the Griffey's, I liked order too. I liked having my own toys and had no problem putting them away at the end of the day. Guess I kind of adopted that into my own lifestyle, huh?" he chuckled.

Bayley grinned as she leaned back on her hands. "Blaise was always so neat. So was my dad. I think I take after my mom, who's kind of a free spirit."

Shoulder bumping her, he agreed, "Oh, yeah, you're a free spirit."

They sat in companionable silence for a moment before she prodded, "There were no more pictures in your album until your high school graduation, and you seemed so much more . . . intense, I guess, by then."

Nodding, he said, "Don't get the wrong idea. I just grew up, that's all. And Uncle Bernie wasn't much into documenting anything. Mom was always the one running around with a camera. I don't know—without Mom and Dad, I didn't really want pictures either."

Feeling her heart break for him, tears stung her eyes. He looked over, surprised at the emotion overflowing. Reaching up, he caught a tear falling down her cheek with his thumb. "Don't cry for me, Bayley. I'm not the only person in the world who had an unconventional child-hood and mine was certainly not without happiness."

"I know, but I feel like you were adrift on a boat in the middle of storm-laden seas and needed an anchor, but no one really provided that for you."

"Wow," he said as a feeling of warmth slid over him. "I don't think I've ever had anyone describe a childhood like that and certainly not about me."

"Don't make fun of me when I'm emotional," she said, playfully slapping his arm. After another moment of thoughtful reflection, she asked, "Things seem good between you and your great uncle..."

"I knew him as a hard-ass Marine from my earliest memories, so I never expected anything else. He wasn't a touchy feely guy, never has been. But when I was living with him, he really made an effort to be involved in my life. He went to school functions, games I was playing in, even helped coach baseball one year. I also think that he was probably more at ease with me as I got older, since he'd never spent much time with kids. The older I got, the more we had things to talk about. I graduated a year early from high school and, back then, with guardian approval, I could join the military at seventeen with a high school diploma."

"I didn't know you were in the military."

"I wasn't. At the last minute, I realized I was about to sign just because I had no idea what else to do. So, I went to college instead, got my degree and went to the FBI academy. Been an agent ever since."

"Was Bernie okay with you not becoming a Marine?"

"Oh, yeah. He always said I needed to do what was right for me. But no one knows what that is when they're seventeen." Hearing her slight giggle, he asked, "Okay, what did you want to be at seventeen?"

"Lots of things—I wanted to join the Peace Corps and save the world. But then I also thought it would be fun to be in the roller-derby."

At that, Nick snorted, eliciting another playful giggle from her. After a moment, she asked, hesitantly, "I was wondering about the medallion around your neck. Is there a special meaning behind it?"

Nick's hand automatically reached up, feeling the pendant lying against his chest, near his heart. "When I was born, my dad bought a St. Nicholas pendant for my mother to have. It seemed fitting with my birth-day, after all." Seeing her head tilt as she waited for him to continue, he explained, "My birthday is December 25."

"Oh, my God, you're a Christmas baby!"

Nodding, he said, "Yep. Kind of sucked when I was little, but my parents always made sure that we had Christmas presents that morning and then that evening, we had my birthday celebration."

They sat quietly for a moment as Nick stared at the water below rushing by. Sighing, he plunged ahead. "I told you my parents were killed in a car accident. They were killed on Christmas Eve. At the hospital, a nurse had taken the necklace off my mother and handed it to me. I slipped it around my neck and have rarely been without it."

Tears stung Bayley's eyes as her heart ached for the little-boy Nick who had to live through such tragic circumstances.

"I once did some research on St. Nicholas," Nick admitted. "It seems that he lived in the third century and, strangely enough, his parents died when he was young. And he was raised by his uncle."

"No way," she breathed, her eyes wide.

"Yeah. Crazy, right?"

After another minute of silence while his tale settled over them, he admitted, "I don't get down here to see him much, and I feel really bad about that. We do talk on the phone every week...like I said, the older I got, the closer we became. He moved out of his house about three years ago and into an independent-living facility. He's got his own apartment, where he still cooks, but takes some of his meals in the cafeteria. They help with cleaning, but after all those years as a Marine, he keeps his place in top-shape."

The memory of Nick's neat habits now made even more sense as Bayley quietly listened. "What will happen now? Now that he needs help."

Shaking his head, he said, "I don't know. I'll have to get that figured out."

"Maybe Vera can help?"

Catching the twinkle in her eyes, he smiled.

15

"When will Ms. Hanssen have the next writer's critique group?" Agnes asked, eyeing Bruce as he continued to type.

Bruce looked over at Daphne. "Hey, where's Bayley? Aren't we having our group meeting tonight?"

Daphne walked over with another cup of coffee for them and said, "Not this week. She had to go out of town for a few days."

"Oh, I hope everything is all right," Agnes rushed to say, smiling up at Daphne.

"She's fine, but needed to go somewhere with a friend." Giggling, Daphne leaned down, whispering, "A really gorgeous friend."

Laughing, Agnes nodded in understanding. "Lucky girl. She certainly had a parade of handsome men in here a few days ago."

"Tell me about it," Daphne rolled her eyes, pretending to be bothered by the security. Grinning, she said, "Bayley was threatened by some man on the street, so her super-secret brother and some of his crew were making sure she was safe."

"Oh, my goodness," Agnes exclaimed, wide-eyed with her hand on her heart. "That sounds so scary."

"Hey, I'm the one who chased the guy off," Bruce countered, inserting himself into their conversation.

Agnes whipped her head around to him, "Did you see the person?"

Grimacing, Bruce replied, "Nah. I didn't even hear him. But I guess just the sound of my footsteps as I jogged back sent him running."

"Well, it's certainly good that Ms. Hanssen was not harmed," Agnes said.

"Yes, and now she's off with her FBI protector," Daphne agreed before heading back to the counter.

Pulling out her phone, Agnes sent a text, a small smile playing about her lips.

Hours later, as Daphne closed the shop, making sure to lock the doors, she waited outside on the sidewalk for a moment hoping her date had not forgotten he was supposed to pick her up at work. Pulling out her phone to send him a text, she saw a car pull up. Grinning, she hurried over as he alighted from the vehicle and opened the door for her.

"I like your manners," she said, sliding into the expensive leather interior.

Lazlo smiled as he climbed behind the wheel. "My mother taught me how to treat a lady," he said smoothly, as they pulled out onto the street.

"You gonna stand there or you gonna come on in?"

Nick walked in, glad to see Bernie's color was better. "Looks like your visit with Vera went well."

"Shut up," Bernie complained, although his color increased as two blush spots appeared on his cheeks. "Meddlin' old woman."

"Awfully pretty woman, if you ask me."

"Well, I didn't hear anyone ask you."

The two men shared a chuckle as Nick settled into the chair by the bed, allowing his gaze to roam around the room, seeing less tubes than before. "Looks like things are progressing."

"They want me to walk some this afternoon...or at least, get up out of bed and stand. Doubt I'll be able to piss by myself, but I'll move around some."

The quiet was interrupted by the continued beeps from the various machines still attached. "You gonna mention that girl you've got with you?"

As his forehead creased, Nick asked, "How do you know about any girl?"

"Seen her walk by a time or two, glancing in, trying to be unobtrusive, but she sure as hell ain't looking at me. Get the feeling she's checking on how you're doing."

"So, who's the investigator now?"

"Hell, boy. Don't take an investigator to see when a pretty young thing is interested." Holding a pillow to his chest as he coughed, Bernie winced in pain. As the spasm abated, he continued, "And Vera might have mentioned her as well."

"She's just part of a case I'm working on."

"That so? I'd say you're either lying to me or to yourself."

Nick looked down, his hands clasped in his lap.

"Boy?"

Nick lifted his head, the instinct to follow Bernie's orders still strong. "Yes, sir?"

"Why don't you talk a bit? I'm stuck in this bed with stuff attached to body parts that make me cringe. Talk and take my mind off all this."

"Anything in particular?"

"Nah...well, tell me about work. What's going on the world of the FBI right now?"

Sighing, Nick leaned back against the hard, metal chair and replied, "I was working on a terrorist case. That's when I was in Alaska a while ago. Then I did some temporary work on a case while another agent was on paternity leave. Just got assigned to a kidnapping case—someone is snatching women. May be tied into human trafficking."

"Damn, boy. Your job covers a lot of ground."

Nodding, Nick said, "But it's interesting. Keeps me on my toes."

After a moment of silence where Bernie's intelligent gaze studied Nick, he said, "Seems to me that there's something weighing on you. FBI no longer the career you want—or is it just this case?"

Rubbing the back of his neck, Nick shrugged, saying nothing.

"You gotta do what works for you, boy."

Slowly nodding, Nick replied, "I don't know if it's a speedbump or a roadblock."

"Does it involve that pretty girl who just walked by the door again?"

Nick swerved around, eyes searching, seeing no one. Chuckling, he looked back at the smiling face greeting him from the hospital bed. "Bet you think you're smart, don't you, Uncle Bernie?"

"I've been around a helluva lot longer than you. Guess I've learned a thing or two. You jerked your head around so fast to catch a glimpse of that girl, I thought your head was going to snap off."

After another protracted silence, Nick said, "She's a possible witness that I need to keep safe and when I got the call about you, she wanted to come with me. It made the most sense at the moment, but maybe I wasn't thinking straight."

"And you got your ass chewed by a superior," Bernie surmised correctly.

Nodding, Nick admitted, "Yeah, but that's not what this is about. Everyone's going to get their ass chewed at one time or another. Hell, I've chewed out some people myself at times. That's just part of working."

"So, what's got you in a knot?"

Nick stared at the man lying in the hospital bed, his lower half covered with a sheet and his chest a mass of stapled incisions and tubes. Bernie had always been so hardcore Marine. "If it hadn't been for me, would you have stayed longer in the military?"

Bernie winced again with another cough before settling his hard gaze on Nick. "What on earth are you asking that question for?"

"I'm just wondering about what all you gave up."

"Didn't give up nothing, boy. Truth be told, I shoulda given up the Corps two years earlier when you first needed me. Lived with that regret for the past twenty years."

Nick stared dumbly at Bernie's confession.

"At the time, I figured you'd be better off with some nice family than an old Jarhead. Wasn't until I got out, visited and, while them people were nice, hell, that place was noisy. I couldn't hear myself think and figured there was no way you could either. Right then and there, I made the decision to settle and get you with me."

"But that wasn't the life you had imagined. Raising an orphaned ten-year old. School projects, ball games—"

"We can't always predict life. I figured I was lucky to have gotten out of the Marines alive. Got in near the end of the Vietnam war, did tours in Iraq, Iran, Afghanistan. By all predictions, I should've been dead years ago. But God kept me alive and I figure, looking back, it was for being able to give us both a home." Bernie's sharp gaze continued to pierce Nick. "Don't you realize, boy? You gave me a reason to live beyond the Marines. I needed you as much as you needed me. Sometimes life changes and you gotta be willing to change with it."

Nick sat silent for a moment, Bernie's words moving through him. He thought about his life with the FBI, never thinking that he would have another career other than being an agent. But the job was changing... *hell, I'm changing.* Maybe Bernie's words were giving him the impetus for making the decisions he needed to make.

The two were silent for another moment before Bernie shifted in his bed. "They want me to try to take some steps today. You ready to help an old man?"

Ringing for a nurse, Nick moved over to stand by the bedside, his hands grasping Bernie's wrists firmly. The nurse and Nick assisted Bernie to stand, steadying him as his knees wobbled.

"Mr. Stone, would you like to try to walk down the hall?" the perky nurse asked.

Shooting her a glare, he groused, "No, I thought I'd go ballroom dancing."

Pinching her lips to keep from smiling, she said, "There's no need to get snippy, Mr. Stone. Your handsome visitor here will keep you in line."

"He's got himself a woman, sitting patiently out in the waiting room, so you keep your eyes in your head, Miss Nursey, and leave my nephew alone."

Laughing, she glanced at Nick. "Looks like he's ornery today. Is this normal for him or should I be worried?"

"Nah, this is Uncle Bernie...ornery as ever."

The nurse and Nick smiled as Bernie tried to hide his grin and grumbled once more. "Thirty years a Marine, missy. Don't be disrespecting me in my hour of need."

After a few minutes of assisting him walking as he became slightly steadier on his feet, they helped him back onto his bed. After the nurse checked his vitals, she left, leaving the two men alone once more.

Bernie leaned back, his eyes closing. "Boy, I'm pooped. You take your pretty woman out to lunch and let me sleep." He drifted off before Nick could reply.

Slipping out, Nick stalked toward the waiting area to find Bayley, smiling as his gaze landed on his pretty woman.

"Got a hit on a possible lead."

"What have you got, Harlan?" Nick stood outside the hospital, his cell phone pressed to his ear as his eyes searched the area, checking his privacy.

"While you were working on the terrorist cases, a group's been keeping an eye on the Russian mafia that's been creeping inward from Norfolk. They used to just run the port, but the agents in D.C. have begun noticing some families moving into the mid-Virginia area. At first, it just seemed a few of them might have been wanting to resettle outside the activities they'd been involved in, but now we suspect prostitution, gambling, money laundering, drugs, and a host of other shit."

"You think this ties into our kidnappings?"

"We wouldn't have been able to make that connection if Ms. Hanssen hadn't been approached. Johan made a huge error, now that she's identified him."

"Yeah, and that makes her vulnerable," Nick groused, his frustration evident as he stalked in a path up and down the sidewalk. "Listen, Harlan, we're gonna be down here for a few more days as I get my uncle settled—"

"Nick, I gotta warn you, Richard's threatening to pull you off the case and considering putting you on administrative leave pending an investigation into you taking a witness with you."

Nick's lips thinned in a grimace as he growled, "And I'm telling you, I've never once given the agency a reason to doubt my integrity—"

"I know, I know—"

"And one more thing," Nick growled, "I've had a lot of time to think lately, Harlan, and if Richard tries anything, I'm taking my skills elsewhere. Talk to you later," he bit out as he disconnected, the thought of becoming a Saint playing more and more in his mind.

"And then the elf said, 'But Santa, who'll make the toys?'"

Nick stood in the doorway of the lobby of the hotel, his eyes easily finding the beautiful blonde sitting in a rocking chair, a group of children at her feet. An open book was in her hands and a stack of other books were on the table next to her. After Vera had visited Bernie again, she volunteered to drop Bayley back at the hotel while Nick and Bernie made plans for the rehab necessary. And now, Nick's eyes feasted on the woman, who in such a short time had become a huge part of his world.

The children clapped with glee as Bayley turned the page, continuing the story in her animated voice. As the story progressed, she laughed along with the children, occasionally snorting, which only served to make the children laugh more. The corners of Nick's mouth tugged upward as he watched her. She was different from anyone he had ever known and, in a few days, she had wormed her way into his life—a place he already realized he wanted her to stay.

As she closed the book, she looked up, her bright eyes landing on him. Giving him a finger wave as she accepted a hug from a little girl, her smile beamed at both he and the children.

"The young woman with you is a great storyteller," a male voice said from behind him. Nick jerked his head around and found himself staring into Santa Claus' face. His white shirt was embroidered with red poinsettias and holly and his red pants were held up with suspenders. Up close, Nick discerned that, indeed, the white, bushy eyebrows and thick beard were natural. Santa's ruddy cheeks came from within and not makeup. Startling, clear, blue eyes peered back at Nick, as though studying him as well.

"She's…well, uh…she's…" Nick floundered, unable to pull his thoughts together while facing the iconic character.

Santa chuckled, his belly bouncing with the hearty laugh. "I felt the same way when I met Mrs. Claus."

Narrowing his eyes slightly, Nick stared at the man in front of him, no idea what to say in response.

"I see you're a doubter," Santa said. Turning his head, he nodded to the other side of the lobby where Mrs. Claus was passing out cookies to the children. "She's my wife…been my wife for a long time. Met her and instantly knew I wanted to spend the rest of my life with her."

The men stood quietly for a moment, their gazes on the two women in the lobby, both surrounded by children, so alike in their mannerisms.

"Life surprises us sometimes, Mr. Stone," Santa said.

Nick knew it would not be hard for a hotel employee to find out his name, but the casual use of it caught him by surprise. He dragged his attention from Bayley to Santa.

"We can be heading down one road and before we know it, we come to a fork. That can really throw us, especially if we didn't see the fork coming."

Nick felt a catch in his throat as his chest rose and fell with heavy breaths. *First Bernie and now this guy.* Replying in defense, "Then...then we look at the situation logically. Analytically. Figure out what's the most practical path."

Santa's smile widened. "Is that so? Well, sometimes, Nick, we need to follow our heart. Throw out our long-held plans and travel the path that takes us into the unknown."

Unable to take his eyes off Santa's face, Nick felt sucked in. "I don't know that's the type of person I am."

Patting his shoulder, Santa replied, "For me, the greatest joy is flying off into the star-filled night sky. That's where I find the wonders of life. You should try it. Saint Nick...it has a nice ring to it, don't you think? You just might find everything you've been missing."

Nick's chest heaved as Santa's words hit him...seriously hit him.

"Hey, Nick...how's Bernie?"

Nick jerked his head around, seeing Bayley walking straight to him, her eyes searching his face. Her smile drooped slightly as she placed her hand on his arm.

"Is everything all right?"

"Yeah, yeah," Nick assured, reaching up to take her fingers in his grasp. "I saw you reading to the kids but didn't want to interrupt, so I was just talking to...uh..."

Shifting her stance, Bayley looked over his shoulder. "Talking to who?"

"Santa," Nick said, twisting his head, seeing no one standing next to him. Whipping his head around, he realized he was all alone by the doorway.

16

"Are you about finished playing with your food?"

Bayley had watched Nick for the past ten minutes as he moved his southern fried chicken around, eating only a few bites. He was distracted and even more tense than usual.

"Sorry," he said, a slight blush rising on his face. "I guess I'm not good company."

"What's on your mind? Bernie?"

"No…well, yes…sort of." Rubbing his hand over his face, he cursed, "Damn, I'm not even talking in complete sentences."

Giggling, Bayley said, "Hey, you've earned the right to babble." Gaining his incredulous expression, she said, "Switching cases, for someone like you, must have been hard."

Nodding slowly, he admitted, "Just seems like things are changing at work and I'm trying to figure out how to stay satisfied in my job."

" 'It's what's in yourself that makes you happy or

unhappy,' " she quoted. Grinning, she confessed, "That's from Agatha's, *A Murder is Announced*." She speared another bite of chicken and added, "You know, hearing about your uncle was so unexpected. And now you're stuck at a holiday resort with a bunch of elves and a goofy woman." She waved her hand around at the heavily decorated restaurant.

His lips curved as he shook his head slowly. "Don't throw yourself into the mix of the craziness of my life right now. You might have been unexpected, but I'm hardly stuck with you."

"Oh, yeah? How would you describe it?"

He watched as the lights hanging from the surrounding trees sent slivers of colors over her blonde hair. Her eyes sparkled with an ever-present glow that he had never experienced until meeting her. "Beautiful...I'd describe you as beautiful. Inside and out."

Her mouth opened and closed several times, unable to come up with a response to his simple, yet heartfelt, compliment. Blushing, she nodded toward his plate. "Go on, eat up. I can't wait to try their dessert. I've heard the Brandied-Candied Cake is divine."

He watched the color stretch from her chest up toward her hairline, the blush in the evening light making her more alluring than before. He fought the urge to lean over and trail his tongue along her blushing skin. With a mental shake, he dropped his gaze back to his meal before thoughts of devouring her took over.

Soon, she began moaning as her lips closed over the fork containing a bite of dessert. "Oh, my God, mmmm-mmm. This is so good. Here, have a bite."

Nick stared at her face, almost orgasmic, and all attempts at not wanting to throw her over his shoulder and disappear upstairs flew from his mind as the blood rushed to his cock. She was holding her fork out to him, the moist cake tempting, but not as tempting as her. Unable to stop himself, he leaned forward and slid his lips over the tines, pulling the cake into his mouth. Hearing another groan, he realized it came from him. He had no memory of ever taking a bite of food off someone else's utensil—much less fruit cake, which he did not like—until now. And both were delectable.

Chewing, he watched as she took another bite, staring at her lips and wanting them wrapped around his swollen erection. Tired of battling his desire and growing feelings for her, he stood suddenly, his hand outstretched toward hers.

Eyes wide, her gaze jumped from his hand to his face before a smile slowly curved her lips upward. Placing her hand in his, she moved from her chair, allowing him to lead her toward the elevators.

As soon as the doors closed, he took a step away, his mind fighting with his heart.

"No," she ordered, plastering her body to his, forcing him back against the wall. Lifting her hands to his cheeks, she rubbed her thumbs over the stubble along his jaw before moving them over his lips. Standing on her toes, she leaned in until her mouth was a whisper away from his. "Don't fight this anymore."

With her name escaping his lips in a groan, he closed the distance, latching onto her mouth like a dying man searching for air. Noses bumping, they moved, sucked, licked as their tongues met and tangled.

The doors opened but they paid no heed until the clearing of a throat sounded behind them. Laughing, Bayley pulled Nick out of the elevator leaving an older couple smiling in their wake.

He fumbled with the card lock, but as soon as the door to their room opened, he whirled her around, pressing her back against the wall. His hands framed her face as he held on, angling her mouth for maximum contact, sucking her tongue into his mouth. Her breasts squashed against his chest and his swollen erection pressed into her stomach.

After a moment...or an eternity, he lifted his head and gazed at her kiss-swollen lips, now red and slick, and her lust-hooded eyes, the sky-blue now stormy with need. Her eyes slowly focused then narrowed in confusion.

"No, Nick, please don't pull away from me. Not now. Not when we want each other so much," she begged, her fingers grasping at his shirt.

"Shh," he said, his hands pulling her from the wall and into his chest. "I'm not stopping...I'm just making us more comfortable. I don't want our first time to be—"

"I don't care," she cried, "Our first time can be hanging from the ceiling for all I care."

Chuckling, he stepped back, pulling her along with him until the back of his legs hit the mattress. Standing next to the bed, he slid his hands to the bottom of her shirt, snagging it and slowly peeling it up over her breasts and her head, before tossing it to the floor.

Dropping his gaze to her pert breasts, rising and falling with each ragged breath, the lace barely covering her nipples. Sliding his arms to her back, he unhooked her bra, letting it fall to the floor, allowing her nipples to harden. Pebbled with the cool air across her naked skin, he reached up and cupped her breasts with both hands, tantalizingly slow before slightly pinching both nipples and giving a little tug.

A groan escaped her lips as the sensation zinged from her nipples to her core, sending shock waves to her sex. Throwing her head back, she clenched her thighs together to try to appease her body's desire for friction. Soothing his palm over her nipples decreased the sting, but continued to send shocks of desire to her core.

Her fingers fumbled with his buttons, finally managing to pull his shirt off his shoulders. Forcing his arms down, she hated to lose the connection, but wanted to feel his bare chest against hers. His shirt joined hers on the floor and, pulling her close, he flamed their desire as skin met skin.

Slipping her skirt over her hips it puddled around her ankles, leaving her clad in only silky panties. "You're over dressed," she whispered, her fingers now tugging on his belt. Pulling it loose, she unzipped his pants, freeing his thick cock. Wrapping her delicate hand around its girth, she felt the groan rumble in his chest as her hand worked him.

Whirling around, he backed her against the bed,

pushing her down onto the mattress, hating the loss of her hand on his cock. Grabbing a condom from his wallet, he shucked his pants after toeing out of his shoes, flinging his socks and boxers across the room before looming over her almost naked body. Snagging his fingers into the scrap of lace at her hips, he drew her panties down her legs, leaving her bare beauty open for his admiration.

Crawling over her, he kissed her calves, up her thighs, moving his mouth over her mound, eliciting groans from her lips. Lapping, first her folds before moving over her clit, he loved the taste of her. Pulling her folds apart with his fingers, his tongue delved deeper.

Replacing his tongue with his fingers, he sucked on her clit while scissoring his fingers deep inside. He slid one hand up to fondle her breast, pulling lightly on her nipple.

Her hips rotated upwards pushing into his face as she felt her core tighten. Feeling the delicious pressure building in her core with the scent of arousal in the air, she desperately sought her release. With another simultaneous tug on her nipple and a suck on her clit, his fingers buried deep, she came, convulsing against his face. Exploding, as waves of bliss pounded over her, she threw her head back, allowing the sensations to carry her away.

Nick grinned as he licked her slick folds once more, the taste of her excitement on his tongue and the delightful view of the smile on her lips. Kissing his way up her body, he moved between each breast, sucking then nipping, then kissing to soothe the sting.

Wanting his lips on hers, she sat up and pulled his head in for a kiss. Warm. Pliant. She licked his lips and he growled his response.

Taking over the kiss, he teased his tongue slowly into her mouth. Exploring. Tasting. Tempting. Cupping her face with his hand, he ran his thumb over her cheek, the soft skin silky underneath his finger. Determined to make the night last, he moved his mouth slowly over hers.

Greedy, she grasped his shoulders, feeling the play of muscles underneath her fingertips. Laying her gently on her back, he bore his weight on his forearms, resting them on either side of her head while gently pressing his swollen cock against her pelvis.

Throughout this exquisite torture, he held her lips, taunting and teasing them with his tongue. She spread her legs so that he could settle between them, his cock nestling into her wet folds that beckoned him.

He grabbed the condom from where he had tossed it on the bed and rolled it on quickly. Keeping his gaze on hers, he deliberately slid his cock into her waiting body. Inch by tortuous inch. Not pounding. Not plunging. But so slow he could feel every twinge of her body. Memorizing her feel. Reveling in the sensation of her body accommodating him.

Once buried to the hilt, he slid lazily back and forth. The friction built just as quickly as if he had been rocking into her. Both arms were on either side of her head again, and their eyes never wavered. Over and over he moved until finally the fevered pitch reached its crescendo.

Determined to hold his gaze, she squeezed his shoulders tightly as her orgasm rushed over her, electrifying her body from her core outwards. Tightening her legs around his waist with her heels against his ass, she pulled him in as he emptied himself into her. His neck was corded with thick, straining muscles until he finally collapsed to the side, taking her with him.

Eyes still connected. Hearts beating as one. Legs tangled and arms holding tightly.

An hour later, Bayley lay sound asleep, her head resting on his chest next to her hand. Nick curled his arm around her, tucking her even closer to his heartbeat, the scent of lemons filling his nostrils. Unable to sleep, the advice he had gotten that day echoed in his mind throughout the quiet night.

17

"Here's the key. Make yourself at home and I'll prepare some tea for us and bring it over."

Vera handed Nick the key to Bernie's apartment then headed off to her own. He opened the door and stepped through, his gaze sweeping the area before allowing Bayley entrance.

She laughed, "I don't think the boogie-man will be here."

Swatting her ass lightly, he said, "Force of habit." As she moved into the kitchen to see if there was food that needed to be discarded, Nick stood in the living room and looked around. It had been two years since he had been back to visit Bernie. The neat home appeared very much as had Nick expected—no clutter, no mess, very functional. And yet, with photographs displayed on the walls and end tables, Nick was reminded that Bernie had never had mementoes out before. Stalking over to the wall, he viewed framed photographs of Bernie in uniform over the decades, all with different friends depending on the warzone he was stationed. Having just seen Bernie lying in a hospital bed, he was struck with the difference he found in him in the various photographs.

"He looks the same, doesn't he?" Bayley asked, coming up by his shoulder.

"Huh? The same?"

"Look at his eyes...the determination. That's the same look that he has now. Determined to get better and get back on his feet."

Staring at the pictures with renewed interest, he realized Bayley was right. The same eyes stared back at him from over the years and he knew then that Bernie was going to be coming home from the hospital. Smiling down at her, he placed his arm over her shoulders, pulling her in slightly.

Moving toward the sofa, he bent to see the framed pictures crowding the surface. Startled, he viewed ones of him and his parents when he was a child and pictures of Bernie and his dad when they were little. There was even a picture of Nick in high school wearing a baseball uniform.

He picked up the frame, saying, "I had no idea he'd taken this picture. He came to my games, but I never saw him with a camera."

Just then, a knock sounded at the door and Bayley opened it, seeing Vera on the stoop with a tray in her hands. "Oh goodness, let me take that." Relieving the tray from Vera, she invited her in and set it down on the coffee table.

"Here we are, making ourselves at home in Bernard's

apartment. Wouldn't he just fuss?" Vera giggled, pouring the tea into mugs.

Nick, glad for the sturdy mug instead of a delicate teacup, smiled. "We never had much company when I was living with Bernie. I take it he's the same now?"

"Oh, he likes to grumble whenever there's some kind of party or little to-do in the clubhouse, but I've gotten him to go out. He says it's just to keep the old geezers around here from trying any funny business with me, but I think he secretly likes it."

Bayley snorted at the description of Bernie. "I just met him and yet I can see him dragging his feet and then glaring at the other men looking at you."

Vera met her smile before shifting her gaze to Nick. "It is true, that I do like your uncle a great deal. I was married to a wonderful man for almost fifty years, until he died five years ago. I moved in here about year before Bernard did and we became friends. I think he knew I wasn't at a retirement home looking for another husband and our friendship seemed to keep the other women at bay." Leaning forward, she whispered loudly, "Some of these women can really work to get their claws into a man, since they are so few and far between!"

"I'm glad for your friendship with him, Vera," Nick assured, setting his mug down. "Can I ask you something?"

"Of course."

"These pictures," Nick indicated with his hand, "how long has he had them out?"

Surprise crossed her features. "As long as I've been coming over. He was…is…so proud of you."

Thinking for a moment, Nick offered, "He was a good man to take me in—"

"He may have taken you in out of a sense of responsibility, but I assure you that Bernard thought you were the greatest thing in his life. Even more than the Marines."

Shocked silent, Nick's mouth hung open. Bernie had mentioned regretting not taking him in right away, that they had needed each other, but he thought maybe the trauma of the heart attack had made Bernie more sentimental.

Bayley leaned over, her fingers linking with his, a smile offered in comfort. Recognizing the need to move the conversation to a less emotional one, she said, "His refrigerator is good. I bagged up the spoiled veggies and poured the milk down the sink. I placed the garbage bag in his container."

"Oh, good," Vera said. "I hadn't even thought about that." She turned back toward Nick. "Does he know what his rehab will look like?"

"He and I talked to the doctor this morning. He will spend at least three more nights in the hospital, leaving ICU and being in a regular room starting tomorrow if he continues to progress so well. The hospital will work with the facility's nursing coordinator here and a home health nurse. If his needs can be met, he'll come back here, with nursing assistance as needed."

"Good, good," Vera nodded, a small smile playing about her lips.

Bayley glanced at Nick, her grin indicting what she thought of Bernie's attentive neighbor. With tea finished, Vera stood and placed the empty mugs on the tray. Refusing Bayley's offer of help, she said goodbye, leaving the couple standing in the living room.

"Was there anything else you needed to get?" Bayley asked.

Jarred back to the moment, Nick dragged his gaze from the family pictures lining the walls, and said, "I need to get some clothes for him to put on when he leaves the hospital. I'll get sweatpants and some t-shirts."

Bayley admired the view of Nick's backside as he walked down the hall toward Bernie's bedroom. "Don't forget underwear," she called after him. "Everyone wants clean underwear when they leave the hospital."

Hearing Nick chuckle from the bedroom, she sighed, waiting patiently until he returned, a small travel-bag in his hand. After returning the key to Vera, he linked hands with Bayley and they climbed back into his vehicle. Back at the hospital, they headed up the elevator to Bernie's floor.

"I figure, once things are settled tomorrow, you and I can start the trip back."

"Are you sure? I don't mind staying longer. Daphne says the shop is fine."

"I appreciate it, but I've got to get back—as long as Bernie is doing well."

"Are you worried about the case?"

Nodding, he admitted, "Not really worried, but I've got some decisions to make." Stepping off the elevator,

Nick said, "Come on into the room with me. I'd like you to meet Bernie."

"Oh, I don't want to take up your time with him—"

"He's been asking about you...he saw you passing the door yesterday and noticed you kept looking in."

It did not take long for the couple to reach Bernie's room, Nick pleased to see him sitting up in bed, his color still pale but less white than the previous days. Bernie's eyes landed on Bayley and he smiled.

"Well, I see my nephew has decided that I'm not too old of a coot to be introduced to his pretty girl."

Laughing, Bayley unlinked fingers with Nick and walked to Bernie's bedside, leaning over to kiss his cheek. "It's so nice to meet you, Mr. Stone. I'm Bayley."

"Bah, with that Mr. Stone stuff. Call me Bernie...or Uncle Bernie, if you're so inclined."

Cutting her eyes over to Nick, who had moved beside her, she said, "All right, Bernie it is."

"I brought you some clothes, Uncle Bernie," Nick said as he opened the bag. "When do you think they'll let you put them on?"

"Hell, right now, if they know what's good for them. I'm tired of my wanker being out for anyone to see!"

"Bernie!" Nick scolded, his lips curving as he observed Bayley's giggling.

Bernie shot a look toward Bayley. "Miss Bayley, I do apologize for my crudeness...I seem to have forgotten my manners since being here."

"It's perfectly fine," she smiled. "I'll step outside and let Nick assist you with whatever clothes they'll let you put on."

Just then the nurse entered the room, eying the sweatpants in Bernie's hands. "Oh, no, Mr. Stone. No pants for you until you are ready to be discharged and that won't be for a few days."

Bernie aimed a narrow-eyed look at her, muttering under his breath. "Shoulda known, you'd be wanting to peek at my—"

"Bernie!" Nick interrupted again, glaring at both his uncle and Bayley, whose giggles rang out once more.

Kissing Bernie's cheek again, she patted Nick's arm. "I'll go back to the waiting area while you and Bernie talk a bit."

Nick watched her delectable ass as it moved away from him before turning back to his uncle, seeing his eyes on Bayley's backside as well. Shaking his head, he decided not to chastise Bernie, sitting down near his bed instead. Nick felt like a bug under a glass as Bernie faced him, his intelligent eyes pinning him to his chair.

"So, talk to me, boy. What have you decided?"

"Decided?"

Nodding, he said, "Uh huh. You know what I mean. That morose expression that's been on your face is gone. I take it good things are happenin' with that pretty Bayley?"

Grinning, Nick met his uncle's blue-eyed gaze. "Yeah, good things are happening." As his smile dropped slightly, he added, "But I've got to decide about work."

"You thinking about leaving the Bureau?"

Nick searched Bernie's face for signs of disapproval, but found only curiosity. "We'll see. I never thought I'd leave. Never thought I'd feel like I needed to. But, I've been offered a lucrative positon with a private investigative firm. I've coordinated with them for a year and have to admit I'm impressed. They get assignments that are right up my alley and aren't...uh...limited by political posturing. And the opportunity to work with a team that I respect. I think I'd like to do something different...more challenging."

"Boy, it sounds like you already have your answer," Bernie pronounced. "Just listening to you and the look on your face...sounds like a good deal."

Shrugging, Nick said, "We'll see. A lot will depend on how things go when I get back." Holding Bernie's gaze, he added, "And speaking of that, I thought I'd head home tomorrow and then come back when you're out of rehab and make sure you're good in your apartment."

"Nope, you and Bayley head on back to Virginia as soon as you can. I'm good here...sure as hell don't need no coddling. Lord knows, Vera'll do enough of that when I get back to my apartment."

Nick nodded slowly, smiling at the thought of his uncle finally succumbing to the ministrations of a good woman. "I'll say goodbye now and then plan on coming in tomorrow morning before we leave. The hospital is on the way out of town anyway."

With heartfelt goodbyes, Nick wrapped his arms gently around Bernie's body, offering what he hoped was his thanks as well as his love. As he pulled back, he noted the tears that had gathered in the older man's eyes, then realized they were in his as well.

Bayley sat quietly, watching Nick's chest rise and fall. She had insisted he lie down after they ate, knowing he needed rest. His lashes were thick against his cheeks, which now held a slight scruff, giving him a dangerously debonair look. His lips were full and, now that she knew how they felt, she longed to taste them again. Wearing only a white t-shirt after shucking his button-up, his muscles were showcased to perfection.

Tiptoeing out of the room, she headed down to the lobby after deciding to buy some snacks for tomorrow's road trip back to Virginia. Stepping out of the elevator, wearing black yoga pants and an old t-shirt, she observed the crowd. Mr. and Mrs. Claus were going to make an appearance in the lobby and the children crowded near the large tree, hoping to have their picture taken. Slipping through the closest doors, she came face to face with Mr. and Mrs. Claus preparing for the afternoon's activities.

Grinning, she greeted, "Hello!"

Santa chuckled as he winked at Bayley. "How lovely to see you again." Nodding toward Mrs. Claus, he said, "We have something for you. Just for you." Mrs. Claus reached her hand into the large bag of presents and pulled out a small box. Stepping up, she smiled, her rosy cheeks shining.

"We thought you would like this," she said, handing it to Bayley.

Taking the red box, wrapped with a silver bow, Bayley smiled. "Oh, my goodness, thank you."

Patting her hand as they prepared to step into the lobby, Santa turned back to Bayley and whispered, "My dear, I think you should go out the door to the side. Avoid the main lobby and I will do what I can to help."

"Wha—what? I don't understand," she protested, but the iconic pair stepped into the lobby to the loud cheers of the children.

Standing for a moment, she looked down at the box in her hand, unwrapping the bow. Opening the gift, she stared in dumb silence as a beautiful silver chain and pendant was revealed. A Saint Nicholas. So much like the one Nick wore. Clutching it in her hand, she held it to her heart before slipping it over her neck.

Turning, she walked to the side door and slipped into the back of the lobby, avoiding the crowd. Walking briskly, with her back toward the gathering around one of the trees, her spidey senses engaged, sending alarm tingles down her spine. Sliding discreetly behind one of the large, snowman decorations, she peeked around the edge of the top hat, spying across the lobby. Carefully moving her gaze slowly from one side to the other, her eyes landed on a man standing near the entrance door leading to the Holiday Garden, leaning casually against a pillar. *Shit!* Recognizing the man who had accosted her, she jerked back behind the snowman.

Heart pounding, she stood in indecision for a moment. Ever so slowly, she squatted before peeking back around the snowman's midsection. At this angle, she could observe him without him seeing her. She noted he was also shifting his view around as though searching. *Good, he hasn't seen me yet!*

Putting her hand in her pocket only to discover she did not have her cell phone, she wasted another moment in indecision. Just then, Mr. and Mrs. Claus called for the children to head out to the Holiday Garden for more games. As the mass of people rushed toward the doors, Bayley looked over the snowman's shoulder to see the man's attention diverted as he attempted to move away from the crush of children. Taking her opportunity, she headed to the stair doorway. Glancing back, her gaze caught Santa's—and with a nod, he winked.

18

Nick jerked awake as Bayley bounded into the hotel room.

"Get up, get up! I just saw him in the lobby. I don't know how he knew we were here, but I saw him!"

On his feet in an instant, Nick's heart pounded as his groggy mind tried to decode Bayley's words while she rushed around the room, throwing items into her bag.

"Your bag's already packed, so that's good. You just gotta grab your toiletries. Or leave them. Yeah, you can get others. You probably have stuff at your house." She grabbed the pile of her clothes lying next to the bed and shoved them haphazardly into her suitcase. "I gotta get my hair stuff. It's kind of expensive, but it'll only take a second." Stopping, she looked up at him, saying, "Nick? Are you listening? Get a move on!"

Stalking over, now fully awake, he stilled her flurry of movements with his hands on her shoulders. "Bayley. Slow down. Who did you see?"

"The man. The man who accosted me. The one you said was some super-duper Russian bad guy. He's down in the lobby!"

"Johan? Johan Serkov?"

Shoving him to the side, she ran into the bathroom as she shouted, "I don't know! I don't know his name. All I know is that he's down in the lobby right now and I don't think he's there to visit Santa!" Rushing back into the room with her arms full of cosmetic bags and hair-care products, she added, "But would you believe that Santa must have known what was going on because he helped me escape back up here?"

Blinking at her nonsensical ramblings mixed in with the facts, Nick halted her again. Holding her face in his hands, he said, "Bayley, you've gotta focus. Please, focus."

She pursed her lips, but nodded obediently.

"Tell me exactly what happened and what you saw."

"Fine," she agreed, and related her observations from the lobby. Finishing, she peered into his eyes, asking, "Are we okay? Don't we need to get out of here? Like now?"

Stepping back, he said, "Keep packing." Pulling out his phone, he dialed. "Harlan? Bayley just saw Johan Serkov in the lobby. Get the security tapes from downstairs and see if you can identify him. Yeah...yeah. We're packing now and will be out of here in about five more minutes. I'm not going to do anything here but get Bayley out. I'd rather he not know that we're on to him. We're going out the back and won't check out. We've got a reservation for two more nights, so it'll look like we're still here."

"How the fuck did he find you there?" Harlan asked.

"Got no idea," Nick replied, scruffing his hair with his hand. "I've used no personal accounts but—" he halted. "Fuckin' hell, Bayley made the reservations."

She stood, eyes wide and whispered, "I used my Expedia account even though you paid for it with your card."

"Damnit!" Nick cursed. "Okay, Harlan, call the Knoxville FBI office and get someone here immediately. I'll call you from the road. We're outta here now."

"Nick, I'm so sorry," Bayley cried, her hands clutching his forearms. "Are we in danger?"

"Baby, I've got you and this is not your fault," he assured, sliding his hand down so that his fingers could clasp with hers. Bending down to capture her eyes, he repeated, "This is not your fault. I never thought about it. Paying with various cards is a habit with me, but I never thought about the reservations. That's on me." He eyed the bag on the bed. "You done?"

"Yeah," she said, her head bobbing, fear clutching at her now that her movements had stilled, allowing her mind to focus on Johan's presence.

"Make sure you've got everything and, for God's sake, go to the bathroom. Once we leave here, we'll slip down the back stairs and make our way to my vehicle. I want to get back to Virginia, where I can guarantee your safety. Harlan will notify the local FBI office, so they can investigate."

The two worked in tangent for another minute, making sure to gather all their belongings and then Bayley ran into the bathroom. Emerging a moment later, she nodded. "I'm good."

Looking at her blue eyes, no longer wide with fright but bright with adrenaline, he stalked over, lifting his hand to the back of her neck. Pulling her in, he latched onto her lips, kissing with the initial intention of offering comfort but, as her tongue tangled with his, it zoomed into pure, white-hot need.

Discipline was the only reason he pulled back, his breath raspy as he observed her stormy-blue eyes piercing his. She licked her lips as her chest heaved. "Now, I'm good," she wheezed.

Smiling as he gave her neck a slight squeeze, he replied, "Yeah, you are, babe."

Fifteen minutes later, they pulled out of the back of the parking lot, leaving the Christmastown Inn behind.

Seven hours later, Nick pulled into his apartment's secure garage. He had sped the entire trip and, even with the three pit stops Bayley needed, they made good time. Glancing to the side, he observed her face, relaxed in sleep. Leaning over, he ran his finger over her petal-soft cheek, watching as her eyes fluttered open.

"Hey. We're home."

Blinking a few times as she regained her wits, Bayley looked at the man whose face was so close to hers.

Licking her lips, she hoped he would kiss her. Moving forward slowly, giving him every indication of her intention, she licked his bottom lip before angling her head to latch onto his firm mouth. He immediately plunged his tongue as they let the nerves of the day morph into desire, now that they were safe. After a moment, they leaned back simultaneously, smiles playing about their lips.

"Let's go in, Bayley. I need to talk to my people and I also need to check in with Jack. I know you want to talk to Blaise as well, but let me fill him in first, okay?"

She nodded, having no difficulty letting him handle this situation. "While you do that, I'll check in with Daphne."

Once in his apartment, Bayley hesitated at the door, wondering if he expected her to stay. *Where should I put my things?*

As he pulled his cell phone out of his pocket to call Harlan, he turned, seeing the doubt on her face. "Put your things in my bedroom...that is, if you're okay with that."

Grinning, she nodded. "Absolutely." As he connected with his fellow agent, she moved down the hall, stepping inside his room. It was larger than the guest room, a king-sized bed against the back wall, flanked with two walnut nightstands. A tall, walnut dresser was against another wall, next to a door leading into the bathroom. His bed was made, covered in a dark grey comforter. A chair in the corner was empty—of adornment and of clothes. Stepping into the master bathroom, her gaze swept the clean counters. Biting her lip, she wondered how she would ever be able to stay in his room without leaving a mess. Walking back to the bathroom in the hall, she set her toiletries inside the cabinet before moving into the guest room and placing her bag on the bed.

Back in his bedroom, she pulled out her phone, dialing Daphne as she sat in the comfortable chair.

"Girl, how are you?" Daphne greeted.

"We're fine, but how's everything here?"

"The shop is fine. You know I would have told you if anything was wrong. The coffee's hot, the customers are buying, and the writers are in their cubicles creating. Don't worry about us."

"Good. I can't thank you enough. I'm heading to my place tomorrow, so that will take some of the work off you at the store."

"Ooohh, spending the night with Mr. TDMB?"

"I hadn't thought of him with that name in a couple of days," Bayley commented, thinking of how their relationship had changed with the trip. Now he was just...*my Nick.*

"And how do you think of him?"

Blushing and glad her friend could not see her, she replied, "Just a really super nice, smart, caring man."

Daphne was silent for only a second before she gushed, "Oh, Bayley, that's so sweet."

"How are things with you and your man?"

"Uh...okay, I guess," Daphne replied. "I mean, he keeps coming around, but I'm not sure he's as into me as I thought."

Sensing her friend wanted a change of subject, Bayley said, "I'll be into the shop tomorrow afternoon so, can you open for me again? That'll give me a chance to talk to my brother and have time to check in with the writers when I get there."

With Daphne's assurance that she would not mind, Bayley disconnected, staring out the window at the sunset. The sound of an angry voice met her ears and she hurried to the doorway, hesitating as she stepped into the hall. Uncertain if she should be listening, curiosity won out and she moved toward the kitchen.

Nick was standing in his living room, his back to her as he stared out the window, his voice raised in frustration.

"The bigger risk was her staying here without me or the Saints able to provide the security we needed. No. No. What the hell, Harlan? I know this isn't coming from you. It's coming from Richard, and I'll be damned if I let him trash my record just because I didn't ask him first on this."

Bayley stepped back, pressing against the wall, her heart pounding as her stomach clenched in nerves. *He's in trouble...because of me.* His voice continued in anger before she heard the phone landing on the coffee table. Licking her dry lips, she stepped around the corner, her eyes searching for him. He stood, still facing the window, his hands on his hips. She caught the instant his eyes found hers in the reflection.

She opened her mouth, but no words came as she continued to stare, the air crackling about the room. He turned slowly, his gaze now directly on her.

"Come here," he growled, and the sound of his voice shot straight to her core.

Her feet moved of their own accord as she hurried to stand directly in front of him. Neither touched for a moment, until he swooped down, encircling her waist, hauling her up against his chest.

She grabbed his cheeks in her hands pulling him in close without kissing him. "What's going on?" she whispered against his lips.

Shaking his head, he said, "I don't want to talk right now."

A slow grin curved her lips as her tongue darted out, moistening them. "So, what do you want to do?"

"I want you...your body under mine...or hell, on top of mine. As long as I'm in you when you come."

His words, rough and needy, speared her sex as she rubbed her core on his jean-clad leg, her clit aching for his touch.

"I feel yucky from the long drive," she claimed. "But your shower is big and huge and I'm dying to try it out."

"I can honestly say I've never had shower sex, but I'm willing to give it a shot."

"I haven't either," she confessed, "but I have it in my books, so—"

"So, this is research?"

Giggling, she nodded against his chest. "Oh, yeah. Definitely research."

Scooping her up in his arms, he stalked to the master bathroom as she squealed, hanging on as he nibbled on her neck. Twisting his body so he would not hit her head or her feet on the doorway, he settled her down on the thick bathmat. Turning on the water, he looked over his shoulder as she immediately shucked her clothes. With her hands on her hips, her naked body had his cock standing at attention. His eyes landed on the pendant dangling at the top of her breasts.

Seeing his curious stare, she reached up, fingering the necklace. "Santa gave this to me just before he warned me to leave from a back door."

Shaking his head slowly, he grinned in amazement. "If you'd told me this last week, I'd have said you were crazy, but now? I'll believe almost anything." As his gaze slid down her body, his lips curved upward. Jerking his shirt off, he threw it on the floor. Her impatient fingers fumbled with his belt as he toed off his shoes. With his cock soon free, she knelt on the bathmat, taking him in her mouth as he slid his pants and boxers down his legs.

His hands grasped her hair, winding the tresses through his fingers as she licked and gently sucked him into oblivion.

Bayley looked upward, heady with power as she watched his head fall back, his face a picture of agony and ecstasy. His cock was thick, long veins running down the length. Her fist worked the base as she sucked while moving up and down his shaft slowly. Building speed, she was surprised when he pulled out quickly, stopping her protest when he grabbed her underneath her arms and lifted her up.

"About to explode, Bayley, and I really want to come inside you." He leaned over to snag a condom, but her hand on his arm stilled him.

Seeing his confusion, she said, "I'm on the pill. Have

been since college. The last guy I was with was over a year ago. So, I guess the only thing is—"

"I'm clean," he vowed. "Got the paperwork, 'cause we have to be tested with the Bureau."

She bit her lip, saying, "Um, I've got paperwork too. I get tested at my annual exam, but the report is at my house."

He reached up and held her face tenderly in his hands. "Bayley, I trust you. Maybe it's rash, but I trust you. And I'd really like to feel all of you around all of me, with no barrier."

"Come on," she grinned. "Let's do our shower sex research."

Entering underneath the spray of water, he pressed her back against the tile. "You got a specific way this is supposed to work or are we just going to wing it?"

With her hands on his shoulders, she said, "In romance books, the guy always lifts the girl in his arms and then enters her with her back pressed against the wall."

His eyes filled with doubt but his cock was tired of the conversation and wanted to get back to business. Lifting Bayley was easy and she immediately wrapped her legs around his waist. He pressed her back against the wet tile, but she began to slip down.

"Here, let me hold on to your shoulders," Bayley said, feeling her ass sliding.

Nick lifted his knee to give her balance, but his foot slipped on the wet shower floor, sending sprays of water shooting directly into her face. As she gasped, sucking in a mouthful of water, her hand flailed about, causing him to press her harder against the wall.

"Nick, this isn't working," she wheezed, coughing as she swallowed several times.

Setting her feet down carefully, he made sure she was steady as he moved so that the water hit his back and was no longer in her face. Staring at each other for a moment, they burst into laughter, water droplets sliding down their naked bodies.

"Oh, God, Nick. In my books, it's so easy!"

"Tell, you what, baby," he grinned. "How about you face the wall?"

Her eyes sparkled as they widened slightly, lust deepening the blue. Turning slowly, she presented her back to him, her heart-shaped ass drawing his attention. With a slight wiggle, she placed her palms on the wall, bending slightly.

He ran his hand from her neck, down her spine, over the globes of her ass, before sliding them up to her front, cupping her breasts. Tweaking her nipples, he elicited groans of pleasure from her lips. Stepping close, his cock nudged her entrance. Using his fingers to spread her folds, he slipped inside her sex with ease. The feeling of skin on skin, the friction of movement, had them both panting.

The angle shot jolts of electricity through her, causing her core to tighten as she raked her fingernails along the hard tile. Holding on to her hips, Nick pumped in and out, knowing he was close. Sliding one hand to her front, he fingered her nub, feeling her fall apart in his arms. With a few more thrusts, his neck muscles tightened as he groaned, his orgasm sending shock waves through his spine and down his legs. Collapsing against her back, he held them up with one hand on the wall beside her head as his other arm wrapped around her waist, pulling her close.

The water was cooling, so he turned it off, holding on to her as they stepped out onto the bathmat. Grabbing a towel, he began to dry her off, batting her hands away as she reached for the cloth.

"I got you," he said. "Let me take care of you."

Resting her head to the side, she smiled as he slowly and carefully dried off each inch of her body. As he finished, he bent to take her lips in a whisper-soft kiss. Pulling back slightly, he said, "Thank you."

"For what?"

"For giving you to me. All of you for all of me. I've never experienced that before. Not like that."

"I've never wanted to be with a man without a condom before," she admitted. "I can't even say exactly why this felt so right."

With his arms wrapped tightly around her, he kissed the top of her head, leaving his lips against her hair. " 'The greatest joy is flying off into the star-filled night sky, into the unknown.' "

Leaning back, she peered up at his face, her brows lowered as she pondered his words.

Shaking his head, he said, "That was something Santa said to me while we were at the inn. I didn't understand it at the time and, to be honest, I was thinking about my job. But now, I realize his words are right for us as well."

"So, we were flying off into the star-filled night sky?" she asked, her lips curving into a wide smile.

Capturing them in a kiss, he murmured, "Oh, yeah. Definitely flying."

19

Nick's boots clicked on the floor as he stalked down the hall to his office. Passing by Margery's desk, he stopped, accepting her greeting.

"How's your uncle?"

"Think his old ticker's gonna keep him going for a while."

She patted his arm, peering into his eyes. "Good... I'm glad, Nick. I was praying for him. Well, for both of you."

Lifting an eyebrow, he asked, "You think I needed those prayers too? Things that bad around here?"

Pursing her lips as Mike walked in, she said, "Things seem to be changing, Nick. It's not the way it used to be. Cases are getting reassigned on the whims of some of the bigwigs. Mike and I just try to stay in our little cubicles, doing the technical investigating. But for those of you on the front lines? It's getting crazy."

"This got anything to do with Richard?"

"According to Harlan, Richard's got a bee up his

shorts when it comes to you. Personally," she said, patting his arm, "I just think he's jealous of your investigative successes."

Nick observed hesitation in her eyes and he tilted his head in silent question. Margery shot Mike a look before she plunged ahead. "You need to know that Richard has reassigned Mike and I to a different case. He says there's nothing here to connect the nightclub snatching with the Russians and since…uh…well, in his words, 'you've fucked up the investigation', he's moving on."

"Fuckin' hell," Nick cursed, his hands on his hips as he turned and faced the wall for a moment until gaining his composure. Sucking in a deep breath through his nose before letting it out slowly, he said, "I need you two to know that I may not be staying with the Bureau. I'm looking at options to make sure that I can continue to work this case."

"You've got to do what's best for you," Mike agreed. "Just don't get burned waiting too long. I'd hate to see you go, but watch your back."

Holding on to his temper, Nick acknowledged Mike's words with a head jerk as he continued to his office. Sitting at his desk, he stared into space for a long time, before picking up the phone.

"Blaise? It's Nick. I know Bayley called you last night but I wanted to follow up. The trip was good until yesterday when she saw the man who accosted her in the lobby. He did not see her and we made it out unnoticed. Listen, I need to talk to you face to face. Can you meet for lunch?"

Making the arrangements, Nick disconnected. Pondering his next move, he dialed Jack. "Hey, man. We need to talk." Coming up with a time to go to the Saints' compound, he tossed his phone to his desk and looked around. The walls held a few photographs of Nick during his FBI career. Pictures he was proud of. Had been proud of. Rubbing his hand over the back of his neck, he turned to his computer and began to type.

Lunchtime found him ensconced in a booth at a small Italian restaurant around the corner from Bayley's shop. Seeing Blaise walk in, he smiled, now recognizing Bayley's features in her brother's face.

Blaise slid into the opposite side of the booth, reaching across to shake his hand. Blaise's blue eyes pierced his as he said, "So, you got something to tell me?"

"Damn, man, you don't mince words."

"Didn't think you did either."

Leaning back, Nick nodded. "You're right. No way am I going behind your back with Bayley, so I gotta tell you that I'm interested. And not just as an agent, but as a man."

Weighted silence sat over the men for a moment, before Blaise smiled. "Bayley hinted as much last night, but I really appreciate you coming to me."

"You got a problem with me being with her?"

"Not at all." Blaise leaned back in his seat, nodding as the waitress took his order. "I've wanted Bayley to be with a good man. Someone who appreciates her...uniqueness."

"And you think I'm that man?"

"Nick, what I know about you, you're as trustworthy as they come. And I've never known you to make a snap decision. So, yeah, if you tell me you want to be with my sister, then I know you'll take care of her." Grinning, he added, "And last night, she warned me that I'd better not stick my nose in her relationship. Then I got off the phone, told Grace, and she warned me about the same thing."

Shaking his head, Nick said, "Your sister's special, no doubt about that."

The two men finished lunch, finding their conversation revolving around the women in their lives and barely touching on the case. As Blaise stood, he shook Nick's hand, saying, "I've said it before and I'll say it again. You want to join Jack, I'll be glad to have you as a partner."

Hiding his irritation over his job situation, Nick just nodded before he headed down the street to check on Bayley.

"Nice to see you again. It looks like you've begun your book."

The dark-haired, pretty woman stood quickly from the table, her hand reaching for Bayley's. "Please, call me Agnes."

Turning to Bruce, with her hand on his shoulder, she asked, "How's the story going?"

Bruce began talking but, as much as Bayley wanted to hear about his manuscript, she could not seem to escape the feeling of Agnes' eyes on her. Excusing herself, she made her way behind the counter, moving straight up to her friend. "Hey, Daphne, has the new girl been coming in a lot?"

"Yeah," Daphne replied, wiggling her eyebrows.

"Come on, what else is going on. I can always tell," Bayley shoulder bumped her, bringing out a smile.

"I think she likes him," Daphne replied, nodding toward Bruce. "She comes in and always sits with him."

"Oh, honey," Bayley hurried to say, "I know you kinda liked him—"

"No worries," Daphne laughed. "I did like Bruce, but my new guy is just as handsome." Looking over Bayley's shoulder, she said, "Shh, here comes Bruce."

"Ladies," Bruce greeted, leaning his forearms on the counter in front of Daphne.

"I told Bayley that you've been coming in a lot with Agnes," Daphne said, her smile faltering slightly.

"Not with her, but when we're here, she does tend to sit at the same table with me." Shrugging, he admitted, "She's okay, but I don't know how serious she is about writing."

"Maybe she just needs more encouragement. I'll talk to her," Bayley said. Before she could move, the bell over the door rang and the trio looked up as Nick stalked over to them. Nodding at Daphne, he ignored Bruce as he walked behind the counter, placing his hands on Bayley's waist. "Hey, darlin.'"

As she twisted her neck to look up at his handsome face, so close to hers, she grinned. "Hey yourself."

"I just had lunch with Blaise."

Lifting an eyebrow, she said, "And…"

"He gives his blessing." Seeing her beam, he queried, "Was there any doubt?"

Playfully slapping his shoulder, she shook her head. "No doubt from me. He likes you…respects you. Hell, he probably hopes some of your neatness will rub off on me!"

"Listen, I just stopped by to see how you were doing. The security is in place here, and you're on the Saints' grid, so they can see what's going on at any time."

Whispering against his ear, her blue eyes sparkling, she asked, "Are you going back to the office now or can I talk you in to heading up to my office for a few minutes?"

Kissing her neck, he groaned. "I wish, but I'm heading out to meet with Jack."

Dropping her smile, she twisted so she was facing him. "Oh…I take it things didn't go well this morning at work."

Nick held her gaze, relishing the intuition and understanding pouring from her. Lifting her chin with his knuckle, his pressed a chaste kiss on her lips. "Don't worry about it. I've got it covered. I'm heading out now, but I'll be back to pick you up this evening."

Bayley's dreamy expression stayed on her face as she watched him walk out the door. She never noticed the stare from Agnes, before the dark-haired woman moved to an empty corner, placing a call.

Am I really doing this? Nick stood on Jack's massive front porch, looking to the mountains in the background. Sucking in a deep breath, he let it out slowly. Just then the door opened, a serious-faced Jack greeting him.

"Welcome back, Nick. Come on in."

The two men shook hands as they proceeded to the living room. The last time Nick had been in Jack's house, the room had been full of Saints and some of their wives or fiancés. The now empty room was just as warm, but much more open as Jack motioned for him to sit on one of the oversized sofas.

"How's your uncle?" Jack began.

Nick noted Jack's full attention was focused on him, giving the impression that he really cared about his relative. Smiling, he replied, "Good. He should be fine and I'll go back in a couple of weeks to make sure his rehab is going as planned."

Silence slid over them before Jack said, "You wanted to meet so, Nick, I'll let you take charge right now."

Clearing his throat, he heaved a sigh. "Hell, Jack, I find myself at a crossroads...one I didn't expect. But, after careful consideration, I'm at the end of my rope. I'm turning in my resignation this afternoon."

Jack nodded slowly, his intelligent gaze steady.

"I like order...I like piecing the investigations together, but I have grown increasingly frustrated with the politics of the job." With a rueful huff, he added, "It used to be about doing the right thing and we all knew what that was. Now, that gets lost behind the politics of some of the people in power."

"What's happened recently?"

"My supervisor has decided he wants me off the kidnapping case. He's into political gain and not into hard-core investigating. In trying to protect Bayley, he thinks I've jeopardized the case. But, to be honest, I think we're bringing them out of hiding."

"So, you're resigning?"

"Yes. Not just because of what has happened with this case, though that has pretty much pushed me over the edge. It's something I've been thinking about for a while now, and the time is right," Nick stated firmly. "And I'd like to discuss coming to work for you. I'd like to stay on this case and bring what I know to your table."

Jack smiled widely, leaning back in his seat. "That makes me happy, Nick. I've thought for a while that your investigative skills would be a real asset to the Saints. You know who we are and what we do, but how about we go downstairs and let you take a look around. I can answer more specific questions then."

Jack led the way down the hall leading from the kitchen. He stopped at a closet door and pulled it open. With a few taps of his fingers on a hidden security pad, he entered the code and the back wall swung open, exposing another set of stairs leading down. Descending the steps, they moved through the door at the bottom, walking into a spacious, open room filled with computer stations and monitor screens on the walls.

Nick stared at the hub of the Saints' company space. He knew Jack had built his business from the ground up, filling the space with the latest equipment and the best men he could find, but this was something else. Jack pointed to the bank of computers at which Luke and Charlie sat, greeting him enthusiastically before going back to work.

"Behind those doors are equipment rooms, firearms, and a variety of other items that we find come in handy," Jack said, with a rare grin. He nodded toward the far wall where a steel door stood and said, "That leads to the back entrance, which leads up to my garage. There are ATVs and a few company SUVs as well."

Nick nodded in appreciation of what he was viewing. "Impressive, Jack. Very impressive."

"My business took almost four years to create, but I was able to lure each of my employees to me. We're able to fly under the radar, using whatever means necessary to accomplish our contracts." He eyed Nick, as he added, "That's the only reservation I have with you, Nick. We are not bound by the same rules that you have been used to. Each of us has had to learn to work in this environment, so I want to make sure you are okay with that."

Nick looked down at the large conference table in the center of the room and took the seat Jack indicated. "I've thought about this, Jack. I'm not making a rash decision here. I've worked with you all for a while now. I've seen how you investigate and, while it was a bit shocking at first, I now am really interested in being able to get the job done without the politics. I like order and process, true, but I want to do things right from now on, not push them under the rug when it suits the big wigs. I want to be proud of what I do again."

"You also should know that most times, we do a lot of the leg work in the investigations but we don't get the glory. That goes to the police or FBI or hell, even the CIA."

Nick nodded, understanding what Jack was telling him. "I get it. All guts and very little glory. As long as we get who we're after, I'm fine with that."

Jack leaned across the table, his hand extended toward Nick. Clasping hands, he said, "Nick...welcome to the Saints."

2 0

"Tell me about your boss," Lazlo said, watching as Daphne walked around the store, readying it for the next day's business.

"Bayley? She's super sweet," Daphne gushed. "She's turned this place into a really cool book store. And she's smart too. She writes romance novels and runs this business. I don't know how she manages to do it all."

"Did I overhear she had some problems last week?"

Daphne paused, her hand on the trash bag. Brows knitted, she asked, "Did I say that?" Shrugging, she said, "I can't even remember. Oh, well. Yes, she had some problems, but she's fine. A man accosted her outside the shop, but he ran off."

"Wow," Lazlo said, his face adopting a concerned expression. "Did she...uh...know who it was?"

Nodding, Daphne said, "She worked with some police artist and, from what I understand, she identified the person. Some kind of mafia man, I think." Smiling at him, she added, "It all sounds so crazy, doesn't it? Like something from one of her books."

"It certainly sounds like she should be more careful."

"Well, she's got some super-hot detective boyfriend who'll make sure no one gets close to her again."

Lazlo turned, barely hiding the grimace on his face.

Later that night, Lazlo closed the door behind him, careful to lock it before walking down the hall. Checking his pants' zipper, he pulled up short at the sight of Grigory glaring at him.

"You shit where you sleep?"

"What?" Lazlo argued. "I steal the girls...why shouldn't I avail myself of the merchandise?"

Shaking his head, Grigory barked, "You need to focus more on your job than fucking the ones that look like that blonde you can't get."

Fingers clenched at his side, Lazlo's hands itched to slam into his brother's face, but he knew that would only bring his parents' wrath down on him. Instead, he bit out, "You take care of your part of the business, sitting behind your big desk, and let me take care of mine." Shouldering past Grigory, he continued down the hall.

Stepping into his office, Grigory walked to the credenza and poured a small tumbler of vodka. Seeing his father's raised eyebrows, he said, "I'm going to have Lazlo watched. He's getting sloppy and less focused on his job."

Milos said nothing, but slowly nodded, giving his silent approval.

———

Bayley stood at the breakfast counter in Nick's kitchen, her elbows resting on the surface as her gaze drifted around the room. An uncomfortable feeling of discontent slithered over her as she viewed the pristine apartment, her coat recently hung up in the closet, her purse tucked to the side of the table next to the front door. Unable to find one thing wrong with Nick's apartment, she nonetheless felt as though they were still at a hotel.

Sighing heavily, she wondered when he might get home from work, before she grabbed her laptop and turned one of the living room chairs around so it faced the large windows. Settling in, she began to type, but found the words stilted, unflowing.

His view was so much better than hers, but his apartment was so sterile, she felt her creativity sliding from her being. Closing her laptop, she laid it beside her, leaning back with a heavy sigh.

———

"You're really doing it?"

Nick stood in Harlan's office, his mind at peace but his heart a little heavy. "Yeah…turned in my resignation, effective immediately, a few hours ago. Richard took no time at all in letting me know that he wanted me out by the end of today."

"Well, Nick, I've known you for a long time and never knew you to make a rash decision, so I'm gonna reckon you know what you're doing."

Looking the older man in the eyes, he nodded. "I do. I admire you, Harlan, but I've been feeling discontent for a while. I used to see the world in black and white, but the longer I've been here, the more I've come to see the shades of grey."

Harlan chuckled as he agreed, "Probably my background as a Marine, but I have always seen the world with such clear decisiveness." The two men were silent for a moment before Harlan asked, "So, the Saints, huh?"

Grinning, Nick said, "I'm excited to make the switch. I saw them as arrogant when I first met them, but the assistance they were able to give on some of our cases made the difference between getting the ones we were after and losing them." Shrugging, he added, "I'm going to like working alongside them without my normal constraints."

"I hear the governor asked for their help."

"Yeah...some of them have other cases they're working, but Jack is putting me on this case full time tomorrow, along with his computer gurus."

"You'll share?"

"Harlan, I want you to know that working with you as a Saint liaison will make my new job so much better."

Harlan stood, extending his hand as he walked around his desk. Shaking Nick's hand, he clapped him on the shoulder. "Well, Nick, I'll be proud to continue to work with you, even if it's not with the same agency."

"As long as the criminals go down, Harlan, it won't matter who we work for."

Fifteen minutes later, Nick turned in his weapon and badge, stopping to say goodbye to Mike and Margery. Walking out to his SUV, only one box of personal items in his arms, he turned and looked up at the brick Bureau building behind him. And smiled. Time to go home...to Bayley.

Something was wrong, he was sure of it.

Nick had not told Bayley yet about his resignation and, subsequently, joining the Saints, wanting to surprise her after dinner. But now he watched her as she sat at the dining room table, moving her mashed potatoes from one side of her plate to the next. Then moving them into a pile. Then flattening them out with her fork, making lines in the top of the now cold mashed potatoes.

Leaning over, he placed his hand on hers, stilling her movement. "Bayley, stop. You've tortured those potatoes long enough."

Jerking her gaze up to his, she looked back down at her plate in surprise, as though she had not even realized what she had been doing. Her mouth fell open, but no words came out.

Sliding his hand up to cup her cheek, he asked, "What's wrong? You aren't acting like yourself tonight."

"I can't stay here," she blurted before slapping her hand over her mouth. "That didn't come out right."

Holding her gaze, he leaned back in his chair, concern in his voice. "So…what do you mean?" Distress crossed her face as she twisted her napkin in her hands before he stilled them with the admonishment, "Don't start torturing the napkin."

A slight grin slipped out before her expression sobered again. Swallowing deeply, she admitted, "I love being with you, but maybe we're just too opposite."

His brows dropped as he waited for her to continue, his heart beating faster.

Her eyes searched his and just as she opened her mouth to speak, Mr. Lickers flew from the hall, running at full speed. "Oh, damn," she cursed, hopping up to run and scoop the litter box.

A moment later, after she had still not emerged from the guest bathroom, Nick walked down the hall, hearing a sniff from behind the closed door. Knocking hesitantly, he called out, "Bayley? Babe, what's wrong?"

The door opened and his gaze landed on Bayley's tearful face, mascara running down her cheeks, a wad of toilet paper in one hand and a tied plastic bag in the other. Pulling her into his embrace, he tucked her face next to his heart as one hand cupped the back of her hand and the other moved slowly up and down her back. His calming motions were met with more crying.

Pulling back, he looked down in concern. "Honey, tell me what's wrong. Whatever it is, I'll make it better."

As she leaned away from his chest, she noted the black mascara smears on his white dress shirt and tears flowed anew. Wiping at the mess, she cried, "I'm a mess and you're not. You're clean and neat. Your clothes are always pressed. You have no stuff lying around your apartment and I walk through and automatically drop everything where it falls. I know you hate Mr. Lickers… he drops fur on your sofa, yaks up furballs on your rugs, and his poop stinks!"

Unable to hold back, Nick looked toward the ceiling as he roared with laughter. Feeling a slight slap on his chest, he looked down, seeing a mixture of remaining tears along with irritation.

"Don't laugh at me," Bayley said. "I'm just trying to save us from a breakup down the road when you get tired of my messes."

Understanding flowed over Nick as he breathed a sigh of relief. Grabbing the plastic bag from her hand, he tossed it behind her into the trashcan. Scooping her into his arms, he stalked back into his living room and sat on the sofa, arranging her over his lap.

"What are you doing?" she called out, sniffling as she wiped her nose with the wad of toilet paper.

"You know, I've got tissues," he said.

Looking at him over the wad as she blew her nose, she replied, "It's all the same stuff. This was convenient. When you feel like crying, you go for whatever is convenient."

Unwilling to argue with Bayley-logic, he grinned. "We need to talk and I'd really like to do it with you here, in my arms, and not through the bathroom door."

"You're right," she agreed, squirming as she settled on his lap, sighing loudly. "It's better to talk face to face."

Suddenly with her watery, sky-blue eyes staring right into his, Nick's words faltered. Sucking in a deep breath, he said, "I resigned from the FBI today." Seeing her eyes widen in surprise, he rushed on, "And I joined the Saints."

Bayley opened and closed her mouth several times, for one of the few times in her life unable to think of what to say. Stumbling, she said, "Oh...uh...are you... well, did you...are you...uh...okay? Is this because of me?"

Giving her waist a squeeze, he nodded, still holding her gaze. "Yeah. I'm fine. In fact, I'm more than fine. And I owe that to you."

Sucking in her lips as she pondered his words, she stayed uncharacteristically quiet as he continued.

"In the simplest terms, for my career, I had become disenchanted with the Bureau and the political grand-standing that goes on. You are not the reason I resigned, but you are the reason I want to move on to something more compelling." Looking toward the window for a moment, he let out a rueful snort. "I never looked out these windows to stare at the mountains and sunset until you pointed out the...what'd you call it? The vista?" Seeing her small smile, he nodded. "Yeah...I never noticed the vista before you came barreling into my life."

She reached her hand to his arm, her fingers lightly tracing the muscles underneath his shirt as she waited for him, recognizing the importance of his words.

"I was existing, but I had no idea how lonely my life was. I had my work, my apartment. My coworkers were not friends...not really. I had Uncle Bernie, who I talked to weekly but, had not been to visit in a while. This place," he swept his gaze around as though seeing it for the first time, "was a place to be, but not really a place to live in. I think I equated neat and calm for satisfying, but having you in my life, I now recognize that it's been a long time since I had a home. A real home."

Stunned at how much he was talking, she continued stroking his arm, relishing the warmth emanating from him as he drew her in.

"Bayley, I want you in my life. What we've started, I want to keep going. I don't give a fuck about this place. We can live anywhere. We can live here and you can make whatever changes you want. Hell, Mr. Lickers is welcome." Hesitating for a few seconds, he added, "Although I do have to admit the furballs on the carpet are a little disturbing."

A giggle burst from Bayley before she sucked in her lips, holding his gaze. Her voice shaky, she said, "Are you asking me to move in with you? We've only known each other a short time."

"Agreed," he acknowledged, "but I know what I feel. We've been living together out of necessity and now, the idea of not having you around doesn't feel right."

"Honestly, I'm such a mess sometimes. My life is not orderly at all. What if we find out we can't stand each other or we rushed things?"

He lifted his hand to cup her face, rubbing his thumb over her cheek. "Baby, I haven't had this—a chance at a real home—in a very long time. So what if you're a mess? Hell, sometimes my life is a mess. Together, we make each other better." Leaning forward, he kissed her lips, soft and sweet, tasting the salty tears that had slid

21

Pulling to the front of Jack's place the next morning, Nick parked next to a couple of vehicles and realized he was not the first one to arrive. He sat for a moment, filling his lungs with mountain air, then looked down at his attire. Jeans, clean and pressed, but still jeans. A long sleeve t-shirt instead of a buttoned, collared dress shirt. A leather jacket, comfortably worn at the seams, instead of a blazer. And no tie.

He waited for a moment, wondering if an uncomfortable panic would ensue but he felt nothing but serene...and ready. As he got out and moved to the steps, two other vehicles pulled up beside his. Bart, Jude, and Cam alighted from one, as Marc, Blaise, and Chad hopped down from the other. The six men moved toward Nick, grins on their faces as greetings rang out in the early morning air.

Shaking hands and accepting back pats, the group made their way up the front steps to the large front porch. The door opened and a pretty blonde hurried them all inside. "Cobbler's on the counter, boys. Help yourself."

Nick hesitated as he watched in amazement as the others hustled toward the kitchen where the scent of peaches and cinnamon filled the room. Looking down, he peered at the petite woman, her honey-blonde hair pulled into a long braid hanging down her back. Her hand was outstretched and he took it in his own.

"You must be Nick Stone," she said. "I'm Bethany, Jack's wife. Welcome to our home and to the Saints. I know Jack is excited to have you join the team."

Expressing his thanks, he watched as Jack walked from the back, sliding his arm around Bethany's waist. "First things first, Nick. Bethany likes to have something for everyone to eat, so make yourself at home and dig in."

Bethany smiled and added, "Monty's wife, Angel, also provides nummies so it's not always just me. She owns Angel's Cupcake Heaven and when she sends in a big white box tied in pink, purple, and teal ribbons, you're in for a real treat."

Thanking her, Nick made his way to the counter, glad to see that the cobbler had not been decimated. Serving himself, he followed the others down to the command center where Luke, Charlie, and Patrick were already working.

Once the welcoming speeches were over, Jack turned to Nick and said, "The governor has us on this case now and, while some of the others will be working out other assignments, I wanted everyone here to listen to what you can tell us."

Nick nodded, thinking over the case before speaking. "I wasn't on the missing girl's case for long, as you know, but what we feared was that she had become a victim of human trafficking, which is a problem in Virginia. Social media makes it so much easier for traffickers to make contact with girls and boys that are loners, looking for friends and attention. Easy to contact, easy to manipulate, easy to hook up with, and then easy to grab."

"And it's profitable," Bart added.

"Oh, yeah," Nick agreed. "Drugs can only be used once. A human can be sold over and over. And many use legitimate hotels for their trade. Unlike drugs, where the dealers will often have to have a certain type of place to process the drugs, and we have trained dogs that can be used to sniff out drugs, the selling of humans can take place anywhere. All it takes is a couple of motel rooms and the pimps start raking in the money."

"How does Amy Willis fit into this?" Patrick asked.

"To be honest, there had been no evidence to tie Amy Willis to any other disappearance, until Johan Serkov approached Bayley." Grimacing, he spared a glance toward Blaise. "While I still kick myself for not realizing she was at risk, it was her, through Faith's drawings, that led us to Johan. We did not know he was back in the states."

Luke spoke up, saying, "Since we've received that information, we've tried to see when he came back into the country and if he is back with the same Volkov family."

"The Bureau was looking into that when I had to leave to go to Tennessee. Since I basically resigned immediately upon return, I am not privy to what they determined." Rubbing the back off his neck, he pierced Jack with his gaze and said, "I need to let you know about something and I hope like hell it doesn't make you regret giving me a position with the Saints."

The group was silent as all eyes landed on Nick. "Obviously, you know that one of the main reasons I left the FBI was because of the political posturing from above. But, recently, it has been more than just posturing. My supervisor, at the state level, hated the governor's use of your organization. He saw it as a threat, instead of cooperation. It didn't matter to him that your investigative findings were always turned over to the Bureau and they got credit."

"Richard Tillman?" Jack asked.

"So, you've heard of him?" Nick countered.

Chuckling, Jack replied, "Yeah. Actually, it was from the governor. He thinks Tillman's a blowhard."

Laughing as he relaxed back in his seat, Nick agreed, "That he is." Sobering, he added, "I just wanted you to know that he was gunning for me once I became the liaison between you and the FBI last year. And the more I worked with the Saints, especially when I came back from Alaska, the more he wanted to put the Saints out of the picture. My opinion is that he's threatened by the work you do and he's got political aspirations that make him paranoid." Shrugging, he added, "I just wanted you to be aware that's why I don't have the latest intel."

"Well, you'll be glad to hear that Charlie and I have

already been working on that," Luke said. Turning to her, he said, "Take it away, babe."

Grinning as she blushed, Charlie flashed Johan's picture on the screen as she said, "We know Johan was associated with the Volkov family, based in Norfolk. They're suspected of extortion, money laundering, shipping guns, stolen goods, drugs, and also in human trafficking. While the police and FBI in the area have been able to nab some of their lower members, Gavrill and his top family members and eschelon have managed to keep their necks out of the noose. It took some digging, but we've discovered Johan came back to the states about five months ago, under a false passport, but he's stayed well under the radar. In fact, I can't find any evidence that he's been back with Gavrill's group. He may be working for one of the other Russian mafia families. But with Bayley's positive identification, we know he's here."

"With his false name, we're working on tracing his movements and following any money trails we can," Luke added. "We're still working on it, but that's all we've got, at the moment, on him."

"Tell me about Gavrill's trafficking business," Nick requested.

Bart replied, "I know we worked on the Chinese traffickers last year, but Gavrill's business is similar. Seems like they will go for teens, runaways, college students. What we don't know is where they are housed before being shipped overseas. With his family's shipping business, he has ready access to ship a few at a time with his other shipments. Easily hidden...not easily traced."

"So why here in central Virginia? What's got them here?" Jude asked.

No one around the table had an answer, as curses were growled under their breaths. Cam leaned forward, his arms on the table, and said, "I got sisters. I got a woman I'd die for. And now I've got a daughter. This shit pisses me off more'n about anything." He pinned Nick with his dark-eyed stare. "I'm all in on this."

Jack said, "Agreed." He moved his gaze around his Saints before landing on Nick. "We've got a few other cases to work on, but this takes priority."

Nick let his breath out slowly, not realizing he had been holding it. Nodding, he said, "Thank you. I appreciate it."

Looking at the clock, Jack said, "I'm going to have you work with Luke and Charlie on the money trail to see if we can figure out where Johan is and who he's now working for."

"You will go with me today," Chessa said, "after we are finished with lunch."

Pinching her lips together, Agnes walked over with the plates, setting them on the table. "I had plans this afternoon."

"You will have time after we check on the new girls."

Arguing with her mother would get her nowhere, so Agnes acquiesced, while inwardly protesting.

"I see your face," Chessa bit out. "You have a problem with my request?"

Knowing her mother's request was actually an order, Agnes shook her head. "No, no, it'll be fine."

"Good. There's no place for insolence in this family."

"Yes, Mama," she replied dutifully, placing the silverware next to the plates.

Chessa walked over, patting her daughter's cheek. "You're a good girl, my Agnes. You'll make someone a good wife."

"What if I want more?" Agnes dared to ask.

Her mother's eyebrows rose as she peered at her daughter. "Life will give you more. Babies will come and there will always be family duties." Agnes remained quiet as Chessa added, "Our place is not to rule the family business...but to serve to help make it profitable."

Nodding obediently, Agnes finished the table setting as her brothers and father walked into the room. The gathering became boisterous as they passed platters and talked amongst themselves.

As the meal came to a close, Milos turned to Lazlo, asking, "Are you making headway? I want that girl who can identify Johan."

"Her employee says she still has some kind of guards around her and she's moved in with a Fed."

"I can get to her much easier," Agnes pronounced, gaining the eyes of all around the table. "I've been in the store. I've seen how the guards watch every man who walks in...even you, dear brother."

At that, Lazlo glared. As he opened his mouth, Agnes

rushed on, "But for me, it's easy. No one suspects a female author just hanging out with a cute man she acts interested in. He's easy to get information from as well."

Milos nodded slowly, cutting his eyes over to his wife. "Chessa, what do you think?"

"I'm taking her to the girls today to check on them since our shipping of the older ones has been delayed a week."

"Yes, but maybe there is work she can do that would be helpful. This shop owner would be more likely to trust another woman." The table was silent as Milos pondered the situation. Nodding again, he pierced his daughter with a stare. "You keep going to the shop and report to Lazlo. He can work on the employee and see if we can get the Hanssen woman away from her protectors."

With that pronouncement, Lazlo preened at having his sister required to report to him, but Agnes still smiled. "Thank you, Papa. I won't let you down." Finishing her meal, she planned her next move, determined to be more than the next wife of Gavrill's organization.

Agnes was surprised with the cleanliness of the room holding the six women. As she and her mother entered, her gaze swept the room, noting the position of each woman as they stood to the side. The small hotel room held three bunk beds, a small table with only four chairs, and a small connecting bathroom with shower, toilet, and sink.

She observed as her mother walked down the line, outwardly inspecting each girl carefully, before saying, "There's been a slight delay in getting upstairs rooms for you so you'll stay here a few more days."

Agnes recognized the flare of hope in the girls' eyes before her mother squashed it by adding, "But don't get any ideas. You will soon be making money for us in the oldest profession."

Chessa turned and walked to Agnes, announcing, "This is my daughter. She will be handling you at times. Make sure you give her the respect you give me or," she pinned them with a hard stare, "you will not like the consequences."

Agnes watched as the girls lifted their eyes to her before dropping them back to the floor. Stifling a smile, she knew this job would be easy. Following her mother out the door, she let the grin slide over her lips.

22

"You know, I don't really need a babysitter or a chauffeur."

Nick looked down at Bayley's upturned face, her nose scrunched as they pulled to a stop outside Blaise's house. "As long as you're still the one who can identify Johan, you're in danger. So, we've got the Alvarez eyes on you, a Saint most of the time, and I'm your private chauffeur."

Grinning, she ran a finger down his shirt and purred, "Well, I guess having you as my *private* chauffeur can have its advantages."

He grabbed her finger in his hand, stilling her movements. "Don't start something we can't finish right now," he growled with a matching grin.

Laughing, she agreed, "Okay, but raincheck?"

"Oh, yeah. In fact, I'll collect as soon as we get this dinner with your brother over with."

Bayley's smile faltered but before he had a chance to

question her on it, the front door open and an attractive, older blonde stepped out onto the porch waving.

"Um, I might have forgotten to mention that my parents will be here as well."

A band tightened around Nick's heart for a second, the light from inside the house shining behind Bayley's mom. He sucked in a deep breath at the idea of the gathering inside.

"We don't have to do this," Bayley rushed. "It's totally okay if we—"

"Shhh," he admonished. "I've got this...we've got this. Hey, I was going to meet them sometime anyway." Leaning over he placed a gentle kiss on her lips before adding, "Wait till I come around."

Moving around his SUV to her side, he assisted her to the driveway before placing his arm around her shoulders as they made their way toward the front door.

As soon as their feet landed on the porch, Bayley was engulfed in a hug. "Hey, Mom," she greeted, her eyes dancing.

Nick stood to the side for a few seconds, until Bayley's mother let go of her daughter and grabbed him in an equally tight hug.

"Oh, Nick, we've been dying to meet you. Bayley's talked my ear off about you this week," she said, finally stepping back, her smile matching Bayley's. "I'm Barbara. Barbara Hanssen. Come on in."

With his hand on the small of her back, Nick leaned down to Bayley's ear, "You been talking your mom's ear off about me?"

Blushing, Bayley conceded, "Maybe a little."

Once inside, Nick's gaze gratefully met Blaise's and the two men greeted with a head nod toward each other. Another beautiful woman, long, dark hair pulled away from her face, walked into the room, holding a baby in her arm. She smiled at Nick as she handed the baby to Blaise and moved forward, her hand out to Nick in greeting.

"Nick, I'm Grace, Blaise's wife. Welcome to our home. We're so glad you and Bayley could come this evening."

Taking her small hand in his, he thanked her before lifting his gaze to Blaise, whose attention was riveted on the small child in his arms. Bayley bounded over to her brother, cooing while patting the baby's back.

A man sitting on the sofa stood and walked toward Nick, extending his hand as well. Tall, muscular, with just a slight bulge around his middle, he appeared to be an older version of Blaise, with his light blond hair slightly grey around the temples. "Good to meet you. I'm Bjorn Hanssen, Bayley's dad."

"Sir, nice to meet you too," Nick replied, the sense of being overwhelmed receding as the warmth of the gathering slid over him. He quickly noted the Nordic heritage between the four Hanssens and, seeing Bayley, now with her arms full of the baby, the thought of their child flitted through his mind. Mentally stumbling at the image, he focused on her as she walked toward him.

"And this is baby Ben," Bayley whispered as the child's face scrunched before settling back to slumber.

Nick, unused to babies, stood awkwardly to her side,

looking down at the cherubic face, the boy's downy hair sticking straight up. His tiny, cupid's bow mouth puckered before twitching into a small smile. Chuckling, Nick lifted his hand and gently touched Ben's cheek, eliciting another smile from the baby.

"Oh, he likes you," Bayley cooed, turning her face up toward Nick's, her eyes alight.

Grace took Ben from Bayley and excused herself so she could place him in his swing. Bayley slid underneath Nick's shoulder, her hand snaking around his waist.

"Dinner will be ready in a few minutes," Barbara announced. "Bayley, will you help me?"

Nick caught Bayley's wink before she followed her mother out of the room, leaving him with Blaise and their father. Unused to family gatherings, he stood awkwardly for a moment until the other two men started down the hall, inviting him to come to the family room as well. Near the kitchen, Nick followed them into a large room, warmly paneled, with family pictures covering the walls. A navy sofa, with red throw pillows, sat against one wall, facing a large screen TV. A couple of comfortable chairs in a red, patterned material sat against the back wall.

A multitude of baby items scattered across the floor, most unidentifiable to Nick, but the clutter screamed *family* to him. Little Ben was asleep in a contraption sitting on the floor and Nick watched in fascination as Blaise plopped down on the rug next to his son and gently moved the device side to side in a rocking motion.

Bjorn took the sofa, nodding for Nick to settle in one of the cushioned chairs. He did, noting how his body sunk in the pillows, relishing the comfort it provided. He could hear the women in the kitchen as they talked and laughed in unison, evidence of the relaxed environment. Sighing in content, his attention was snagged as Bjorn spoke.

"I understand my daughter is in some danger?"

Blaise, still on the floor, chuckled. "Way to cut to the chase, Dad."

Bjorn shook his head, answering, "No reason to beat around the bush." Shifting his gaze to Nick, he added, "You look, to me, like a man who likes to get down to business."

Nodding, Nick agreed. "Yes, sir, I do. I don't know how much Bayley has told you—"

"It's not what my daughter has told me," Bjorn interjected, "it's digging through all the extraneous details she adds in, that makes it hard to discern exactly what the hell is going on."

Nick battled a grin at the description of Bayley. Clearing his throat, he explained, "She met me one night while I was working..." He suddenly hesitated, unsure what her father knew about his changing career path. "Uh, I was still with the FBI at the time."

Bjorn, seeming to catch Nick's reticence, encouraged, "I understand. I know you've just joined the Saints."

"Yes, sir. Well, she talked to me that night and was taking a lot of selfies, or rather shots of the nightclub for her research. Unfortunately, someone was there who didn't want their picture taken." Seeing Bjorn's hard expression, he hastened to add, "She was able to identify the person who approached her the next night, but he has not been caught. Between me, the Saints, and another security firm, we've got her covered around the clock."

"How the hell that girl gets herself in these messes—"

"Dad! Stop telling stories on me," Bayley cried from the kitchen.

Nick, surprised, looked first to Blaise and then to Bjorn, as Bayley continued to mumble from the other room.

Bjorn, ignoring his daughter, continued, "She had some freaky fan stalking her on Facebook for a while last year, until Blaise set him straight. Then there was the model she used on the front of a book cover and damned if that son of a bitch didn't start sending her flowers and shit, wanting to have a relationship with her."

Blaise, still rocking his son, looked up and added, "Don't forget about that elderly neighbor she had that left notes about how he was now on Viagra so she and he could date."

Nick's eyes widened but before he responded, Bayley rushed into the room, a dishtowel draped over her shoulder. Planting her hands on her hips, she glared at her father and brother. "Stop right now," she demanded. "You're going to have Nick thinking there's something wrong with me!"

Unable to contain his mirth, Nick threw his head

back in laughter, then "umphed" as she plopped down in his lap. Wrapping his arms around her waist, his gaze landed on her bright eyes as she leaned in close, her hands clasping around his neck.

"Don't believe them. Those were isolated incidents that were nothing more than an inconvenience."

"Hell, girl, you end up in the strangest situations," Bjorn continued, before clamping his mouth shut as Barbara walked into the room shooting him a warning look. "Fine," he mumbled. Looking back at Nick, he said, "Just tell me that you and Blaise have got her."

"Sir, I promise," Nick vowed. "I would protect her with my life."

The others smiled in response to his declaration but Bayley sobered, hoping the words would not come true.

———

Grigory walked into the opulent room noting his brother's face. "What's wrong with you?"

Lazlo, leaning back in a dark, burgundy, leather chair, a cut glass tumbler in his hand, grimaced. With a quick shake of his head, he bit out, "Nothing. Leave it." The quiet of the evening penetrated his grim thoughts and he looked over, where Grigory had sat in a matching chair opposite of him, staring. Shooting a glance toward the door, he asked, "Where're Mama and Papa?"

"Upstairs."

Nodding, Lazlo, said, "It's that girl." Seeing Grigory's

unspoken question written on his face, he added, "That bookstore girl."

"Oh, the one you've taken out—"

"No, the one Johan approached. I knew we shouldn't have sent him. He's gotten too old to trust with a job like that. One that should have been handled with finesse."

"And you would be the one to have applied just the right finesse?" Grigory smiled.

"Yes," Lazlo bit out, his lips pursed. "She's different."

"You like her? You're used to taking your fill of the women who have no choice. You think you have a chance with an independent woman like her?"

"So what? It's not a crime to be interested in someone," Lazlo retorted in defense. "You're getting ready to settle down."

Grigory pierced his brother with a stare. "Seriously? You're comparing the two? Portia is from one of us. Her family is subservient to us. That shop owner—who, I might add, is now dating that agent—is hardly one of us."

Grigory stood, pouring a drink into a tumbler before sitting back down. "Forget her. She was never meant for you. Let Father handle Johan and you just see if you can romance information from the counter girl you've got on a string."

The two brothers sat quietly, not noticing Agnes standing just outside the door.

"I'm so impressed. You know Mom doesn't make her Norwegian Almond Cake for just anyone! I mean, she says she didn't even make it for Dad until their third date and here you get it the first time she meets you. Of course, she might have held off for Dad since he used to brag about his mom's cooking. Could have given my Mom a complex or something."

Driving home, Bayley talked incessantly, her conversation bouncing between her nephew, her latest novel, her shop, and the dessert they just had. The grin on Nick's face had remained for hours, unable to remember the last time he had had such a good time.

"What did Dad say to you as we were leaving? You know, when I was off saying goodbye to Mom?"

Looking to the side, he asked, "Can't a man have a secret?"

"Nope, not when it's about the person in your life and her dad is the one doing the talking." Seeing his lifted eyebrow, she rushed, "And I'm pretty sure that's a relationship written rule somewhere."

Chuckling, Nick repeated, "A relationship written rule?"

"Stop evading the question," she complained.

"To keep you from having a conniption fit, I'll tell you. Your dad said that he was glad that I had joined your brother with the Saints."

Bayley's face fell as she slumped back in her seat. "Oh," she mumbled.

"And..."

"I knew it!" she said, her face resuming its former smile. "What else did he say?"

"He wished us a pleasant evening."

"You are so full of it," she groused. "I know he said something about us."

Nodding, he said, "You're right. I'll stop teasing. He said that he was proud to have me dating his daughter and that his sentiments had nothing to do with keeping you safe."

A satisfied expression crossed her face as she turned to face him. "That's so sweet. I knew my parents would like you." Reaching over to link her fingers with his, she added, "I'm so glad you were comfortable with my family. I was afraid it might be overwhelming."

Walking into his apartment a few minutes later, Nick thought back to Blaise's home in comparison. Blaise and Grace's den no longer seemed chaotic as flashes of his former foster home returned, the warmth from laughter, smiles, conversation, and playtime filling his mind. His own staid apartment now seemed bare and cold. Looking down at Bayley's upturned face, her eyes alight and her smile wide, he realized he wanted a real home...with her.

23

"Where would you like to live?"

Bayley rolled over, opening her eyes, then immediately squinted as the bright sunlight peeked through the blinds. "Huh? What are you talking about?"

"I want to know where you would like to live," Nick repeated.

Pushing a tangled mess of hair from her face, she blinked a few more times, willing her sleep-fogged mind to follow his question. "Are you kicking me out?"

Rolling over her body, resting his weight on his forearms planted on the mattress, he pressed his lower body onto hers. "Does this feel like I'm kicking you out?" Kissing her lips, he asked, "I just want to know what kind of place you see us living in. I was going to tell you to fix this place up any way you want, but after being with your family last night and seeing Blaise's home, I thought that maybe you'd rather live in a home like that."

Staring up at his face, the dark stubble on his jaws

only serving to make him appear more dashing, she smiled into his deep, brown eyes. "I...I...well, I guess I haven't really given it any thought. Until recently, I was just satisfied in my little apartment and dreaming of when I could afford something with a view."

Chuckling, he brushed blonde tendrils from her forehead, memorizing her face. "Well, I've got a view but, let's face it, compared to Blaise's home, this is pretty boring."

"I like your place," she said, uncharacteristic hesitation filling her voice.

"Hey," he said, kissing her nose. "What's got that doubt in your eyes?"

Licking her lips, she shrugged, moving her hands up his arms to wrap around his neck. "Does it seem too fast?"

Leaning back slightly, he cocked his head to the side. "Too fast?"

"Nick, what we have is really good and I want to keep it really good. I like your place, and if you don't mind me bringing some of my things here, I'm fine with this being our place for now."

"For now?" he repeated, fear sending cold sliding down his spine. "As in *only for now*?"

"No, silly," she admonished. "I mean, for now until we decide that another place, or even a house, would be better."

Relaxing, his breath left his lungs in a whoosh. Leaning over again, he nuzzled her nose before sliding his lips over her cheek.

Warmth slid to her core as she lifted her hips

slightly, his cock pressing against her thigh. His whisper sent shivers as his breath tickled her ear, "Baby, you do whatever you want to this cold place and I promise I'll love it."

"I could say the same to you," she moaned, undulating against his cock. "You can do whatever you want to me and I promise I'll love it."

With a growl, he slid down her body, grabbing her pajama shorts, covered in green frogs with smiling faces, and jerking them off her legs. She pulled her hot-pink camisole off before lying back, completely naked, with her arms held out to him, beckoning.

Disposing of his boxers, he rolled back, staying to her side as he latched onto her lips. Determined to go slow, his hand moved over her body, memorizing every curve, from her neck, with the wildly throbbing pulse, down over her breast as he palmed the fullness. Flesh against flesh spurred him on as his hand continued its exploration over her slightly rounded stomach and full hips.

The feel of his hand moving torturously over her body made Bayley feel beautiful, but needy. The light touch of his fingertips sent electric shocks from her skin to her core. As he slid his lips from hers, she moaned in protest until his lips sucked the pulse point at her neck. Sucking in a gulp, she clutched his muscular shoulder with her fingers. His lips suckled down her collarbone to her breast, where he latched onto one nipple before moving to the other.

"Nick," she whispered, her voice an unrecognizable croak. "I need you."

"Patience," he mumbled, his mouth still working her breasts.

"No patience."

As he chuckled against her body, she felt the rumble deep inside. "Please…"

His answer was to slide between her legs, pulling her calves up on his shoulders, opening her sex to his view. Her folds were slick and his nostrils filled with the scent of her desire. Kneeling between her thighs, memorizing her taste as he had her curves, he licked, nipped, and sucked his way around her folds, finally latching onto her clit.

Crying out his name, the sensations poured over her body from her core outward. Bucking her hips upward, she felt his large hand press down on her stomach, holding her in place. More than sex, she felt connected to Nick in a way that defied description as the exquisite torture continued. His tongue moved inside her sex and as he moaned, she felt the vibration deep inside. His morning scruff scratched her sensitive skin as her body wound tight, her fingernails digging into his scalp as her heels slipped off his shoulders opening herself even more.

He moved back toward her clit, sucking it into his mouth while his hand slid up from her stomach to her breast and rolled her nipple between his fingers.

That was all it took for Bayley to come apart, her hips bucking once more as the orgasm vibrated deep inside, spreading outwards. She felt owned by him… loved by him. At the thought of love, she jerked her eyes open, staring at his face peering up at her from between her legs. Heat rushed over her face but she was not sure if it was from her orgasm or emotion.

Nick crawled up her body after lowering her legs, releasing his arms. He kissed his way to her stomach, her breasts, giving each attention, to her lips, where she tasted her essence on his tongue.

Sliding his eager cock to her entrance, he plunged in to the hilt with one, firm thrust, feeling her body jerk with the movement. Halting, he groaned, "You okay, baby?"

"Yes, yes, don't stop," she bit out, her fingers digging into his shoulder muscles with more force than before.

Grinning, he began to thrust as her tight, slick channel molded itself to his erection. The sensation of ultimate pleasure trickled down his spine as the friction built. He wanted to slow down, make it last, but as his balls tightened, he knew he was close.

Her face was awash with her own pleasure and her eyes snapped open as he growled, "You close? Don't think I can last."

Nodding, she shifted her hips upward slightly, increasing the contact of his thrusts on her clit. "Almost, almost," she grunted against his thrusts.

Pulling out quickly, he flipped her over onto her stomach before grabbing her hips and pulling her delectable ass toward him. Plunging back in, he grinned as her initial grunt turned into groans of pleasure.

This angle provided a different sensation and Bayley lowered her head as her fuse began a slow burn. She loved the possessive feel of his hands on her hips as he moved them together as one.

Looking down at her perfect ass, he palmed the pale globes before sliding one hand to the front, pressing on her clit. With a final roar, he came, his orgasm pulsating inside her sex as he felt her channel grabbing his cock.

Thrusting until the last drop was wrung from his body, the two crashed down on the mattress, his chest against her back. She grunted with the force but the heavy weight felt comforting. As he gained consciousness, he rolled slightly to her side, one of his thighs still across hers. Pushing her now tangled hair off her damp back and away from her face, he grinned.

Opening her eyes, she pretended to glare. "And just what are you grinning about?"

"Someone looks satisfied."

"Just satisfied?" she prodded.

"Well fucked, I'd say."

Snorting as she giggled, she said, "Well, you must be looking into a mirror, buddy, 'cause from where I'm lying, you're the one who looks well fucked."

Chuckling as he leaned in, placing a sweet kiss on her nose, he added, "I'd say that describes both of us."

Purring as she nodded, she said, "I'd say you're right." Placing her hand on his stubbled cheek, she whispered, "But honestly? I feel worshiped."

His eyes warmed as they peered over at her, the feel of her gentle touch on his face a signal of her sincerity. "You were, and are, worshipped, baby." Seeing the smile on her face, he leaned in to kiss her lips, soft and sweet. "Never doubt, I plan on worshipping you every day."

After a moment of recuperation, she giggled and

said, "I'd also say we're both a mess. How about a shower?"

"We get in the shower together, no telling what'll happen," he cautioned.

Sitting up with a sly grin on her face, she said, "I'm counting on it!"

———

Daphne rolled over in bed, smiling at the dark-haired man sleeping next to her. She wanted to reach out to touch his hair but, remembering his orders from last night, she kept her fingers still. She stretched, her body sore from the rousing session of dominant sex. As the sun peeked through the blinds, she slipped from bed and padded into the bathroom. Naked, she perused her body in the mirror. Bite marks tattooed her body from her neck, across her breasts, down her stomach and thighs. Sucking in her lips, she fingered a few of the darker bruises, hating to admit they were sore. She hated how he always seemed to ask questions about Bayley right after they had sex but, then, he had said he only wanted to get to know her better and that included her job. Daphne's gaze shot back to the bed where she heard him stirring. Convincing herself a man like him was worth the slight pain, she plastered a smile on her lips and moved back into the bedroom.

———

Agnes walked down the hall alone, stopping outside one of the doors. Using the key, she opened the door, announcing herself as she stepped inside. Grimacing, she immediately held the medical mask to her face. All six women were lying in bed, the sound of sniffling and coughing the only noise in the room. The faint putrid stench of vomit greeted her nostrils, even as she sucked in air through the mask.

"Please," one of the women said, struggling to sit up in bed.

Agnes eyed her coldly. "No need to beg, I'll have the doctor who initially checked you in come back. But make no mistake, as soon as you are well enough to begin your service, you will be moved from here."

Slamming the door and locking it behind her, she looked up at the guard prowling along the hall. With a head jerk toward the room she just left, she ordered, "Give them extra water and food for now. Ill, they are of no use to us."

With his nod of understanding, she turned and dumped the mask in the nearest trash can on her way out the back door.

Luke walked into the compound's main room, seeing Charlie already at work. "I didn't hear you leave our bed this morning."

She looked up and smiled at her fiancé. "You were up so late last night that I didn't have the heart to wake you this morning. I grabbed a bowl of cereal and headed over here."

Knowing her penchant for working through problems in the dark of the night, he asked, "You have an idea?"

Nodding, she said, "Yeah. I started going through Gavrill's associates from the Norfolk area, but wanted to go back over his list of businesses. Something kept coming back to my mind and I wanted to get in to look at it."

Walking over to peer over her shoulder, Luke's interest peaked. "What've you got?"

"I followed the money and he's got several front businesses that are just for money laundering. Restaurants, a hotel, a casino. And they are all up and down the east coast. I decided to look at his family interests and found that he has a distant cousin that has received money from him. And they own a hotel…in Richmond. It looks legit, but I'm curious."

Squeezing her shoulders, he kissed the top of her head. "Good work, babe. As soon as Nick and the others get here, let's see what we can pull together."

24

Nick sat at the table, eying the screen on the wall with the other Saints. With Bayley taking a rare morning off from the shop to get some writing completed before the rescheduled critique group that night, all the Saints were at the table.

"What I've worked on," Charlie said, "was digging into Gavrill Volkov's businesses that might be in this area. I'm basing this on Bayley's identification of Johan, who was last working for Garvrill's organization in Norfolk."

"What have you got?" Jack asked.

Nick leaned forward, his body tense as he awaited Charlie's results, having witnessed her ability to follow a money trail way beyond what he had witnessed in the FBI.

"Back when we, especially Bart, were investigating Ivan Krustas' family in Norfolk, we came across his cousin, Sergio—a particularly nasty individual who has no moral compass at all."

Bart snorted at the description, remembering his dealings with the black-hearted mobster when he interviewed him in prison.

"And, Bart has also interviewed Gavrill Volkov, another nasty leader of the Russian mafia, who seems to be of like character to Sergio. Because these two leaders have no compunction dealing in human lives, I've been digging into their finances to see if there are any ties to this area."

"Gavrill's managed to make inroads with some of the docks and Sergio, while still in prison, manages to lead his own family business. Together, they've been suspected of not only smuggling girls in their cargo ships to Russia, where they'll be sexual slaves, but also having them serve the ships and docks on the way there."

"Why the fuck haven't they been stopped?" Bart growled.

Nick heaved a sigh and replied, "The FBI, police, Coast Guard, Homeland Security...hell, even the CIA all try to take these guys down, but they've got a long reach. They manage to launder their resources so many times before ending up in off-shore accounts, it's almost impossible to trace. There is also the loyalty issue. No one comes clean. And I mean no one. If a member of the Russian mafia is caught, they keep quiet or they know their life will end and it won't be pleasant." Sighing again, he said, "I never worked in that district but I knew it was a helluva place to try to investigate." Turning back to Charlie, he asked, "So, have you been able to get us closer?"

Grinning, Charlie said, "I have been able to follow the money trail slightly. Gavrill owns a couple of hotels in the Virginia Beach area, all legit on the surface, but it seems he has a small monetary interest in a hotel closer to us. Again, appears legit, but I don't trust anything that even hints at him having his name attached to at all."

She projected a hotel on the screen. "This is the Belvue in Richmond. As you can see, it looks nice... expensive. In fact, there are senators and congressmen who frequent it. Even the governor has hosted a ball here. Everything appears legal and proper."

"I used to work undercover in Richmond and know the area. This hotel is in a ritzy block and I've never heard of a problem there. So, what's the catch?" Cam asked.

"It's owned by a company with the money coming from the Cayman Islands, so that is suspicious. But it's run by a Gruzinsky family. Milos Gruzinsky and his oldest son, Grigory. None of them caught my eye until I ran across an article about the opening of the hotel about ten years ago. Milos Gruzinsky was pictured with his wife, Chessa. And her maiden name was included. Chessa Volkov Gruzinsky. In doing some checking, I discovered Chessa is a cousin of Gavrill."

"Hot damn," Jude exclaimed. "So, we've got a connection."

"Yes, but without any proof of anything else, it's not illegal to be a cousin of a crook," Nick replied. "Otherwise, we'd have an easy time arresting suspects."

"So, what about the hotel makes you suspicious?" Chad asked. "Other than just the familial connection."

Charlie sighed. "Sorry, guys, that's all I've got right now. But, I'm still working on following the money."

Luke jumped in, "I've been working on the social media aspect. We know Amy Willis had been posting about going out with friends to Neon before actually going. When I checked her Facebook account, emails, and phone texts, I didn't find anything specific, and I'm just checking out her dating site profile."

"How the hell did I not find this?" Nick growled, his mouth twisted in anger. Looking at Jack, he shook his head. "I know, I know...that's why you get results. You've got the equipment and the manpower." Rubbing his brow, he added, "I had to take days away from this to check on my uncle and thought the case was still being worked the way it should have been. It was only when I got back that I realized it had stalled."

Jack leaned forward, his forearms on the table, and pierced Nick with his glaze. "I get that...I know it sucks. But you gotta put that out of your mind and focus on what we can find out now."

Nodding, Nick sucked in a deep breath, clearing his mind. "Got it," he acknowledged. Turning back to Luke and Charlie, he asked, "What else have we got?"

Luke continued, "Right now, we've got nothing to tie any of the Russian mafia or their families to Amy Willis or any of the missing girls. All we've got is conjecture and possibilities. I'm working on getting visuals of the hotel, their security, and blueprints. It'll take a bit, but this is our number one priority."

"I need a better way to murder someone."

"Yes, but is there a way to do it so that the police can't catch you?"

Bayley pondered the question before answering, " 'Every murderer is probably somebody's old friend.' " She looked up at her group before laughing as she added, "Yes, dear old Agatha!"

"So, I should make the murderer the victim's friend?" Bruce asked. "But that still doesn't give me a good way to do it."

Agnes looked askance at the people sitting around the table, their laptops open in front of them, all discussing murder. Bayley observed the newcomer's surprise and said, "Don't worry, Agnes—you'll get used to us."

"I suppose it's because I'm not writing a mystery," she replied.

Sitting down next to the dark-haired beauty, Bayley said, "I write romantic suspense, which isn't pure mystery, but I love to have a good murder or kidnapping to cause the tension for the hero and heroine."

"Well, I'm not writing romance, either," Agnes confessed. "I suppose I don't really know what genre I'm writing in."

"Would you like me to read over your story to see where you are?" Bayley asked.

Before Agnes could answer, Bruce jumped in. "Oh, she won't let you see it. I've been asking her to let me read what she's written, but she won't."

"It's my first work," Agnes protested. "I'm not ready."

"That's fine," Bayley said, jumping to her defense, making a face at Bruce. Turning her gaze to Sally, she added, "You and Bruce need to put your heads together to come up with the perfect murder."

The group soon settled into their writing and the next two hours passed quickly. A knock on the front door startled Bayley, but her surprise morphed into a huge smile as she saw Nick in the doorway. "Okay, guys, it's time to pack it in."

As the others gathered their laptops and books, Bayley unlocked the shop's door and greeted Nick enthusiastically. Becoming more accustomed to public displays of affection, he returned her kiss with equal enthusiasm.

As the writers filed out the door with goodbyes ringing in the air, he noted a few new faces in Bayley's group. Several stared at him unabashedly, but a few kept their faces turned away. Bayley locked the door after they left before turning back to Nick.

"You got new people?"

"Yeah. I think since Bruce works at the college, a few students have heard about us. I want to make sure we don't grow too large, but having about ten people is really nice." Squinting her eyes in thought, she commented, "But you always ask questions with purposeful intent, so why are you asking?"

Laughing, Nick repeated, "Purposeful intent?" Watching as she walked over to the counter to grab her purse and laptop case, he admitted, "I guess that's the investigator in me."

As they stepped through the door and Bayley locked it again, she pressed, "So...why'd you ask?"

"I just noticed that a couple of them seem to be avoiding looking at me."

"Oh, and the handsome agent is so used to women looking at him that he wonders when it doesn't happen?" she laughed, pretending to pout.

Slapping her ass playfully as she hopped up into his vehicle, he said, "No, missy. But I just always get suspicious when someone doesn't look me in the eye."

As he climbed into the driver's seat, she looked over at him with a grin on her face. "Well, I happen to love looking into your eyes. In fact, I think I noticed your eyes right away." Tapping her chin with her forefinger, she shook her head. "No that's not right...it was too dark. I first noticed your profile. You've got such a classic profile...kind of like Al Pacino in the Godfather movies—"

"What is it with you and the Godfather movies?"

Shrugging, Bayley's forehead wrinkled as she thought. "I don't know. I've watched them a million-jillion times, so I guess I've got them imprinted on my brain. Such a brilliant portrayal of gangsters."

"And your Agatha Christie?"

"Oh yes! I've watched all her mysteries too. But you know the difference? I prefer reading her books and confess that the Miss Marples in my mind don't look like the ones in the movies. But with the Godfather, when I read that book, Al Pacino is in my mind."

Pulling out onto the street, Nick shook his head in

wonderment of the way Bayley's conversations managed to move all over the place.

Stepping from the corner, Agnes pulled her phone out of her pocket, sending a quick text.

Chessa walked out of the basement room with the doctor, locking the door securely before lowering her mask and turning to him. "How soon?"

"It shouldn't be long now."

"We are losing money every hour, you know. My husband leaves the girls' care to me and I'm failing the family at the moment."

The grey-haired doctor patted her shoulder. "We cannot rush these things, Mrs. Gruzinsky. If these girls pass on illness to your customers, especially the ones that pay well for the privilege, your business won't be worth anything."

She pinched her lips together in frustration, glancing over her shoulder as Agnes walked down the hall toward them.

"News?" Agnes asked.

"The same," her mother bit out. "Dr. Kovenov says they need a few more days."

"And the upstairs girls?"

"He just checked them and says the same thing. Whatever virus they have, it takes days to work through their system. Your father will not be pleased."

Shrugging, Agnes said, "It's only a few more days. Then we can ship the upstairs girls to your cousin and these girls can move into their place. You will see, Mama...it will be all right."

With narrow eyes, Chessa glared at both her daughter and the doctor. "Bah! Tell that to your father and Grigory when they look at the books and see how much money we are losing. And my cousin gets impatient with waiting. The ship cannot be held in port indefinitely." Stomping down the hall, she left the two in her wake.

"Your mother has little patience when things do not go her way," Dr. Kovenov said, his voice weary.

Agnes watched her mother as she moved through the door leading to the back stairs of the hotel. "New ways are coming, my good Doctor. And with it, a new way of doing things." With an enigmatic smile, she slipped her arm through his as they followed Chessa.

Several minutes later, Agnes stood outside the closed door of her father's office, recognizing the raised voices from inside. Hearing a noise behind her, she watched as Lazlo moved to her side.

"What's going on?" he asked.

"The girls are still sick. Mama was checking with the doctor and he says another few days before they can be shipped or put back to work."

With anger in his eyes, he opened the door, walking inside. Milos glowered as his youngest children came into the room. "What is this? A family meeting that I did not call?"

Agnes, keeping quiet, stood near the wall, her eyes cast down. Lazlo, unheeding of his father's ire, said, "I hear the girls are ill. Who cares if they are sick? They can lay on their backs, can't they? Who gives a fuck if they don't feel well?"

Chessa opened her mouth, but Milos' hand in the air silenced her. Standing, he placed his fists on the desk, his voice low and dangerous. "Have I raised an idiot?"

Lazlo flinched, but his father continued, "We do not run a whore house, you fool. We provide our clientele with what they want. They want a virgin, we give them that. They want a child, we give them that too. What we do not do, is give them an illness! You are a fool!"

Grigory, silent as usual, spoke, "We need to get them well as soon as possible, Papa, before news gets out about them being ill. We're losing money each day and Gavrill is growing impatient."

Whirling around, Milos growled, "You think you are telling me something I do not know? Are both of my sons idiots? And just how do you expect us to do that?"

The room was silent for a moment, before Agnes lifted her gaze to her family. "We could get rid of these girls and then we will be ready for a new crop."

No one spoke...the silence deafening. Agnes wiped her sweating palms on her skirt as she waited for their reaction. Lazlo scoffed but, like Grigory, did not speak, looking to Milos instead. Chessa stared at her daughter as though seeing her for the first time. Finally, Milos' lips curved into a slow smile.

"Ah, so the one with the solution is my daughter. Perhaps I have underestimated you." He stared at her speculatively. "And just how do you propose this happens? Twelve women in all. Twelve bodies?"

Swallowing deeply, Agnes replied, "I'm sure Dr.

Kovenov would be able to inject something...uh...effective. No mess, no problems. Once...dead, we could load them at night using the laundry trucks and get them to Gavrill. He'd have ways to dispose of them with one of his tankers in the middle of the ocean."

Once more, the silence in the room snaked across the occupants. Milos walked around his desk, stopping in front of Agnes. She stood her ground as he lifted his hand, his knuckles caressing her cheek. "My little one, you might have just solved our problems."

Lifting her eyes to him, she smiled. "Would you allow me to take charge? Prove to you that I can be part of what needs to happen with this family?"

Grinning a white-toothed smile, he nodded. "Yes, but you will work with Lazlo."

Emboldened, she added, "But he needs to focus on replacing the sick girls. Twelve girls are a lot to replace."

Nodding, Milos agreed. Turning to the others, he said, "We have work to do. I suggest we all get busy."

Letting out a breath she had not realized she had been holding, she turned and walked out of the room, feeling change in the air. Her brothers thought they had the family business locked up when her father died. Grinning, she knew they had met their match.

25

Bayley looked up in surprise as Nick bolted through the door of her shop. Stalking over, with a nod toward Chad sitting near the front, he said, "We need to talk."

Chad immediately stood and followed Nick and Bayley as they moved to the service area and the stairs leading to her office. Once there, Nick closed the door and whirled around, saying, "Johan Volkov has been arrested."

Her breath left her lungs in an audible *whoosh* as her knees threatened to give out. Nick's hands whipped out, grabbing her upper arms, steadying her as he assisted her to a chair.

"Wow," she said, unable to think of anything else to say.

"Who picked him up?" Chad asked.

Nick replied, "I got a call from Harlan, one of my former FBI superiors who knew I would want to know.

Seems the Chesapeake FBI office got him in a routine sweep of the dock area."

"Will I need to testify against him?"

Smiling down at her, Nick's hand slid to her back, rubbing circles in comfort as he said, "I don't think so. They've got him on so many other charges that accosting you is actually low on their list of things he'll have to answer for."

"What about Gavrill and the family here?" Chad continued to prod.

"From what I hear, Gavrill is working to disengage himself from Johan, but the Feds'll be trying to go after him as well."

"Good," Bayley announced, standing. "So, it's all over. I don't need any more babysitting."

"Whoa, baby," Nick said, placing his hands on her shoulders. "I'm not ready to make any assumptions right away."

"But, whoever hired him to get to me now has to realize that I'm no threat. I thought the only reason I needed protection was from him, in case I identified him."

Chad chuckled, shaking his head. "You've got your own mind, don't you, Bayley?"

Rubbing his chin, Nick said, "I take your point and I know we don't need a Saint with you, but I still want to pick you up at the end of the day, especially when it's dark outside."

Bayley grinned as she slipped her arms around his waist. "That can be arranged."

"Okay, you two, I'm outta here," Chad waved as he headed back down the stairs.

Stepping away from Nick, Bayley moved to the door, locking it with a firm click. Turning, she leaned against the door, a seductive smile on her lips. "You want to celebrate the good news?"

His lips curved in answer and his eyes lit as she sashayed his way.

Hating paperwork, Bayley stood from her desk several hours after Nick had returned to work, and stretched. She grinned as she thought of the initiation they had given her office before he left. Looking down at the spreadsheets of her monthly accountings, she closed her laptop, deciding to send them to her accountant the next day.

Moving to her window to view the store below, she smiled. Children were moving in and out of the kids' reading room and the coffee counter had a small line of people waiting for their beverage. Customers were milling about, searching for books or reading. Bruce and Sally were ensconced at their table, both typing furiously. Thinking of the small printer in the corner reminded her that she wanted to ask the accountant if she could afford to purchase a larger printer for the shop.

From her vantage point, she could see a couple standing behind one of the tall bookshelves. Curious, she stepped a few feet to the left to have a better vantage point. Agnes was facing the man, but it did not appear to be a happy conversation as her arms waved about and the man pointed his finger at her. Just as Bayley was about to go downstairs to ask the couple to take their heated discussion elsewhere, the man turned around and made his way to the coffee counter, plastering a smile on his face as he approached Daphne.

Eyes wide, Bayley watched Daphne greet the man with an attempt to kiss, but he turned his face away at the last second. She noted Agnes peeking at the couple from the corner of the shop. The man left just as Agnes moved back to the table where Bruce was busy at work. Biting her lip, Bayley wondered what she had witnessed. Realizing she had not spent much time with Daphne in the last week, she headed down the stairs.

"It's nice of your boyfriend to bring us here," Daphne said, popping another French fry into her mouth.

After checking to see that Daphne was available for dinner, Bayley called Nick to see if he would drop them off at a restaurant near his apartment. Taking a huge bite from her hamburger, she chewed and swallowed before replying, "It's no problem. He still wants to keep an eye on me even though that guy was arrested."

Shaking her head, Daphne said, "I still say your life has turned into one of your novels."

"Crazy, isn't it?"

The two women fell into a comfortable silence as

they continued to eat. Bayley finished her hamburger before playing with the rest of her fries.

"Okay, girl, spill it," Daphne ordered. "I can always tell when you have something on your mind."

"I was just wondering about the guy you're seeing. The one who was at the bookstore today."

"You saw Lazlo?" Daphne asked, her eyebrows raised in surprise. With a laugh, she added, "Oh, that's right—you were in your office."

"I wasn't spying, honestly," Bayley rushed. "It's just that I saw...uh—"

Blushing, Daphne said, "Oh, you saw me hug him. I'm sorry. I know it wasn't professional of me. I'll make sure not to anymore."

"No, no, it's not that," Bayley responded. Daphne blinked her eyes in confusion as Bayley hesitated. "Okay, here's the thing. I know you were upset when Agnes started coming to the shop and writers' group, monopolizing Bruce's attention, though I still say he's not interested in her romantically. But anyway, I knew you were seeing someone else and, today...in the shop... before he came over to you...he was...well, I don't know exactly what—"

"What are you trying to get out, Bayley?" Daphne accused, her eyes full of a mixture of disbelief and irritation.

"It's just that he and Agnes were behind one of the bookcases and they were having some kind of discussion."

"Discussion? That's it? That's all you've got to report

from your snooping?" Tossing her napkin down, Daphne glared at Bayley.

"I told you I wasn't snooping. I just went to the window to check on business and I saw them having what looked like an argument."

Daphne pinched her lips together as she stared down at her plate.

"It's just that I realized they knew each other and I thought it was strange, that's all." Silence greeted her. "I just don't want you to be hurt."

"Look, I know Lazlo's totally different than Bruce. He's very dominant, but he likes me as a lover, unlike Bruce, who just seems to like me as a friend." Looking up at Bayley, she added, "It feels like you're trying to stir up trouble where there doesn't need to be trouble. Maybe she was just in his way as he looked for a book. You don't have to make everything seem like such a big mystery." Pushing her chair back, Daphne said, "I need some time to myself, Bayley. I'll see you tomorrow."

Before she could apologize, Daphne stalked away from the table, leaving her alone and feeling miserable. Slumping in her chair, she played with her French fries a little more before leaning back, sighing. " 'Instinct is a marvelous thing. It can neither be explained nor ignored,' " she said, looking at Daphne's empty chair. Standing as she paid the bill, she wished Agatha Christie had more words of wisdom for her.

"Can I ask you something?"

Lazlo rolled away from Daphne, stalking to the bathroom to dispose of the condom, assuring it held firm. The last thing he wanted was some bitch claiming to be pregnant by him. Unless it were *her*. The idea of the beautiful Bayley carrying his child flamed his lust. Hearing Daphne calling out to him again, he grimaced. Sex with her was bearable—somewhat uninspiring—but she proved to be submissive enough. But *her*...it was Bayley's face he thought of when he was on top of Daphne. Staring into the mirror, he whispered to the empty room, *"Some day...she will be mine."*

"Lazlo? Are you coming back to bed?"

Wiping the grimace from his face, he walked back into the bedroom, bending to snag his boxers and pants off the floor.

Daphne watched as he began to dress and sat up in bed, letting the sheet slip to her waist. "I thought you might stay the night with me."

Looking at her, his dick stirred at the sight of her perky breasts, but he zipped his pants instead. "You know I don't stay the night."

Sighing, Daphne pulled the sheet up to her chin, his callous demeanor while dressing making her self-conscious. "Will I see you tomorrow?"

"I have meetings for most of the day. If I can come by tomorrow night, I will."

"If you want, I could come to your house sometime," Daphne offered, her smile hopeful.

Piercing her with his dark eyes, Lazlo said, "I come to you, when it suits. Not the other way around." Continuing to stare, he asked, "Is that a problem?"

Shaking her head quickly, she replied, "No. No problem."

Hearing the click of the door as he left, she slid down, grabbing the pillow as her tears flowed.

"I think I screwed up."

Nick was sitting on the sofa, Mr. Lickers lying next to him as his hand rubbed the cat's chin. Having just finished a conversation with Bernie, he was relaxed and satisfied with his uncle's recovery. Looking up as Bayley walked into the room, her t-shirt was emblazoned with a large owl on the front, its eyes wide open and placed over each breast. Her sleep shorts were covered in dogs and, distracted by her ever-changing array of sleepwear, he just stared.

"Nick, did you hear me? I said I think I screwed up."

Blinking away from the owl staring at him, he said, "How so?"

Plopping down on the sofa next to him, she rubbed Mr. Lickers absentmindedly. "I upset Daphne."

"You two have been friends for years," he said. "I'm sure whatever you said, she'll be fine."

"I don't know. It was about the new guy she's dating. He seems kinda weird and I brought this up to her."

"And she didn't take it well."

Shaking her head, she said, "Nope. Not well at all."

"I thought she was dating that writer in your group?" Nick asked.

"Bruce? She was really interested in him and I think

he still likes her, but she met this other guy, who doesn't come around much, now that I think about it. And that's fine with me because, quite frankly, when he does, he gives me the willies. And then Agnes—that's the new girl writer that you swear never looks you in the eyes—anyway, when she started coming, she always hung out with Bruce. I never saw that either of them was interested in the other, but Daphne felt left out, so I think she started really focusing on this new guy."

"Wait, he gives you the what?" Nick asked, attempting to follow Bayley's story.

"You know…the willies. Kind of like the creeps only less creepy."

"The willies," Nick repeated.

"Are you going to let me tell my story, or just keep interrupting?"

"Is your story going to start making sense?"

Snorting out a giggle, Bayley shook her head. Nick twisted his body toward hers and apologized. "Please go on. Tell me about how this guy gives you the less creepy creeps."

Shooting him a pretend glare, she said, "He doesn't come into the store usually. I've only met him a couple of times and he's dating my best friend. He picks her up outside and the few times he has been in the store, it's as though I can feel his eyes following me around."

At that statement, Nick sat up straighter, his intuition triggered. "Go on."

Shrugging, she said, "Well, this afternoon when I was working in my office I happened to look down from my window and saw he and the new girl, Agnes, behind one of the bookcases—" Seeing his raised eyebrow, she hastened to explain, "No, no, not like that. They appeared to be arguing. I mean, you don't argue with a complete stranger...well, not unless they cut in front of you in line or something like that. Although sometimes, I've wanted to fuss at people who are acting like a jerk out in public—"

"Bayley."

"Oh, yeah. So, I figured they must know each other which is weird. Then he goes over to speak to Daphne after slapping a smile on his face. I brought it up to her when we had dinner and I think I insulted her...or her boyfriend."

"You want me to check out this guy? I don't like the idea of someone in the store that gives you the willies."

"Oh, he's harmless, I'm sure. I just wish Daphne would go back to Bruce." Shrugging, she added, "And I hope she doesn't stay mad at me."

Mr. Lickers hopped down from the sofa and padded into the kitchen to root in his food dish, so Bayley slid into his vacated spot, next to Nick. He wrapped his arm around her, pulling her in close. Kissing her head as they embraced, he assured, "I have no doubt that Daphne will show up tomorrow, all anger forgotten... all back to normal."

"I hope so," Bayley yawned, purring as she snuggled closer to his warmth.

"I'm uncomfortable with this."

Agnes jerked her eyes over to Dr. Kovenov. "We don't have a choice. We need to get the girls out of here before new ones can be brought in. And we can't take any chances on getting caught. This is my chance, don't you understand? My chance to finally make a statement."

Turning his watery, grey eyes toward the young beauty, he pressed, "Are you sure?"

"I'm sick of their patronizing way of looking at women. I can do more…I can be more."

"But your mother has a role in the business. She is treated well," he protested.

Rolling her eyes, she glared at him. "My mother is treated that way because she married into another family. And she brought the Volkov name with her."

At the mention of the name *Volkov* he winced. The fierce name of Gavrill's family was well identified with his ruthlessness.

"We will do this and we will make a statement," Agnes said, her voice strong. "I'll be known, over my brothers, even over my parents. But, I need your help."

Sighing, knowing he could not persuade the determined woman, he nodded. "Okay, I'll help. But once the girls are dead, how will their bodies be disposed of? Who will help you?"

With a sharp shake, she said, "No. I have to handle everything myself. That's the only statement that I can make to assure complete success."

Nodding, he agreed. "I'll get the drugs. I'll be ready tomorrow. Ingestion will be quick. But you need to be ready." He turned to walk away and then stopped, stepping closer. Peering into her eyes, he added, "And not just ready to handle the situation but ready to deal with what you are doing. Getting rid of the girls...you might not be ready for—"

"Don't worry about me," Agnes interrupted, lifting her chin. "I can handle this." She observed as he nodded before walking down the hall, a sly smile curving her lips.

Bayley looked up from the counter as Daphne walked into the shop, her eyes red-rimmed. The two women stared at each other for only a second before Bayley ran around the counter and engulfed Daphne in a hug.

"I'm so sor—"

"No, I'm sorry," Daphne said, cutting off Bayley's

apology. "I was super sensitive and you have always had my best interests at heart."

"But I should have never interfered."

Daphne wiped a new tear from her cheek as she shook her head. Allowing Bayley to lead her toward the back, where they could sit in the employee lounge, Daphne said, "I'm going to end things with Lazlo."

"Oh, no, please don't based on what I said," Bayley pleaded.

"It's not you...honestly. The truth of the matter is, he really doesn't treat me very well. I thought he was just private. You know, the kind of guy who doesn't like his business out there for everyone. Last night..." she swallowed hard, "I felt like the only thing missing was him putting money on the nightstand."

Eyes wide, Bayley soothed, "Oh, honey."

"I mean, I know that's how a lot of people are. Just sex and nothing else. No talking, no cuddling, no public displays of affection. But even a fuck-buddy has the word *buddy* in the title. He made me realize that I was nothing more than convenient sex."

Holding her hand, Bayley cried, "You are worth so much more than that. Please tell me you know that."

Nodding sadly, Daphne replied, "I do. That's why I'm letting him know today that I don't want to see him anymore. I'm going to wait until the end of the day. He'll probably come pick me up and I'll tell him then." With a slight lift of her shoulders, she added, "I don't think he'll care."

"That, right there, tells me he's not worth the worry," Bayley declared, leaning over to hug her friend, hoping

Daphne was right. A sliver of concern slid through her at the thought of Lazlo not being the type of man who liked to be dumped.

The Saints all moved to their seats in the conference center. Nick had arrived early to work with Luke and Charlie, attempting to find some connection between the hotel the Gruzinskys owned and Gavrill's nefarious businesses.

Nick reported, "I've been in touch with the U.S. Coast Guard. They've been investigating and watching Gavrill's ships for the past year, waiting for the right time to board. So far, Gavrill's managed to slip by them, not having human slaves on the ships they've spotted. Gavrill's got a ship in his port now that should have already sailed, but the dates have changed twice. The only reason given that there has been a hold up of goods being delivered. I have no idea if that's tied in to what we're looking at, but the Coast Guard is at the ready."

Luke added, "While we know the familial relationship between the two families, I've found no money coming from Gavrill into the Gruzinsky's business, but we've been able to trace an account going in the other direction."

"Payout to the head of the main family?" Marc asked.

Monty, the other Saint that was former FBI, nodded as he said, "While the old mafia ways have changed over the years, the idea of making payments to the ones in charge is still very much in force."

"I've been pouring over the security tapes from the Gruzinsky's hotel and from the lobby, to the back alley, to the floors, I'm not seeing anything suspicious," Charlie reported. "Luke's been looking at the floor plan, and we've determined there is no security camera in the basement, beyond the staff rooms. There also appears to be a block of rooms on the first floor, near the back, away from the elevators. Six rooms. And there is no camera there either."

"What kind of staff rooms?" Jack asked, looking up at the screen where the blueprints of the hotel were being shown.

"There is a large staff breakroom in the basement," Luke said, using enhancements to change the color of the room his was referring to. "On the west side, there is a men's locker room and on the east side, there is an equal women's locker room. There are security cameras in there, except for the toilet and shower areas. We've been watching the tapes and have seen no unusual comings or goings there."

"What else is down there?" Bart asked.

"Supply closets, mostly. But here is where it gets interesting. The blueprints show more space beyond where the cameras provide security. So, there is the possibility of something else there that we can't see."

Cam grinned, "Time for night stalking?"

Hell yeahs rang out from around the table. Jack grinned as he looked over his eager crew. "Let's get it planned."

Nick leaned back, his heart pounding. This was what the Saints did. Not hampered by legalities. Not worried about search and seizure regulations. But able to find out what needed to be discovered. Looking up, he saw all the eyes in the room staring at him, unspoken questions in their expressions. Grinning, he said, "You heard the boss…let's get it planned."

"Time to eat."

The Saints had been planning for the next evening's recognizance mission when Jack interrupted the meeting with his pronouncement.

As the group stood and stretched, Jack added, "Bethany's got something for everyone upstairs. That way we can eat here and keep planning."

"Hell, she didn't have to fix food for us," Charlie said, knowing how much these men could eat.

Chuckling, Jack said, "Don't worry about it. You'll see what I mean when you get upstairs."

Filing up the stairs, the Saints laughed as they walked into the living room, hearing chatter. It appeared the Saint women were gathered and ready to eat. The huge dining room table and kitchen counter were filled with warming trays of chicken, asparagus, new red potatoes, vegetable lasagna, bowls of salad, platters of rolls, and on another table set up near the couches stood a decorated cake.

"What the hell is this?" Nick wondered aloud.

Shrugging, Bethany explained, "There was supposed to be a wedding last night at my venue and as the bride got to the head of the aisle where the groom was, he looked over the crowd and said he found out, and had proof, that she had been having a long-time affair with his best man and it was still going on. So, he walked back down the aisle, looked at me and said, since his family had more money and had paid for the reception instead of the bride's parents, he did not want them to have the food."

"You brought it all here?"

"No, we packed up as much as we could in my truck and took it to the homeless shelter in town. But we couldn't carry it all and the shelter has a rule about not accepting food after a day, since it might not pass the health inspectors, so what we couldn't carry we brought here. Believe me, this is only a scrap, compared to what the shelter received."

The Saints greeted their wives, children, and fiancés. Nick was surprised to see Bayley in the midst, but hustled to her side. Kissing her sweetly, he said, "How'd you get here?"

"I can drive, you know," she teased. "But, Bethany called and said that Faith would pick me up from the shop since it was on her way." Looking around the huge gathering, she grinned. "This is a great group, isn't it?"

Nick dragged his gaze from her shining smile and gazed around. The eclectic group appeared to be at ease with each other, laughter filling the room. Giving Bayley a squeeze around her waist, he agreed, "Yeah, you're right. It's a great group."

"No regrets?" she asked, her voice soft, eyes searching his.

Smiling back, he shook his head. "No regrets."

An hour later, stomachs full and laughter still going, Bayley set her empty paper plate on top of Nick's and watched as he went into the kitchen to throw them away. The men offered to clean up since the group had decimated the leftovers. Bayley felt a nudge on her foot and startled as she looked at the perpetrator.

Grace, sitting on the floor with Ben in her arms, grinned back at her. "Yep, you've got it bad, girl."

"What?" Bayley pretended not to know what her sister-in-law was talking about.

"I can recognize love when I see it."

"Oh, you can say that again," Bethany laughed. The other women chimed in, all agreeing, but it was when Bayley's gaze landed on Faith's penetrating stare and she saw the small curve of her smile that she leaned back against her chair, for once no words coming. But warmth slid over her heart.

"So, are you going to move in?"

Bayley was sitting in one of Nick's comfortable chairs turned to face the wide window, her feet propped up and her computer in her lap, the sunset providing the perfect view. Her fingers stilled their pecking, halting over the keyboard. Looking over, she stared at Nick, lounging on the sofa, Mr. Lickers curled up at his side. Her gaze dropped to the cat, whose fur he was rubbing. Grinning, she asked, "Are you talking to me or Mr. Lickers?"

Matching her smile, he replied, "I kinda figured you two were a package deal."

Nodding, she agreed, "Yeah, we are." Sobering, she sucked in her lips. "Are you asking for real?"

"Sweetheart, we may have only known each other a short while, but have you ever known me to not be serious, especially about something that matters so much?"

Setting her computer onto the floor, she stood and walked to him, sliding onto his lap. Wrapping her arms around his neck, he enveloped her waist with his hands. Peering into his eyes, she said softly, "I know you said we could live anywhere, but I've got another two months on my apartment's lease. Why don't we just stay like we are for now and make up our minds when all the craziness surrounding our lives settles down."

He said nothing for a moment, his eyes not leaving hers. "What you're saying makes sense but I get the feeling there's more behind those words. Come on, Bayley. Give it all to me."

"I know how I feel about you, Nick, but you've seen my apartment. What if I move in and our styles clash?"

"You know how you feel about me?"

Huffing, she replied, "Yes, but that's not the point."

"It's exactly the point." He slid one of his hands over her shoulder, cupping her jaw. His thumb caressed her smooth cheek. "Tell me...because, Bayley, it's everything."

Heart pounding as the momentous thoughts slammed into her, she whispered, "I'm falling in love with you, Nicholas Stone...or more accurately, I've already fallen. I think I might have fallen in love with you the moment I saw you sitting at Neon's bar, all stiff and out of place. And then when you walked me to my car and I looked up at you, the light from the streetlight beaming down on you, I felt struck by lightning. And I've never said this to anyone before." Having spoken her thoughts, her breath left in a *whoosh* of exertion. Swallowing deeply, she felt the heat of blush on her face as she waited to see his response.

The edges of his lips curved slowly upward until his smile reached his eyes and was all she could see.

"I love you, too, Bayley Hanssen. I think I fell in love with you the moment you told me you named your car Prissy. And not even the streetlight could compete with the illumination from your smile shining up at me."

Her sob caught in her throat as he pulled her in, his lips crashing into hers. She heard moaning but was unable to tell if it came from her or him. He deepened the kiss and she reveled in the feel of his tongue plunging inside, swirling with hers. Drinking him in, his distinctive taste filled her senses. Barely aware of being lifted, she wound her arms tighter as he carried her down the hall, hearing the click of the door, keeping Mr. Lickers at bay.

Setting her feet gently on the floor, Nick peered into her lust-filled eyes. "Tell me again."

Smiling, she whispered, "I love you."

Matching her grin, he kissed her nose before sliding his lips close to her ear and whispering back, "And I love you." With those words, he took her mouth once more, pressing her tightly to his chest. He felt her nipples pebble and the desire to taste them was over-whelming as he snaked his hands to the bottom of her shirt. Pulling it over her head, he admired her breasts, pushed up in a black, lacy bra. His lips moved from hers, trailing kisses down her neck to the top of her breasts. Moving from one to the other, he sucked her nipples through the lace until he thought he would go mad with want. As though she had read his mind, she slid her hands from his shoulders to her chest, where she pulled the cups down, exposing the perfect, rosy-tipped mounds.

Unsnapping and tossing her bra, he greedily sucked as he backed her against the mattress, gently laying her down. Settling beside her, he filled his hands, molding the fleshy orbs, taking one nipple deeply into his mouth before giving it a gentle bite.

Writhing against his jean-clad knee, she sought the friction to relieve the need building inside her core. Pushing on his shoulders, she flipped him onto his back, straddling his hips, feeling the distinct bulge in his pants.

"I need you." She pulled his face in for a kiss, plunging her tongue in, tasting all that was him. "Now," she mumbled against his lips.

Moaning, he flipped her back over, standing quickly. She moved to unzip her jeans, but he took over, sliding them down her legs, taking her black, lace panties with them.

"Perfection," he said. His hands reached for her feet and he lifted them in his hands. Sliding up her legs, he pulled them apart, exposing her pink folds. Kneeling on the floor between her legs he kissed from her knees upward until his mouth covered her folds. Sucking hard, he licked, lapping her juices until he pulled her clit into his mouth. His cock swelled painfully in his jeans, but growling against her quaking body, he was determined to ignore his own needs until she came.

She arched off the bed, the tantalizing sensations creating the urge to move, but he reached one large hand up and placed it on her pelvis, holding her still.

She began to writhe more, her hips undulating upwards, seeking sweet relief. Slipping a finger into her core while still sucking on her clit, he watched her fall apart.

Moans escaped her as she climbed higher, finally crying out his name as the tremors overtook, shattering her into a million pieces.

He licked her juices and then rose up from the floor, placing his finger in his mouth, not wanting to miss a single taste. Jerking his t-shirt up and over his head, his hands then went to his jeans, unbuttoning them as quickly as he could.

As he shucked his jeans, her eyes traveled down from his wide shoulders to his naked chest. He was defined, with chiseled abs and a tight stomach that ended in a perfect V that traveled downwards. By the time her eyes had moved to the end of the V, his jeans and boxers were off and her eyes feasted on his cock.

He saw her expression go from sated to excited. Leaning over, he crawled up her body until his eyes peered directly into hers. "Baby, I want you to know," he said, "I've never once been in love. I've never loved any woman. You are my one and only." He looked deeply into her crystalline blue eyes, seeing the light that was her shining out on him.

Bayley stared into his eyes, seeing sincerity blazing from them. "I love you," she whispered. "I've never lived with someone before. I've only had a few boyfriends, but I've never been in love either. I write about it all the time, but began to wonder if love was only in my books and wouldn't ever be in my life." Sighing, she added,

"I've seen my parents' love and how Blaise is with Grace. But until you, I had never experienced it."

Laying on his side with her next to him, he began to explore every delicious curve. Bayley felt the electric shock from her nipples to her womb and down to her sex once again. As he moved his finger through her slick folds, he lifted himself over her, placing his engorged cock at her entrance.

He gently entered her, slowly, wanting to feel each delicious inch. She moaned at the fullness and the pressure that immediately began to build. With a final push, he was in all the way, pumping slowly.

"More, I need more," she said in a whisper and that was all it took for him to begin moving faster. The friction was soon sending her over the edge again as the shock waves pulsated from her inner core outwards.

Flipping her again, she was once more on top. "Ride me, baby," he begged.

Bayley placed her hands on his shoulders and as her orgasm flooded her senses, she raised up and down, riding his cock. He felt her inner walls grab his dick and her natural juices made the movement easier. Her breasts bounced in rhythm to her rocking and he palmed the full flesh, tweaking her nipples.

She lowered her face, whispering, "I love you," as he took over, thrusting upward. Nick captured her lips once more, imitating the motion of his thrusting with his tongue. He could feel his balls tightening and knew that he was close. Throwing his head back, he powered through his orgasm, pulsating deep inside as her channel tightened around him again.

She crashed on top of his sweaty body, both still shaking with the intensity of the moment. Neither spoke for several minutes, the emotions of the act too overwhelming. Too important.

As they slowly recovered, the cool of the night finally penetrating the heat they had generated, Nick tucked her in tightly to his body as he jerked the covers over them. Pushing her sweaty tendrils away from her face, he grinned. "So...about moving in?"

Laughing, she said, "All right, all right. You know, Daphne said she needs a change...maybe she'd move into my place. She could have the stuff I won't bring here. I just need to make sure I find the right spots for what I will bring so that nothing gets out of place."

"Already told you, but I'll keep saying it until you believe it. All I care about is you. So, bring your stuff, your clothes, your makeup and hair stuff. Bring pillows, lamps, pictures, rugs...whatever." He kissed her, this time sweet and soulful. "I'm serious, Bayley, all I want is you and I want all of you."

"I love it! Are you sure?"

"Absolutely."

Bayley and Daphne walked around Bayley's small apartment the next day, looking at the furniture. "I'll leave all the big furniture," Bayley said, eyeing what she would like to take and what to leave. "Nick's got a few lamps but, honestly, after the sun goes down, I think his living room is kind of dark. I'll take the two lamps from here and you can bring in your own. I'll get my pictures down and anything that's personal." Turning to look at her friend, she said, "I'm so glad you are moving in!"

"Are you kidding?" Daphne replied, throwing her arms around Bayley. "My roommate is getting married and I need a place to live. Not to mention, considering Lazlo went ballistic when I said I didn't want to see him anymore, this comes at a perfect time...it keeps him from showing up at my front door."

"Good, well, why don't you just plan on staying here from now on. It's Sunday, the store's closed, and I'm grabbing my toiletries and the rest of my clothes, stuffing them in Prissy and taking them over to Nick's."

"I'll go home and get some of my things to bring over and I'll take you up on the offer," Daphne enthused.

Sitting in his car across the street, Lazlo watched as Daphne walked to her car and drove away. Having watched both women go into Bayley's apartment, he knew she was now there alone. With a smile on his face, he started his car and drove away after sending a text.

Tonight.

Bayley Hanssen would be his...tonight.

28

Daphne stepped out of the bubble bath, reveling in the sweet scent in the room. Grinning, she peered into the mirror, stunned at how her rotten day had morphed into a good one. Her old apartment did not have a bathtub and, as soon as she viewed the large tub in Bayley's apartment, she knew exactly how she would be spending the evening. "Out with the old and in with the new," she told herself, as she toweled off. In the bedroom, she quickly donned her pajamas, not concerned at the early hour. She was determined to spend the evening relaxing.

Standing in front of the bedroom window, she looked out, realizing Bayley had been right when she complained that her apartment did not have much of a view. But, Daphne did not care. The place felt perfect— her own fresh start. With a deep, cleansing breath, she walked toward the kitchen to get a glass of wine before settling in front of the TV.

A moving shadow in her peripheral vision caught

her eye and she gasped as she turned, seeing a hulking figure stepping close.

"Come with me quietly," he ordered, grabbing her arm.

A scream froze on her lips for an instant until, breaking free, the screech filled the air. The man clamped his huge hand over her mouth, stopping the noise. As she struggled, another figure stepped into the room, hustling over and quickly pricking her neck. She felt her body slump against her will before blackness overtook everything.

Nick, dressed in the same dark clothing as the other Saints going on the mission, stepped into the equipment room. He had been given a cursory tour when he joined, but the wealth of devices at his fingertips added to his appreciation of Jack's business. Weapons, kevlar, night vision goggles were just a few of the items he grabbed.

With the mission planned, the Saints stepped back into the main conference room, going over the fine points of details one more time. Jack, Luke, and Charlie would remain in the compound, monitoring the mission. Marc and Chad would drive the vans to the hotel, staying with the vehicles while the others did the searching. Nick, Monty, Cam, and Bart would be the first into the building, searching the basement. Patrick, Jude, and Blaise would monitor the outside of the back alley of the hotel.

Final plans in place, the Saints made their way up

the back stairs, to the oversized garage and into the waiting vans. Looking out the window as they pulled out onto the road, Nick watched the scenery go by, a smile sliding across his face as the thrill of the hunt ensued.

———————

I didn't expect to be back so soon. Bayley, in Prissy, was driving back into her neighborhood to grab a few more things from her old apartment to take to Nick's place. She had not planned to return so soon, but when he had called to let her know he would be late, she thought she'd be proactive. Determined to put her stamp on his apartment, she made the decision to run back to her apartment and grab a few more things. Daphne had not answered her phone, but Bayley hoped she was home. If not, she still had her key.

Pulling into the parking space next to Daphne's car, she sat for a moment, soaking in the reality that this would no longer be her home. *I'm moving to Nick's...in with Nick. A man I've only known for a few weeks.* The enormity of her decision gave her pause and she leaned her head back against the headrest, closing her eyes, waiting to see if panic or indecision would overtake her. Nothing. Nothing but excitement and a sense of rightness.

Smiling, she reached forward to open her door, when movement to her far left caught her eye. Two large, suited men were walking out the side door generally used by residents going to the laundry room, and they appeared to be supporting a woman in between them. Bayley leaned forward even more, wondering if the woman was intoxicated. When she realized the woman was dressed in what appeared to be pajamas she started to get suspicious. As the men opened a black sedan with dark windows and maneuvered the woman into the back seat, her head flopped back. Bayley's heart leaped as she recognized Daphne. *They've got Daphne!*

Shutting down the instinct to run after them, she forced her breathing to steady as she started Prissy, pulling out just after the sedan. Reaching inside her purse, she dialed Nick. No answer. Dialing Blaise, she received no answer from him either. Remembering Nick said he would be late, she wondered if he was with Blaise. Trying Nick again, she left a message.

"Nick, I just saw two men carrying Daphne from my old apartment to a dark car. I think they drugged her. I'm following. Don't worry, I'm not stupid enough to do anything but I just want to see where they're taking her, so I'm following."

Hanging up, she continued to track them, from a distance, as they left town. Several minutes later, she thought of the Saints' compound. *Jack had said to call if there was something happening and Nick was unavailable.* Fiddling with her phone, she pulled up the number he had provided.

"Bayley," Jack's deep voice answered.

Momentarily stunned that he knew who was calling, she quickly recovered. "Jack?"

"Yes."

"I tried calling Nick. I went back to my apartment

and saw two men take a friend who is staying at my place. I'm following them, but don't know what else to do. I can't get hold of Nick or Blaise—"

"Bayley."

The one word from Jack calmed her, while at the same time she recognized it was a gentle command. "I'm sorry," her shaky voice squeaked out.

"Don't apologize," he said, offering assurances. "I'm putting you on speaker phone—"

"Oh, is Nick there?" she interrupted.

"No, he's not. But I need you to listen and follow my directions. Can you do that?"

Sucking in a deep breath before letting it out slowly, she noticed the dark sedan taking the exit leading to the highway. Nodding, she realized Jack couldn't see her so she verbally affirmed, "Yes, I can do that."

"Good. Luke and Charlie are here with me. We're monitoring a mission Nick and Blaise are on. But, I promise, you are not alone, Bayley. I need you to succinctly, but accurately, tell us what you saw and where you are."

"Okay...I have a friend who is taking over my apartment. She moved in earlier today. I know Nick was going to be gone most of the evening, so I drove back over to my old place to grab a few more things. When I got there, I saw two men in suits carrying a woman in her pajamas to a car. As they got closer, I saw it was my friend."

She halted her speech as she changed lanes, careful to stay in the distance of the sedan, yet close enough to make sure she could follow. Once sure, she continued, "I have no idea what's going on or who they are, but I'm on the highway following them."

Charlie asked, "Bayley, who else knew that your friend was staying at your place?"

"No one, not even Nick. It was kind of spur-of-the-moment. She needed to move and Nick had asked me to move in with him. Which I know is soon, but we both felt like it was right...augh, I'm babbling!"

"No, no, you're doing fine," Jack assured.

Understanding dawned on Bayley and she rushed, "Oh, my God. You think, that they think, they have me?"

"We don't know, but it's possible," he said. "If someone sent the men to take you, then they would expect the woman inside to be you."

Bayley's heart dropped at the thought that Daphne was now in the hands of kidnappers. "Jack? What will they do when they find out she's not me?"

"Not going to let that happen," his terse reply came back.

"Bayley, it's Luke. Can you see a license plate number?"

"No, I'm too far back. Do you want me to get closer?"

"No!" came the combined shout from Jack and Luke. "Just tell us where are you now?"

"We've gotten onto 64 east heading toward Richmond."

"We've got an idea where you might be heading and we're following you closely," Jack said. "I'm working with the Saints in the field who are not far from you.

But listen to me, do not, and I repeat, do not attempt to go after them if they stop."

"O…okay."

"Bayley, you've got to promise. We need to be able to stay in contact with you, so you have to stay with your phone and the safest place is in your car."

Nodding again, she agreed. "Yes, yes," she vowed. "I won't try to play heroine."

"Good girl," he said. "Now stay at a distance and keep talking us through where you are."

"Okay," she said, glad for the evening daylight that allowed her to see the sedan. Letting out a shaky breath, she focused on the men in front of her, praying Daphne was all right.

———

Stepping inside, Agnes' gaze swept the room, seeing the wide-eyed expressions of the women inside. Dr. Kovenov followed her, setting his medical bag on the table.

"The doctor has the medicine that will make you well again," Agnes said.

Amy interrupted, her voice shaking. "What is the point of being well, if we are…are…"

"You have no control over where you are or what you are doing. That, lies solely with me," Agnes ground out. "But sick, you are no help to us."

Just then, one of the burly guards stepped inside the room, crossing his massive arms over his chest. Agnes watched the light of defiance drain from the girl's eyes. "Good, I see we understand each other."

Dr. Kovenov reached inside his bag, pulling out several small, plastic, measured cups, as well as a vial of liquid. Stepping up to the first woman, he asked her weight before measuring out a small amount of the pharmaceutical. She drank it obediently and followed his direction, lying back on her bed.

"The medicine will make you sleepy," he explained, "but it will make you feel better." Moving down the line, he gave the drug to each of the women, repeating the procedure that he and Agnes had just done with the women in the hotel rooms above.

Within fifteen minutes, all six women were lying on their beds, their chests no longer rising and falling.

Agnes, her palms sweating, looked at the doctor, noting his shaking hands. Lifting her eyes to the guard, she jerked her head toward the hall. "Get the cart," she ordered. "And do it carefully," she added, as her eyes moved over the now-still women. Swallowing back the bile threatening to rise, she whispered, "Even in death, they deserve some dignity."

Within a few minutes, the room was empty, all six women placed in oversized laundry carts and wheeled out to the waiting moving truck parked in the alley, ready to join the women's bodies from upstairs, already there.

Dr. Kovenov picked up his medical bag and turned to Agnes. "I think, perhaps, it is time for me to retire." His rheumy eyes swept the empty room. "I'm not as young as I used to be. And, this...this is not what I became a doctor for."

Patting his arm, Agnes smiled benevolently at the older man. "I agree, Dr. Kovenov. I think you should. But not until we have completed our task. I still need you. Then...I will make sure you are taken care of."

"Nick?"

Jerking his gaze up, Nick realized his name came from his earpiece. Looking at the others, he could tell they were tuned in as well.

"Yeah."

"Got a call from Bayley. You and Blaise need to keep your shit—"

His heart stopped beating for a second as the other eyes in the van leaped to his. Before his brain managed to form a question, Blaise spoke up, "What the hell's happening?"

"Focus," Jack ordered, and Nick blanked out all thoughts, including Bayley's brother in the van behind them, and curtly replied, "Go ahead."

Jack outlined what Bayley had told them, assuring both men that she was following the sedan at a distance. He also explained that Luke was monitoring her positon as she called it in, so they had an idea where Daphne was being taken.

Nick's heart continued to pound out an erratic beat, his thoughts tangled at the idea of Daphne in trouble and yet relieved it was not Bayley. Closing his eyes, he forced himself to listen carefully to every word Jack said, glad the other Saints would have his back.

Just then, Luke came over the headset. "Bayley's stopped and you won't believe it, but she's just a block from the Gruzinsky's hotel."

"Our location?" Bart confirmed.

"Yes."

Nick breathed out, "Then, this changes everything... we're no longer on a reconnaissance mission—we're on a fucking rescue."

The air crackled with a mixture of tension and excitement. Before the Saints had a chance to speak, Jack said, "I'm calling in your buddy, Harlan, at the FBI, Nick. The governor has placed him as our contact. And you're right...we can now go in as a rescue."

29

"**W**hy the fuck is she here?"

Lazlo stood in his private room in the hotel, staring at the woman lying on his bed. His eyes jerked from the slack expression on Daphne's face, her body sprawled on the bed, to the two men standing nearby.

"It's the girl you told us to get," one said.

Sucking in a quick breath, Lazlo growled, "She's not the right one."

The two men glanced at each other, confusion, as well as concern, sparking between them. "She was the only girl in the apartment. She had just changed clothes and was heading into the kitchen when we got there."

Rubbing his hand over his face, Lazlo realized Daphne must have been staying at Bayley's apartment, for some reason. The idea of Bayley staying with the bastard she had been with made him see red. Looking up at the two men, he bit out, "Well, she's not the right girl."

Hesitantly, one asked, "Uh…so what do you want us to do with her, boss? Take her back?"

"Are you fucking stupid?" Lazlo all but yelled.

Wincing, both men stood silent, waiting to see what he would order. Pacing the room, he cursed his bad luck. Unable to figure a way out without his brother or father discovering his fuckup, he whirled around, his face red with rage.

A knock on the door stilled the three men, gazes jerking back and forth, panic in their eyes.

"Mr. Gruzinsky?"

Recognizing the voice of one of the men working in the hotel, Lazlo let out a breath. Attempting to hide his relief, he called out, "Enter."

A tall, thin, older man entered, his eyes taking in the scene in front of him, but he appeared to ignore it as he said, "You wanted to know what your sister was up to, sir."

Receiving a curt nod, the man continued, "She and the doctor have completed their task and she is talking to your father and brother right now. It's my understanding that the truck behind the hotel will be leaving shortly. With another head jerk from Lazlo, the man left the room, closing the door behind him.

Sucking in a deep breath, he turned back to the sleeping, drugged woman lying on the bed. He knew if she awoke here, in his room, she could compromise their entire operation. Rubbing his hand over his face, he stood staring at his feet for a moment.

Lifting his head, his voice hard, he ordered, "Take her down. Use the special stairs and get her outside. Get her in the fucking truck out back." Piercing them with a glare, he insisted, "Don't talk to anyone on the way. If someone sees you, just say she had too much to drink."

"What about—"

"Do not second guess me! Just get her to the truck." He straightened to his full height as he lifted his chin. "Or do I need to get someone else to do your job?"

"No, sir," they said in unison, both bending to grab Daphne underneath her arms.

"You've done well. To be honest, I had no idea you had it in you."

Agnes' lips curved in a small smile as she bowed her head slightly, in deference to her father.

"You have taken a problem and found an answer that had, I confess, eluded the rest of us for a bit," he added.

Chessa stared at her daughter, no words of praise coming, rather, studying her carefully.

Agnes asked, "Is Lazlo going to start filling our needs soon?"

This time Grigory answered. "Yes. According to him, he has already contacted several and will take some men this weekend and begin gathering a new crop of women to service our needs."

"He had better think with the head on his shoulders and not what is between his legs. Lazlo will need to fill our coffers as well as take care of my cousin," Chessa said. "Gavrill is not happy with our latest situation. Having to fill his shipping container with dead women to dump at sea instead of live women to market has made him very angry."

Milos pinched his lips as he sent a glare toward his wife. "We are well aware of what we need to do." Smiling down at Agnes, he praised, "But, for our very smart daughter, we will have a way to rid ourselves of the problem."

Grigory watched Agnes, his wary gaze thoughtful. "Did the doctor ever figure out what made all the women sick, even though they were on different floors?"

Shrugging, Agnes answered, "He just said it was probably viral. Perhaps passed from the kitchen to their food."

Chessa stood, her words laced with venom. "I shall talk to Dr. Kovenov myself. If we do not know what made them sick, we are taking a risk that bringing in a new batch of girls will have the same effect."

Milos, glad for his wife to have a duty, nodded. "Good, good, Chessa. I will entrust you to this." Turning to Agnes, he said, "And what will you do to celebrate a successful venture?"

"Oh, I'm accompanying the truck to Norfolk." Seeing the surprised expressions on her family's faces, she added, "Do you think that I would risk a problem before seeing them delivered to the ship personally?"

Grigory stood, surprise in his voice as he said, "Are you crazy? What if there's a problem? If you're stopped...and then caught with a truck of a dozen dead bodies?"

"And who do you trust?" she bit back. "A driver who

can be bought? Someone who would blackmail the family? Or me? I'll get them to Gavrill's docks and see the deed done. Then, and only then, can I rest."

Without waiting for an answer, she turned and walked out of the room. Alone in the hall, she leaned against the door, waiting for her heart to settle. The thought of accomplishing her mission sent a smile across her face. *Even Gavrill will be impressed with what I've done..*

Grigory sat at his desk, now alone, pondering the family's situation. Rubbing his chin, he leaned back in his chair, the squeak of old wood and leather the only sound in the room. Decision made, he jerked forward, grabbing his phone.

"Yes, boss?" the deep voice answered.

"Agnes is leaving. Follow her. Report back to me."

"Got it."

Dialing Gavrill, he said, "She's on her way. I've got someone following."

Hanging up, he leaned back, a heavy sigh leaving his chest.

Bayley sat in her car as the evening sky darkened. Her last communication with Jack told her the Saints were about five minutes away and she once more promised to stay in her car. She looked around, wondering if she would see them drive up.

A white paneled truck pulled out of the alley behind the hotel and she caught the name **Lomar's Commerical Laundry** painted on the side. As it turned to drive past her, she saw Agnes in the driver's seat with an older man in the passenger side. Blinking to focus, she stared, unable to believe Agnes would be driving a large, laundry truck. The hairs on the back of her neck prickled as she started Prissy and did a u-turn in the street to follow.

Dialing Jack, she rushed out, "I'm on the move. I just saw Agnes, a woman I know, driving a truck away from the hotel. I have no idea why, but she sure isn't a truck driver—"

"Bayley!" Jack bit out. "Slow down and explain. And please, keep it succinct."

Sucking in a deep breath, she said, "I was parked outside waiting, just like you told me, when a laundry truck, Lomar's Commerical Laundry, came out from behind the hotel. The driver is a woman named Agnes, who comes into my shop. And I recently saw her in a deep conversation with Lazlo, Daphne's former boyfriend. The one who gives me the creeps."

"Okay," Jack said. "Go on."

"You said Nick was close to the hotel and I want to see what's going on with Agnes, so I pulled out and am following her."

At the compound, Luke piped up, "I've got her on the traffic cams. Looks like the truck is heading back to

Highway 64." He looked over at Jack and said, "I can't tell if it's east or west yet—"

"It'll be east," Jack said. "I wouldn't be surprised if they were going to Norfolk."

Charlie responded, "Got lots of road cams there. I'll get that set up to follow them."

Nodding, Jack reiterated, "Bayley, just like before. Stay at a distance but let us know where you are going."

"Okay. Let me know what's happening with Daphne, please," she begged.

"You got it," he promised.

Slipping into the dark hall, Nick stepped cautiously ahead, seeing two doors at the far end. No other sounds greeted the Saints as they maneuvered their way closer. Cam, first at the door, ready to pick the lock if necessary, found it unlocked. Swinging it open, he stepped inside, Nick and the others on his heels.

The room was empty, bunk beds still sloppy and unmade. The sight of handcuffs on each bed made Nick's stomach roil. The scent of the toilet wafted through the room as Jude opened the adjoining door. A few bowls on the table showed the residents had left recently.

Bart stepped up as the others swept the room. "You think the inhabitants of this room are in that truck? The one Bayley's following?"

Nick, calling into Jack their findings, relayed,

"There's enough here for the Bureau to be called in. Get hold of Harlan. Tell him what we're seeing and have him get his investigators over here. I want to get to Bayley. There's no sign of Daphne but we've got more to search."

"I've got Harlan on stand-by. He's ready to send in a team of forensic investigators."

Just then Nick's gaze landed on a green blouse, wadded in the corner of one of the beds. "Jack, I've got an article of clothing that looks like what Amy Willis was wearing the night she was taken."

"Harlan's team is on their way. He's got to keep a previously scheduled meeting, but says his team will be there in about ten minutes."

Jack ordered one van of Saints to stay at the hotel to rendezvous with the FBI when they arrived, and told the others to hit the road. "Bayley just called in. The truck took Highway 64 West."

"West?" Nick questioned, looking at the others hearing the same information.

"For some reason, it's not heading to Norfolk…or the driver knows they're being followed and are trying to shake the tail."

"Get Bayley off the tail!" Nick shouted, his wide eyes meeting Blaise's.

"I've already told her to pull back. She says she's keeping her eyes on the truck until she knows what's happening."

A noise in the hall had the men going silent, signals given by eye movement. The hallway filled with two, large, suited men holding a slumped woman between them. At the sight of the others in the room, one man dropped her as he went for his weapon, quickly finding six weapons pointed directly at him.

"Don't move, assholes!" Nick shouted, recognizing Daphne. With a quick glance, knowing the other Saints had them under control, he lunged toward the slumping woman. Picking her up gently, he turned to Blaise, the medic of the group. Maneuvering into the hall, Nick placed Daphne on the floor.

Pinching his lips, Nick looked at the others. "Time to split up. I'm going after Bayley."

30

Bayley watched as the truck in front of her turned off the highway, making its way along several winding turns, eventually pulling into a long, narrow road. At the end, a large, metal building appeared. She sat in indecision for a moment before driving closer. Not seeing the truck, she turned her headlights off, glad for the moonlight. Calling her location in to Jack, she pulled to the side of the road, parking Prissy in a location she hoped would give her vision and secrecy. Her stomach rolled at the uncertainty of what was happening, trying to keep Jack's warning in her mind. *He said Nick's coming.* Straining her eyes toward what appeared to be an old warehouse, she saw a small, lighted window on the side. With her hand on the door handle, she fought an inner battle. *Stay with Prissy.*

The area around the building was wooded and she realized they had not passed any houses for several miles. She had followed the truck west for at least twenty miles before they turned off the highway, so she was glad, and also really amazed, that Luke would be able to figure out where they were from her descriptions alone.

Slipping her hand into her purse, she pulled out her gun, the familiar weight a slight comfort, and exited her vehicle as quietly as possible. *What am I doing? "If you place your head in a lion's mouth, then you cannot complain one day if he happens to bite it off".* Ignoring Agatha Christie's voice in her head, she stealthily made her way to the nearest window of the building, partially hidden by trees. Peeking inside, she could see the laundry truck parked alongside a dark SUV, its windows just as dark. Agnes stepped around the side from the back and approached a man. Unable to see his face, Bayley leaned closer.

"I got them here but don't know if I was followed," Agnes said.

Bayley watched as the man nodded, his hand rubbing over his military short, grey hair. Something about him seemed familiar, but she could not place where she had seen him.

"I've got responders on their way but a wreck on the highway has shut it down and they can't get here right now." The man jerked his head toward the truck. "Can he do the job for now?"

Unable to hear Agnes' response, Bayley tried to see into the truck. Ducking down, she slipped around the corner, peeking into another window, this one facing the back of the truck. Eyes wide, she gawked at the sight before her. The back of the truck was open, with what appeared to be bodies lying inside, an older man standing at the entrance.

Whirling around, her back plastered to the building's wall, Bayley clapped her hand over her mouth, keeping the scream from bursting forth as her chest rose and fell with each forced breath. Her mind racing, she pulled her phone from her pocket. "Jack," she gushed in a hoarse whisper, "I know I shouldn't have, but I peeked in a window. There are bodies in the back of the truck. I don't—"

"Bayley, we're on our way. Get out of there," he ordered.

She glanced back in, seeing the older man in the truck bending over a woman's body. *Oh, hell no!* Disconnecting, she dropped her phone into her pocket as she rushed to the front of the building.

Nick, in the van driven by Marc, sat in the back with Blaise. Chad sat in the front passenger side, communicating with Luke. "Turn here," Chad ordered Marc, who deftly maneuvered the van off the highway.

A moment later, Jack came over their speakers, his words sending a chill down Nick's spine. "Bayley called. Seems the truck has bodies inside. She was cut off, but Luke's got your ETA as twenty minutes. Can you make that shorter?"

"Got a fuckin' accident on the highway that's got all the lanes closed. Just got off and we're taking backroads."

"Get there but get there safely," Jack ordered.

"Done," Marc bit out, stepping on the accelerator.

Nick and Blaise shared a heart-ripping look before both gazed out of their respective windows, keeping their fears to themselves.

The side door to the warehouse opened and Bayley rushed inside, gun in hand and pointed at the inhabitants.

"Get away from her!" she shouted as she rounded the back of the truck toward Agnes and the suited man. She watched as Agnes' face registered surprise, then anger, as she came closer. The man standing next to Agnes, his familiar face also hardened as his eyes jumped to her.

"Shit," Agnes said, her mouth in a tight line.

"What the hell?" the rumpled man asked, his hand going to his waist.

Bayley viewed a weapon holster on his belt and, next to it, a badge. *Badge.* Gaze lifting to his face, she remembered where she had seen him. *In a picture with Nick on the wall of the FBI building.* "Harlan?" she breathed.

Harlan's eyes shifted to hers, surprise in his as he heard his name from her lips.

"Get him away from that woman," Bayley ordered, jerking her head toward the truck and the man still there.

"You don't understand," Agnes said. "He's a doctor. He's helping!"

"H...helping? You've got a truck full of bodies and

he's helping?" Bayley's voice rose with each word. Jerking a glance to the side, she saw the man identified as a "doctor" staring at her, wide eyed, his hands raised in the air.

"We can explain," Harlan said.

"Keep your hands where I can see them!" Bayley shouted again. With one hand holding her weapon steady, she reached in her pocket for her phone, but her fingers found nothing. Grimacing, she realized it must have fallen out. "Nick is on his way. Remember Nick? Your supposed friend?"

Harlan shook his head as he took a step forward. "You've got this wrong, Ms. Hanssen. You've got to let the doctor do his work."

A moan came from the back of the truck and Bayley watched, heart pounding, as a woman staggered from the back, leaning on the arm of the doctor. Sucking in a gasp, she cried out, "Oh, my God! Amy Willis!"

The doctor stepped forward, letting the still-drugged woman slide to the ground, supported by the side of the truck. "Miss, I am a doctor. I've got to give the antidote to these women."

"Antidote?" Bayley asked, her mind racing with a tumble of thoughts, nothing making sense.

"The girls aren't dead," Agnes said, taking a step forward, but halting as Bayley swung her weapon back toward her. "They're drugged. It slowed their respiration down just long enough for me to get them into the truck."

"Why?"

"I had to get them out. Out of that place," Agnes cried, her face tortured.

"She's working with me," Harlan said. "I was supposed to bring some medical personnel with me, but they're caught on the highway at the accident. That's why we need the doctor to work on the women."

Fighting to steady her breathing, Bayley glanced down at Amy Willis who, still dazed, appeared to be waking from a long sleep. Looking up at the doctor, Bayley gave a curt nod. "Fine, but I'll be watching," she warned.

Looking toward Agnes, she said, "Why were you in my store arguing with Daphne's ex-boyfriend?"

"That was my brother."

"Your brother?"

"Lazlo."

Gasping, Bayley looked on in disbelief. "Lazlo...your brother?"

"Yes, well, don't hold my family against me," Agnes said. "They are why I am risking my life to save these girls."

Blinking slowly as understanding dawned, Bayley shifted her attention back to Harlan. "Why didn't you say anything? You could have told Nick."

"That's on me," Agnes said. "I worked out the deal. I'd get the girls out and to him and then I'd disappear. I'd come back to testify against my family but, other than that, I'm gone."

Staring at her a long time, Bayley saw fear in the other woman's eyes. Fear...and honesty. Shooting them all a look, she said, "Nick'll be here in a few minutes—"

"But that will be too late, won't it?"

The inhabitants of the warehouse stared as the deep voice came from around the truck, a gun pointed at them. The man turned to Bayley and ordered, "Drop it."

Thinking fast and furious, still, no plan came to mind and, as the man with the gun stepped toward her, he shifted his aim to Amy, still sitting propped up by the truck. With no good choice available, she placed her gun on the ground and pushed it towards him, watching as he bent slowly, picking it up before sliding it into his pocket.

Agnes looked behind her at the man with the gun and Bayley saw recognition flare in her eyes. "What are you doing here?" Agnes asked.

Chuckling, the man said, "Grigory told me to follow you. Guess he figured you were working on a deal all by yourself." Looking at Harlan, he asked, "Who's he?" As the man stepped to Bayley's right, the gun still facing her, his gaze dropped to Harlan's waist. "Fuckin' hell! You're talking to a Fed?"

In a flash, he moved his arm and fired, hitting Harlan in the arm. Pushing Agnes out of the way before he fell, Harlan shouted for her to get out. Twisting, Bayley shoved the man to the side, causing him to trip over a box on the floor. Agnes rushed forward, grabbing Bayley by the arm, pulling her behind the truck.

In a split-second decision, they made a run for the open door, hearing gunfire as they ran outside, ducking as they went. "Where's your car?" Agnes whispered.

"We can't leave them!" Bayley cried, pressing her back against the building.

Agnes whirled around, getting directly in front of Bayley. "He wants *me*! He needs *me*!" she said, pulling on Bayley's arm. "He follows orders and his orders are to get me. I'm the one that can take my family down."

Nodding, Bayley ran toward the woods, followed closely by Agnes. Both women jumped into the car as Bayley fished for her keys. Starting Prissy, she had just touched the accelerator as a bullet hit the back window.

"Shit!" both women screamed at the same time.

Hitting the gas, Bayley roared away, shooting down the gravel road past the warehouse, cursing that the gunman's vehicle blocked the way out. "I don't know where this road leads!" she yelled.

"Me either," Agnes said, still ducking in case more gunfire came at them. "But we've got to get out of here to get help."

Marc skidded to a stop outside the warehouse, lights burning brightly from inside with the wide doors open. Having been warned by Jack that Bayley left her vehicle, the Saints jumped from the van, weapons raised as they raced inside, cautiously but quickly.

The laundry truck had the back open, an older man looking up at them, his face a mask of fear. Raising his hands, he quickly said, "Don't shoot. I'm Dr. Kovenov. Don't shoot!"

Nick observed several women slumping in the back of the truck, their drunk appearance cause for concern.

"Keep your hands where we can see them!" Blaise shouted.

Nick's gaze swept the room, desperate to find Bayley. Unable to locate her, he turned to the doctor, calling out, "Where's Bayley? Where's the blonde who was here?"

The doctor's confused expression slowly morphed into understanding. "The one with the gun?"

Blaise answered, "Yes!" as Nick's heart sank at the idea of Bayley having to use her gun.

"Over here!" Chad shouted.

Nick and Blaise sprinted to the front of the truck, seeing Harlan lying against a box, his arm bandaged but still bleeding.

"What the fuck are you doing here?" Nick asked, dropping to Harlan's side.

Before an answer came, several ambulances careened to a stop outside the warehouse. Chaos ensued as rescue workers and FBI swarmed the area, immediately moving to assist the women in various stages of drugged stupor.

Recognizing Amy Willis moving slowly, Nick rushed to her, checking that she wasn't gravely injured. Hearing a noise behind him, he stood, allowing an EMT to move in to evaluate her. Blaise stepped up, his face full of concern.

Dr. Kovenov looked at Marc and confessed, "There were too many. I lost some."

Marc turned and glared at the much smaller man. "What are you talking about?"

"I drugged the women to make them appear dead and as I was waking them up, one got frightened and wandered off. I couldn't get to them all and patch up the lawman over there."

"Fuckin' hell," Marc growled, turning to Chad. Pulling out his phone, he placed a call to Jack, giving him the quick and dirty intel. "And we need Nathan, that tracker friend of Blaise's. Get him here immediately with his dog."

Harlan called out weakly, "Nick...you've got to get her."

Nick stomped over, grabbing Harlan by the shirt, disregarding his injury. Several agents pulled their weapons, but Nick still held his up to Harlan's chest. "You better start talking right fucking now. I don't give a shit what you were involved in. Where the hell is Bayley?"

"She was here. She followed Agnes and the truck. I had a deal with Agnes to get the women out. She would testify against her family and I'd give her immunity."

"I don't fuckin' care!" Nick roared. By now, the other Saints has circled around, the tension between the agents and Saints palpable. "Where is Bayley?"

Harlan's pain infused eyes cleared, as he groaned, "Jesus, Nick. She and Agnes ran. One of the Gruzinsky's men came after Agnes and then took off in his car after them. He's got to kill Agnes to keep her from turning against her family. And he won't mind taking Bayley out either."

"Where did they go?"

Shaking his head, Harlan said, "I don't know. But I heard cars behind the warehouse."

Staring at the crowded warehouse, the chaos now somewhat organized with agents and EMTs handling the women and Harlan, Nick looked at the other Saints and darted out the door with Blaise on his heels.

Prissy's headlights only pierced the dark woods so much, leaving Bayley having to lean forward in hopes of staying on the road. Agnes twisted her head, still seeing the headlights behind them. Neither woman spoke, Bayley gripping the steering wheel as Agnes clung to the dashboard, every bounce on the rutted farm road sending grunts from them both.

The gravel road had climbed upward, twists and turns making the driving difficult but, with limited visibility, Bayley had no idea where they were. "I don't know if we're going to get off this," she groaned, stepping on the brakes as another turn in the road had Prissy fishtailing.

"He's getting closer!"

"I know!"

Prissy's tires tried to grab onto the gravel when Bayley went into another curve but this time, she was unable to stay in control. Both women screamed as Prissy slid off the side of the road, and down the ravine, landing with the passenger side pressed up against a tree.

Dazed and heart pounding, Bayley looked quickly at her passenger, thankful to see Agnes looking back at her. "You okay?"

"Yeah, you?"

"Shaken, but I'm okay," Bayley acknowledged. Looking out her window, she saw headlights at the top of the ravine. "We've got to get out of here."

Trying her door, she sent a prayer of thanks when it opened. Seeing Agnes' door propped against the tree, she said, "Come out here."

Agnes unbuckled and crawled across the console and followed Bayley out her door, falling next to her on the leafy forest floor. The dark night was only illuminated by Prissy's headlights still shining a beam out into the woods. A shot zinged over their heads and they grabbed each other's hands as they scrambled around the car and into the woods.

With a huge oak trunk shielding them from the road above—and hopefully any flying bullets—they pressed their backs against the bark, their breaths ragged.

"What now?" Agnes asked, turning her face toward Bayley's.

Bayley, chest heaving, shook her head for a moment. "No cell phone...no gun—" Another shot pinged off the bark on the other side of the tree. "Shit! Come on."

Bolting deeper into the woods, the two ran, tripping over tree roots and slick leaves. Unable to see where they were going, they managed to dart between thick trunks and through underbrush that snagged their clothing, attempting to get away from the danger. Stopping in another clump of trees, Bayley tried to hear if they were being chased, but their heavy breathing was all her ears could discern. Clamping a hand over her mouth to lessen the sound, she motioned for Agnes to do the same. From the distant left, she heard sounds of someone moving through the leaves.

Whispering, "Come on," Bayley led the two deeper into the woods, their steps more measured and soft.

Nathan Washington gently led the missing woman back toward the warehouse, now lit with searchlights, spotlights, headlights, and just about any other type of light to be found. Patting the head of his bloodhound, he called softly, "Good girl, Scarlett. You did good." With his arm around the woman, he made his way inside the building, relieved to have found her quickly and not too far from the area.

Marc approached as an EMT immediately took the woman from Nathan's care and led her away. Several more of the Saints walked over as well, head jerks acknowledging each other. "You want to tell me what the hell's going on here?"

Rubbing his head, Chad said, "A royal cock-up. How's that for an explanation?"

"It looks like it." Nathan's gaze moved over the swarming mass of Feds, emergency personnel, women looking worse for the wear, and a group of angry Saints.

The sound of Blaise's voice came over their earpieces. "Need Nathan. Is he there?"

"He's here," Marc replied.

"Take the road behind the warehouse and get him here. Bayley's car went off the road and there's someone else here. We can hear shots in the background but can't find the girls."

Glad to leave the warehouse to the Feds and have a new mission, the Saints fled to their vans, calling for Nathan to follow. With a light tug on her collar, he looked down and said, "Let's go, Scarlett. Got another job for us, ol' girl."

The wrinkly brow and droopy jowls of the beautiful,

red-coated hound obeyed, trotting alongside him, her tail wagging.

Crawling on their hands and knees up a steep ravine after crossing a small creek, Bayley and Agnes stopped to catch their breath in a cave-like hiding place at the base of some fallen trees. Shaking from cold as well as fear, they huddled together, steadying their breathing. Settling in, Bayley knew Nick would come for them. Other than a few nighttime critters, they heard nothing out of the ordinary for nighttime, deep in the woods. No sound of footsteps following. No gunshots.

Wiping her hands on her pants, Bayley looked next to her, trying to discern Agnes' facial features in the dark. Her mind swirled with all the information from the last hour. "Why?" she asked, her words coming out in a hoarse whisper. She had wanted to ask more but, at the moment, the one word was all she could conjure.

"Why? Jesus, the better question would be *why not?*" Receiving no response, Agnes continued, "I grew up in the heart of a loving family. The little sister treated like a princess. But I always wondered what it would be like to have the respect that was given to my brothers, just because they were men."

Both women listened again for sounds of being followed, but only the crickets filled the night. Leaning her head back against a tree, Agnes continued, "When I got older, my mother decided that I could help with the family business…in the way that a *woman* could help. I learned a bit about the hotel, but it was the rooms in the back that fascinated me. The other rooms held guests, but there were back rooms that only some men were led to. Always escorted. When I was fifteen, my mother allowed me to visit with her, checking on the occupants. I couldn't wait to see what was inside."

Bayley turned her head to face Agnes, hearing the agony in her voice as it shook. "What did you see?"

"Just a plain bedroom with a small bathroom. And the only occupant was a woman. Pale. Thin. Her face looked...haunted. She barely looked at my mother, keeping her eyes down the whole time we were there, but when my mother placed the food on the table and turned away, I saw her look at me." A long pause slithered between the two, before Agnes whispered, "Haunted...her eyes were haunted."

"What did you do?"

"Nothing. I did absolutely, fucking nothing."

was zipping his pants and laughing. He was followed by one of his friends and they were laughing about her. By then, I was old enough to know what was going on."

Bayley opened her mouth to speak, but found no words came out. Trying to understand the world Agnes lived in, she came up blank.

"I kept quiet...but I watched...learned. I was smart and realized that I was smarter than either brother, but especially Lazlo. I watched my father, mother, and brother run a family *business* that included the buying and selling of women."

"How did you live with that knowledge?" Bayley shifted her body so that she faced Agnes, desiring to see her face as well as she could in the dark.

"For a long time, I had no idea what to do with the horrible knowledge. It haunted my dreams...like living in a nightmare. In my family, women are second class. Oh, believe me, my mother was feared as her honored place as wife and mother and I was certainly treated as a favored child. But I was only expected to marry, preferably someone with a Russian heritage, and make babies." Shaking her head, she added, "Most would never believe that the old ways still exist." She lifted her gaze, staring straight into Bayley's eyes, "But I plotted and planned. I discovered that they had basement rooms where they brought in new girls. Kept them there until they could be checked out by the doctor, made a little hungry, and a lot scared. And then moved upstairs. And the upstairs girls were shipped off to our relatives in Norfolk who used them however they wanted."

A suspicious sound quieted the women, so they slunk down, barely breathing as they listened. Sighing, Bayley said, "We're stuck out here until someone comes to find us or daylight lets us see where we're going."

Shifting slightly to ease her back, Agnes nodded. "God, what a mess."

"What happened?"

"I had no problem getting the doctor to help me when I finally realized he hated what he was doing. We came up with a plan to sneak the women out in the laundry truck, but had to figure out how. We came up with the idea that if they were all sick, they couldn't be around any clients. So, he started giving them some drugs that induced nausea and then we claimed that we had no idea what was happening but that they had to be quarantined. My family was scared they might get sick so they stayed away. That was the easy part. Then I had to play the part of the ultimate bitch…the planner of a scheme that my family would go along with. Claiming to be uninterested in the women, I suggested we kill then and then ship them off. Our cousin in Norfolk was pissed to not get live women, but he would take them out to sea and dump them."

Bayley's eyes widened in shock. "You're kidding, right? Your family believed you would do this?"

"Over the past couple of years, I have perfected the cold bitch persona and made it no secret that I wanted more of the family business responsibility. So…they believed it. Plus, Lazlo was screwing up, so my parents were willing to take a chance on me. Of course, as I now know, they sent someone to follow me." Shrugging, she added, "The doctor drugged the girls to slow down their respiration, we got some of the family's hired men to take them to the truck, and the doctor and I drove away."

"And Harlan?"

"I made contact with an FBI agent." Giving a rueful chuckle, she said, "I was so naïve, I can't believe I wasn't caught. I actually called from a payphone, managing to get hold of someone who believed me. He was in on the plan. We were to meet at the warehouse and he would have medical personnel to assist with the women. But the accident, shutting down the highway, made them late. And, of course, we didn't expect you to be following. Or the man my family sent." Sighing once more, she whispered, "What a mess."

"Asshole's been winged," Nick growled to the other Saints as they arrived, all looking down as Blaise tightened the tourniquet over the bullet hole to Gruzinsky's man, illuminated by their headlights.

Standing, Blaise bit out, "That's it for what I can do. One of you can get him back to the EMT and tell them to get a unit here.

Nathan stepped up, shaking Blaise's hand before being introduced to Nick, who had retrieved Bayley's purse from her car. Holding it out, he glanced down to the hound sitting obediently at Nathan's feet. "Does he need something to sniff?"

Grinning, Nathan nodded, then introduced his dog. "This is my girl, Scarlett, and don't worry...me and Scarlett will find her."

"There are two women out there, but we're going to assume they're together," Blaise said.

"Then let's go."

Nathan gave Scarlett the lead and she took off, nose to the ground with Nick, Blaise, and Chad on her heels.

"What was supposed to happen?"

Agnes looked at Bayley before answering. "After the agent took possession of the women and got them to safety, he was going to take care of me."

Cocking her head to the side, Bayley asked, "How?"

"Witness protection."

"Oh," Bayley breathed, knowing what an enormous risk Agnes was taking, reaching out to grasp her hand.

"You might not understand how I could be willing to testify against my family, but I had to. I couldn't live with myself knowing that the very clothes on my back...the very food on my plate, came from the buying and selling of women against their will." A tear slid down her cheek but she swiped at it harshly. "I love my family...and I hate them."

Bayley stared out into the night, thinking of Agnes and all she had endured. " 'You've had a long life of experience in noticing evil, fancying evil, suspecting evil and going forth to do battle with evil.' " Looking over at Agnes, she smiled ruefully. "I know it's stupid, but I love the writer Agatha Christie. It seems she always knows what to say to me...or rather I find that her quotes are so apropos to life."

A noise from the distance halted their conversation. By now, Bayley's eyes had grown accustomed to the woods surrounding them in the light of the moon, and she leaned past the clump of trees, peering into the forest. "I hear something...I hear a dog baying."

"It sounds like a wolf," Agnes whispered, her voice laced with fear.

Turning back to Agnes, Bayley grinned, "My brother knows all kinds of animal people. He even knows a tracker. I'll bet they've got one looking for us."

Agnes' eyes held hers as she said, "You...they would be looking for you. No one will come looking to save me."

"No, no," Bayley protested, her hand squeezing Agnes'. "They need you too. For everything you've done. For the risks you've taken. For—"

"No, Bayley. I can't go back with you. Not now. You get away from here and, when it's daylight, I'll make my way back to the road. I'll get hold of my contact and go into protection. But now, there will be too many eyes on the women and the warehouse. I'll never get by unseen. I don't want to be found with you...it's too dangerous."

"Bayley! Bayley!"

The sound of men's voices ringing through the night reached both women, their eyes locked on each other.

"Go, go," Agnes ordered. "If need be, send the tracker

back for me and I'll deal with just him. But you have to go. If you see the agent, tell him I'll be in touch."

"But he was shot—"

"He'll still take care of me. I just know it."

Bayley threw her arms around Agnes' neck and they embraced tightly. Whispering, she said, "I don't really understand why you won't come with me, but I trust you to make your own choice."

"Bayley!"

That time, she recognized Nick's voice, blending with Blaise's as they came nearer. With a final hug, she jumped up and stumbled out of their hiding place. Just then, a large bloodhound came into sight, its bay calling out.

"Over here!" she screamed, dropping her hand to pet the dog. A rustle behind her caused her to whip her head around as she saw Agnes take off running further into the woods. Sucking in a deep breath, her mind racing with all she had learned, she looked down at the dog and said, "Take me outta here."

Scarlett bayed before trotting toward Nathan and Bayley followed along, crying as Nick came into view.

Nick pushed ahead of Nathan, scooping Bayley into his arms, unfamiliar tears stinging his eyes. Blaise, his breath coming in pants, wrapped his arms around the back of her, creating a Bayley sandwich.

Bayley's body shook with fright and adrenaline, glad for the support, knowing her legs would not have held her steady. Feeing Nick's chest shaking as well, she said over and over, "It's okay. I'm okay."

Finally setting her feet on the ground, Nick glanced

around and asked, "The other woman. Agnes. Wasn't she with you?"

Licking her lips, she shook her head. "We were together, but got separated in the dark." Hating to lie, she looked up at Nathan. "Uh, maybe you could try to find her?"

"I don't have anything for Scarlett to use for a scent," he replied, "but I'll see if she can pick up something."

The two headed back where Bayley had come from and she prayed Scarlett would find Agnes' scent trail, breathing easier when she heard the baying in the distance.

Looking back at Nick, his arms still wrapped around her, she said, "Take me home."

Kissing the top of her head, he replied, "You got it, babe. No where else I'd rather be with you."

Nathan approached Scarlett, observing his dog's stance, alert and still. Looking through the trees, he saw a figure in the moonlight.

"Agnes?"

The woman, whose face was hidden in shadows, replied, "Yes. Please stay where you are. I was supposed to meet the FBI agent, Harlan, but he was shot."

"I know. What can I do to help?"

"I need protection and he's the only one I trust."

Nathan rubbed the back of his neck with one hand while the other stroked Scarlett's head, wondering what to do.

"I was going into witness protection. I don't trust anyone other than the man who I had contact with."

Pulling out his phone, Nathan called Blaise. "I need you to do something but no questions."

"You got it," Blaise assured.

"Get to Harlan, the agent, and tell him to call my number. That's all."

"He's probably headed to the hospital."

"I know, but I need you to do this."

"I'll take care of it," Blaise promised. Turning to Nick, he asked for Harlan's phone number.

Pulling out his phone, Nick rattled off the number of his former supervisor, watching as Blaise repeated it to whoever was on the line. He trusted Blaise...he trusted all the Saints. Looking down at Bayley, he smiled, knowing he was right where he belonged.

Agnes waited patiently, knowing the call would come. She and Nathan passed the time, barely speaking but, she had to admit, the sound of his voice soothed her frazzled nerves. Her stomach ached and she wondered, not for the first time, if she had an ulcer.

She watched him as he knelt next to his dog, his hand caressing the fur. Scarlett. A small smile slipped over her lips. She loved that name. "Is she named for *Gone with the Wind*?" she asked, softly, her voice barely above a whisper.

He looked toward her and smiled, finding the feminine, yet husky, voice to reach through the dark woods and encircled him. "I loved that movie. My grand-mother used to watch it when it would come on TV and one Christmas, when my parents bought her a video player, I got her that as her first movie. We'd watch it over and over." Ducking his head, he laughed. "I guess that sounds kind of whimpy for a teenage boy, doesn't it?"

The wind blew gently, rustling the leaves overhead. Agnes swallowed deeply, suddenly fighting tears. "I think it sounds beautiful." She wanted to add that it sounded just as beautiful as he looked, but she refused to go there. Men like him were too good to ever be associated with a woman as tainted as she.

Twenty minutes later, Nathan's phone rang. Answering it, he said, "Here she is," and he handed his phone to Agnes. She stepped forward, still in the forest shadows and took it from his outstretched hand. She said very little, agreeing to whatever Harlan was laying out. Disconnecting, she handed the phone back.

"What now?" Nathan asked.

Agnes fiddled with the bottom of her jacket for a second as she wondered how much to tell him. Realiz-ing, she trusted Nathan, she said, "I need to get back to the road where we were run off. Harlan will have someone there to meet me."

"You sure you can you trust him?"

"Yeah. He told me who to look for and, well, I've got no other options."

"So, you're going into witness protection?"

Nodding slowly, Agnes replied, "I have no choice. I have to make things right." Shaking her head, a groan slipped out. "Bayley quoted Agatha Christie just before she left. It fit so perfectly." Seeing his quizzical gaze, she repeated, " 'I've had a long life of experience in noticing evil, fancying evil, suspecting evil and going forth to do battle with evil.' " Sighing heavily, she added, "I've got to see this through. Or else evil wins."

Nathan's heart pounded as her words hit him and he was struck with the realization that the woman in front of him was the bravest person he had ever met. Unable to think of anything to say that would come close to touching her strength, he stood silent, cursing his inadequacy.

Her gaze dropped to Scarlett, still sitting next to Nathan, with her tongue lolling to the side. "I'd like for you and Scarlett to lead the way back and I'll walk behind."

Brows drawn down, Nathan asked, "Why? Why can't I see you?"

"I'd rather stay a bit of a mystery to you...it feels safer that way."

With a short nod, he turned, deciding that to give her what she needed was the best way for him to honor her strength. Looking down, he patted Scarlett's head. "Come on, girl. Let's go back."

With his dog happily jogging along in the woods, Nathan followed at a pace slow enough for Agnes to follow. As they approached the road, he saw a dark SUV parked with two men standing next to it, their dress and demeanor screaming FBI. They approached Agnes and hustled her into the back seat. As the SUV made a three-point turn on the narrow road, it headed back

33

After the adrenaline wore off, all she felt was bone weary. The Saints' vans drove into the compound at almost two a.m., but Jack, Luke, and Charlie were there to greet them. Bethany, there with Grace, offered hot chocolate and sandwiches. Blaise immediately greeted his wife, telling her she should not have come.

"Oh, hush," she scolded, leaving his arms to offer a hug to Bayley. "Your mom and dad are over with Ben, but they're sitting up, anxious for news about Bayley."

"I didn't know they knew," Bayley said, her voice showing her fatigue.

"They had been trying to call your cell. Then, when they couldn't get hold of Blaise, they figured something was up. I've already let them know you are safe and sound."

Nodding her thanks, Bayley's eyes traveled to the table, more famished than she realized. Nick, with his arms wrapped around her, guided her to the food as they all plopped down in chairs for their late-night snack before each would head home.

Bethany looked up, seeing another man standing on the porch, a large bloodhound by his side. "Come in, come in. It's fine to bring your dog."

Jack shook Nathan's hand and introduced him to his wife, as well as Luke and Charlie. Nathan smiled his greeting and gratefully accepted a turkey and ham sandwich to share with Scarlett.

Bayley moved over to the beautiful dog, bending to scratch her ears. Scarlett's tongue lolled out as she panted her doggy breath, making Bayley laugh. Looking up at Nathan, she said, "I'm sorry, but I don't think I ever thanked you for finding me and...uh...me."

Nathan's warm smile settled over her, letting her know he would keep her secret about Agnes. "No thanks necessary, ma'am."

Laughing, she said, "Please, call me Bayley." Squatting down, she hugged Scarlett, running her hands over the thick fur. "And is this beauty a Saint as well?"

"Oh, we're not Saints."

"Not yet," Jack said, his dark eyes holding a twinkle. "So far, he manages to come when we need him, but who knows? I might just talk him into joining us. We always seem to need a good investigator and Scarlett's got special skills."

The other Saints joined in with "here, here" ringing out. Nathan simply nodded and with a shrug, just said, "I'm thinking about it."

Soon the drinks and sandwiches were gone and goodbyes were said amongst the group, everyone trudging home to their wives, fiancés, and families. Blaise, Grace, Bayley, and Nick were the last to leave.

As Jack walked them to the door and stepped out onto the porch, he shook Nick's hand and said, "I know this case was...or became, personal for you. But any regrets about leaving the Bureau and joining with us?"

Nick's gaze roamed to Bayley's upturned face smiling gently at him before lifting his eyes to the clear, night sky dotted with a million stars. Inhaling a deep breath of cool, mountain air he shook his head as he turned back to Jack. "No regrets." With a last nod, he wrapped his arm around Bayley, tucking her in closely and together they walked into the night.

Bayley rolled over in bed, staring at the beauty in front of her. Tall, dark, mysterious, beauty. Not getting home until the wee hours of the morning, they were exhausted but too keyed up to sleep. After a hot shower, forgoing another attempt at shower sex, they crashed into bed together, where they burned up the sheets in an effort to wipe clean the fears from the previous hours. Finally falling asleep, tangled up in each other's arms, Bayley was not surprised to see that it was already late morning.

Slipping from his embrace, she headed to the bathroom and then into the kitchen. As the dark coffee streamed from the Keurig, she inhaled the aroma, sunlight streaming through his windows. Looking out over the city with the mountains in the background, she sipped the hot brew after doctoring it with cream and sugar.

"Hey."

Nick's warm voice slid over her as his breath washed by her ear. His arm snaked around her middle, pulling her back into his body tightly as his other hand reached for her coffee, taking a liberal sip.

"How do you stand all that milk and sugar, babe?"

Twisting her head up, she grinned. "I've got a cup of black for you on the counter."

With a squeeze, he stepped back and retrieved his cup. Following her out onto the balcony, they sat in companionable silence for a few minutes.

"I get you following the guys who took Daphne," he said eventually. "You saw that, you knew something was happening. You wanted to help your friend until you could get to us."

Bayley looked over at him, but he did not seem to be searching for an explanation...just stating the obvious. He slowly looked toward her, his brow furrowed, and asked, "But the laundry truck. Why follow that? Just because you saw Agnes in it?"

She allowed her eyes to roam over his face, mesmerized at the intensity of his gaze. Smiling, she simply said, "Instinct."

"Instinct?"

"It seemed incongruous that she would be driving a truck. The pieces of what I knew about her did not fit with that observation."

"And that was all it took to become suspicious?" he

asked, setting his coffee cup on the ground and gently pulling her into his lap.

Straddling him, she kissed him, long and sweet. She cupped his scruffy jaw as he held her soft cheeks. Leaning in, a whisper away, she quoted, " 'Instinct is a marvelous thing. It can neither be explained nor ignored.' "

Laughing at her ability to produce yet another Christie quote, Nick swung his legs over the edge of the chair and, with her in his arms, stalked back to the bedroom. Holding on, she threw her head back and giggled.

"And what does your instinct tell you about what I'm about to do?" he asked as they fell onto the bed together.

Staring into his dark eyes, she replied, "Fun... passion...and..."

"Love," he added, holding her gaze.

Nodding, she agreed, "Yes...love."

"I see you took my advice and flew into the star-filled unknown."

Nick looked at Santa standing next to him, both men watching the two women playing with the children in the Reindeer games. He and Bayley had returned to the Christmastown Inn when they traveled back to Tennessee to check on Uncle Bernie. They found him happy and healthy as he sat with his arm around Vera on his sofa, a teacup balanced on his lap. Four months had passed and Nick assumed the Santa character would not recognize or remember him. He should have known better.

Nodding, he replied, "Yes, I did." His gaze traveled from the children's activity to Bayley, her bright blues eyes shining, leading the little ones in a game before passing out candy canes.

Santa's eyes twinkled as he shook with laughter. "Easiest way to find love, my boy. Just let go and celebrate the season of love wherever it finds you."

As Bayley's eyes searched the crowd, landing on Nick's, her light shone in his direction, warming his heart, and he knew Santa's words rang true.

One Year Later

Bayley left the shop early for lunch, walking down the street to meet Nick. The sun was shining and she lifted her face upwards, allowing the warmth of the day to engulf her. Opening her eyes, she was momentarily blinded by the brightness and almost ran into another pedestrian.

"Oh, I'm sorry," she exclaimed, steering clear at the last second from walking into a woman with dark blonde hair, streaks of reddish-gold highlighted in the sunshine. The woman's dark eyes dropped quickly as she continued to move down the street.

Bayley turned to watch her as she walked away, the

spidey senses filling her making her think that she knew the woman. But the hair was different. The eyes were a different color. The nose may have even been slightly thinner. But…

"Hey, sweetie," Nick called out, jerking Bayley's attention back in front of her. Nick placed a soft kiss on her lips then pulled back, his eyebrows raised. "Are you okay?"

"Did you see that woman? The one I almost ran into?"

He immediately lifted his gaze to peer down the street, but saw no one suspicious on the busy noon-time street full of pedestrians. Shaking his head, he looked back down into Bayley's eyes. "I didn't notice anyone. Who was it?"

Looking back, she shrugged slightly. If it was not who she thought, it would not matter. And if it was who she thought, they did not want to be noticed. "'Very few of us are what we seem.'"

"Huh?"

"Oh, nothing…just me and my quotes. It was no one, I'm sure," she replied, looking back up into Nick's beautiful face. Slipping her arm through his, she added, "Taking me to lunch? I'm famished."

Laughing, he tucked her in closely as they continued down the street.

From the opposite corner, the woman watched the couple as they walked away and she smiled. Turning her face to the warm sun, she sighed. Sometimes she was lonely. Sometimes doing the right thing was not easy.

She had not needed to testify against her family with the evidence the FBI had found in the hotel, along with the rescued women. So, no witness protection for her, but with the assistance of Harlan, she had managed to make changes. He worked with a special group he knew to give her a new identity. He had never explained, but supposedly the group was able to pull off about anything needed, so she had a new birth certificate, new social security card, new driver's license.

She had hated using any of her money, knowing it was from her family's business, but nonetheless took out just enough to afford to disappear—plastic surgery on her nose to alter her appearance slightly and a small apartment. With new hair color and clothes bought from a thrift store, she was able to stay hidden. From what, she was not sure since her whole family had gone to prison. Harlan suggested she move far away—across the country or across the world. But she felt the pull toward the Blue Ridge Mountains. Maybe because they had given her refuge when she needed it. Maybe because the mountain man with the beautiful dog was nearby and even if she could not see him, it gave her comfort knowing he was close.

A gust of wind blew briskly, bringing her thoughts back to the present. She still struggled with what she had to do, but today, seeing Bayley's happiness, she felt less lonely. In the last year, she had had a lot of opportunity to read and found herself devouring a great deal of Agatha Christie, having been intrigued by Bayley's words. And as Agnes turned to walk back down the street, she softly reminded herself, " 'I like living. I have sometimes been wildly, despairingly, acutely miserable, racked with sorrow; but through it all I still know quite certainly that just to be alive is a grand thing.'"

Two Years Later

Nick drove into his driveway, his gaze landing on the two-story Colonial in the family neighborhood. The homes were built back in the time when each house was individual in design and he loved the brick façade, complete with green shutters and a green front door. Walking to the porch, he waved at Grace standing in her front yard across the street, little Ben toddling at her feet as she watered flowers.

He came home early, tip-toeing into the house attempting to keep noise down to a minimum. His gaze swept the front living room, a baby swing in one corner, baby blanket on the floor, laundry folded in a basket sitting on the sofa, and Mr. Lickers curled up in a sun-spot on the chair. Passing the kitchen, he noted the washed bottles lining the counter and the breakfast dishes in the drying rack.

Smiling, he continued to tip-toe up the stairs, hearing a slightly off-key lullaby being sung. Turning the corner at the top, he moved into the doorway of the nursery, his gaze finally landing on the objects of his desire. Bayley sat in his mother's rocking chair, nursing baby Bernard. Just like his uncle, his son would be called Bernie. Bayley insisted on the name and Nick had to admit, it was perfect. His son had a set of lungs on him and when he cried, his face turned beet red and his eyes squinted as he bawled. Uncle Bernie claimed he had the makings of a Marine Drill Sergeant.

Bayley looked up, her beaming smile hitting Nick right in the chest, just as it had that first night in the nightclub. Baby Bernie's mouth was slack against her breast as his little fist curled up over his mother's heartbeat.

Nick walked over, assisting her from the beloved rocker, and kissed the top of his son's head before she placed him in the crib. The two of them slipped from the room, arm in arm, and he steered her toward the master bedroom.

"Oh, honey," Bayley protested, "I've got to finish putting the laundry away and I know the dishes are still in the drying rack in the sink."

Continuing to guide her to the king-sized bed, he turned her toward him, kissed her head, and then gently pushed her shoulders so that she plopped down on the mattress. Crawling over her, he said, "All that stuff can wait. It doesn't matter. You need to rest when you can and right now, with Bernie asleep, this is the perfect time for a nap."

Her tired eyes grateful, she snuggled up next to him, soon the two drifting into sleep.

Ten Years Later

"Bernie, don't run," Bayley called out as her arms were full of four-year-old Bryce, while also holding the hand of seven-year-old Brooke.

Nick dropped their luggage as he grabbed Bernie's shoulder. "Whoa, slow down there, son. We'll all get to see him in just a minute."

As a door elf welcomed them into the entrance of the Christmastown Inn, the children squealed at the sight of Mr. and Mrs. Santa Claus. Bayley laughed as she walked over, hugging both while keeping an eye on her rambunctious children.

"It is so good to see you again," Mrs. Claus exclaimed, embracing each child, now standing in rapt attention receiving their candy-cane.

As they walked over to the tall, stone fireplace to warm their fingers, Santa stepped toward Nick, extending his hand in greeting. Nick shook his hand, while staring into the face that had become so familiar. Cocking his head to the side, he noted that Santa had not aged one bit in the last thirteen years.

Seeing Nick's perusal, Santa laughed, his belly jiggling. "Oh, you know me, Nick. Me and Mrs. Claus are always the same. Been that way for as long as I can remember."

No longer doubting what his mind could still not

perceive, Nick smiled, glad for the familiar face. The two men turned to watch Mrs. Claus, Bayley, and the three children laughing with glee at the decorations.

"You've got a beautiful family, Nick," Santa commented, his blue eyes twinkling.

Nodding, Nick agreed. "You once told me to celebrate love wherever I could find it." His eyes never leaving his family, he said, "I have. And I celebrate the love that is right in front of me every day."

With a jolly clap on the back, Santa led Nick over to join the others as Bayley beamed up at him, warming his heart.

For the next exciting Saint and the continuation of Nathan's story:
Searching Love

Cael

Jaxon

Jayden

Asher

Zeke

Cas

Lighthouse Security Investigations

Mace

Rank

Walker

Drew

Blake

Tate

Levi

Clay

Cobb

Hope City (romantic suspense series co-developed

with Kris Michaels

Brock book 1

Sean book 2

Carter book 3

Brody book 4

Kyle book 5

Ryker book 6

Rory book 7

Killian book 8

Torin book 9

Saints Protection & Investigations

(an elite group, assigned to the cases no one else wants…or can solve)

Serial Love

Healing Love

Revealing Love

Seeing Love

Honor Love

Sacrifice Love

Protecting Love

Remember Love

Discover Love

Surviving Love

Celebrating Love

Searching Love

Follow the exciting spin-off series:

Alvarez Security (military romantic suspense)

Gabe

Tony

Vinny

Jobe

SEALs

Thin Ice (Sleeper SEAL)

SEAL Together (Silver SEAL)

Undercover Groom (Hot SEAL)

Also for a Hope City Crossover Novel / Hot SEAL…

A Forever Dad by Maryann Jordan

Letters From Home (military romance)

Class of Love

Freedom of Love

Bond of Love

The Love's Series (detectives)

Love's Taming

Love's Tempting

Love's Trusting

The Fairfield Series (small town detectives)

Emma's Home

Laurie's Time

Carol's Image

Fireworks Over Fairfield

Please take the time to leave a review of this book. Feel free to contact me, especially if you enjoyed my book. I love to hear from readers!

Facebook

Email

Website

ABOUT THE AUTHOR

I am an avid reader of romance novels, often joking that I cut my teeth on the historical romances. I have been reading and reviewing for years. In 2013, I finally gave into the characters in my head, screaming for their story to be told. From these musings, my first novel, Emma's Home, The Fairfield Series was born.

I was a high school counselor having worked in education for thirty years. I live in Virginia, having also lived in four states and two foreign countries. I have been married to a wonderfully patient man for thirty-five years. When writing, my dog or one of my four cats can generally be found in the same room if not on my lap.

Please take the time to leave a review of this book. Feel free to contact me, especially if you enjoyed my book. I love to hear from readers!

Facebook
Email
Website

Made in the USA
Coppell, TX
21 January 2022